PHANTOM

H. D. CARLTON

Copyright © 2025 by H. D. Carlton
All rights reserved.

978-1-63893-337-3 (Paperback)

Cover design by Collin Estrada
Formatting by Designs by Charlyy

Distributed by: Zando, LLC

10 9 8 7 6 5 4 3 2 1

Manufactured in the United States of America

MORE BY
H. D. CARLTON

PLAYLIST

THEME SONG:

Bad Omens—"Bad Decisions"

Ariana and the Rose—"Honesty"

PVRIS—"Old Wounds"

Emmit Fenn—"Painting Greys"

Iris Temple—"Typhoon"

Wolves at the Gate—"Waste"

The Word Alive—"Burning Your World Down"

Benji Lewis—"Fast Forward"

Hailee Steinfeld—"Afterlife"

Bad Omens—"Like a Villain"

Point North (feat. Kellin Quinn)—"Into the Dark"

1940S PLAYLIST

Bing Crosby—"Just One More Chance"

Fedora Mingarelli—"Un'ora sola ti vorrei"

Oscar Carboni—"Tango del mare"

Alfredo Clerici—"T'ho vista piangere"

Glenn Miller—"Elmer's Tune"

Cesare Andrea Bixio (sung by Beniamino Gigli)—"Mamma son tanto felice"

Tommy Dorsey and His Orchestra—"All the Things You Are"

IMPORTANT NOTE

This is a dark romance with triggering situations such as stalking, cheating (not between love interests), graphic violence and murder, graphic language, on-page rape and domestic violence (not between love interests), alcohol addiction and codependency with an addict, mentions of infertility and traumatic labor, and explicit sexual situations.

There are also kinks such as degradation, breath play, and fear play.

Please heed these warnings seriously.

Your mental health matters.

AUTHOR'S NOTE

First, please keep in mind that this story takes place during the 1940s. Not only was the language slightly different then but the value of the dollar was also vastly different from what it is now.

While I tried to stay accurate to the time period, some liberties may have been taken for the sake of the story.

Second, if you are reading this after the Cat & Mouse Duet, then you are familiar with Gigi's diary. Please note that Gigi wrote in her journal *every day*, so there are hundreds of entries detailing events and information that you may be unaware of.

Happy reading!

GLOSSARY

Belly-up: Bankrupt

Big earner: Someone who makes a lot of money for the family

Bird: A pretty woman

Blabbermouth: Someone who talks too much

Broad: A woman

Bum rap: A false accusation; being blamed for something you didn't do

Bust your chops: To scold or chastise someone

Cafone: An embarrassment to himself and others; a phony

Capo: Short for *capodecina*, the family member who leads a crew

Capo di tutti i capi: Boss of bosses

Clock: To keep track of someone's movements and activities

Come heavy: To arrive carrying a loaded gun

Consigliere: A member of the family who serves as an adviser to the don and resolves disputes within the family

Contract: A murder assignment

Crew: A group of soldiers that takes orders from a *capo*

Cugine: A young criminal looking to be inducted into the Mafia

Dip: An idiot

Don: Head of the family

Enforcer: A person who threatens, maims, or kills someone

Empty suit: Someone with nothing to offer who tries to hang around with mobsters

Floozy: A common name for a sexually active and oftentimes promiscuous woman

Fuzz, the: A cop

Gobbledygook: Talking nonsense

Godfather: A powerful crime boss in the Mafia

Hoosegow: Jail

Jalopy: An old car

Large: A thousand, a grand, a G

Made man: An indoctrinated member of the family

Mafioso: A member of the family; a mobster

Magazine: An ammunition storage and feeding device for a firearm

Make one's bones: To gain credibility by killing someone

Numbskull: A dull, stupid or dimwitted person

Omertà: The code of silence and the vow taken when being sworn into the family

Pinched: To get caught by law enforcement

Problem: A liability, likely to be murdered

Rat: A member who violates omertà and snitches on the family

Sauced: The state of being drunk or intoxicated

Section hand: A railroad worker

Singing like a canary: To give someone, usually the authorities, a lot of secret and often illegal information

Sound, the: Puget Sound, the body of water surrounding Seattle

Take a powder: To leave

Tribute: Giving the boss a cut of the deal—violation is often punishable by death

Underboss: The second-in-command to the boss

War-tax stamps: A postage stamp used to raise war revenue

Whack/ice/burn/pop/clip: To murder

May 26, 1944

My mother always told me I was different. She would spit the
word at me like it was rotten fruit on her tongue.
I thought it was because of my deep love for gothic literature.
She had trouble getting my nose out of Mary Shelley's
Frankenstein, or my favorite Edgar Allan Poe stories.
As a child, I told her I wanted to live in a house that was
built to look like the inside of their brains. Gothic. Dark.
Spooky, I'd even say. My mother recoiled at that and called
me crazy. She called me many other despicable names, but I
won't give her the satisfaction of repeating them, even in ink.
But what would she think now?
She passed away when I was twenty-three, but even from the
grave, I can feel her judgment.
Letting a man into my home, and kissing him. A man who isn't
my husband.
A man who stood outside my window for weeks, watching me
from afar.
There is something wrong with him.
Clearly there is something wrong with me, too.

PROLOGUE

"What's your name?" I ask again breathlessly.

"Ronaldo."

"Do you want to hurt me, Ronaldo?"

"Never," he answers. "I only want to cherish you, Genevieve."

"How do you know my name?"

"I know everything about you. Just as I know you will love me, too."

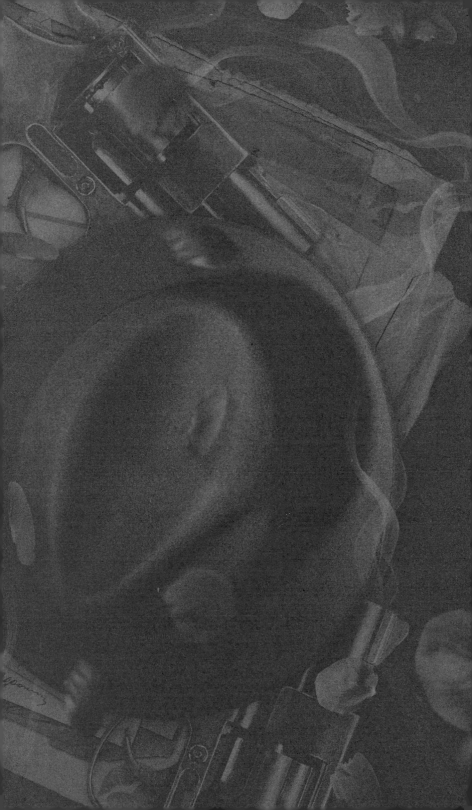

CHAPTER 1

THE PHANTOM

March 18, 1944

T his will be the third man I've whacked today, and I've run
out of patience for their useless begging.

Typically, I leave this job to the enforcers in the Salvatore
family, but ending a man's life offers a release unlike any other vice.
Cigarettes, whiskey, birds—none of them have the same effect.

It's their damn talking that threatens the peace I find after making
a heart stop.

"No, no, wait! Let me explain!" the kid pleads, his nasally voice
cracking from terror. It's past midnight. The biting air and thick fog have

settled around us on the Aurora Bridge.

His desperation gets the best of him, and he attempts to land a blow on my left side. The kid is stupid to think I'm not used to men attempting to take advantage of my disability. I slap his fist away easily, then pop him in the nose for daring to try.

Blood spurts from his nostrils, and while he groans and mutters insults beneath his breath, I loop ropes around his ankles and tie them into a tight knot. Sweat and grease mat his overgrown hair to his forehead, and motor oil stains his navy-blue coveralls, now joined by the blood pouring from his nose. By trade, he's a mechanic, but his interests have always been in the Mafia. His mother had ties to a family in New York City, but she refused to raise him in the family business. He's a cugine. For the past few months, he's strived to be made and has pledged his loyalty to the Salvatores.

A pledge he failed to keep.

Which is why I've tied cinder blocks to his feet. If anyone discovers his body, they'll find a bullet through his mouth—a clear message of his crime.

"You're a rat, Worm. You were feeding information to the Baldellis," I remind him dryly. Angelo nicknamed him for his pinched facial features and grating voice. Not sure what his real name is, but I'm sure his obituary in the *Seattle Times* Sunday newspaper will confirm it, assuming he's ever found.

The media will recognize the message and know his death resulted from organized crime. And the public will undoubtedly look at the Salvatores.

Angelo has owned Seattle for the last two decades and been declared the *capo di tutti i capi*. He's allowed other families to conduct business in Seattle with his permission and, of course, with the understanding that he'll receive a cut of their profits.

However, five years ago, Don Manny Baldelli found an issue with that. He claimed his great-grandfather migrated from Sicily to Seattle first, making him the rightful owner of the city. After which, word got out that Manny was withholding Angelo's tribute and dealing guns under the table. Since then, war has broken out, and men are getting burned left and right. Families are choosing sides, and to this day, several bodyguards surround Angelo at any given hour.

It's a dangerous time, and none of us walk the streets without checking over our shoulders.

"You're givin' me a bum rap!" Worm insists vehemently. "I ain't no rat, Ronnie; you know me! The Baldellis forced me in that car, but I didn't tell them nothin'. Please, you have to believe me!"

One of our crew, Lloyd, spotted him getting into a Baldelli car two nights ago, and it just so happens Worm showed up in an expensive suit yesterday with a brand-new Rolex on his wrist. The timing wasn't a coincidence, and the kid made it obvious that the rival family had paid him off.

"Don't call me Ronnie," I clip.

It's the only response I bother to give him. There isn't any point in arguing with the kid—he's already marked. If I'm not the one to ice him, one of Angelo's enforcers will.

Worm opens his mouth again, preparing to plead his case some more, but I take the opportunity to shove my revolver in his mouth and pull the trigger. A car passes, but rather than slowing, they hit the gas.

I make quick work of removing the Rolex from his wrist and stuffing the piece in my pocket. Later, I'll return it to the Baldellis to let them know their investment has been wasted.

Next, I slump Worm over the railing and lift the cement blocks, tossing them over. His body careens over the edge and into the canal, the following splash echoing in the night air.

Finally. Some goddamn peace and quiet.

I roll my neck, relieving the tension gathered in my shoulders. Not only is their begging useless but quite bothersome, too.

Heading back toward my car parked on the other side of the bridge, I whistle the tune to "Just One More Chance" by Bing Crosby.

March 18, 1944

"The numbskull got sauced and lost three hundred dollars to Tommy, but did that stop him from playing another round? Of course not! Now, he owes Tommy five hundred."

It's late in the morning, and I'm on my way to report back to Angelo about completing Worm's contract last night, when Santino's words catch my attention, his voice ringing out from the family room in Angelo's estate. Quickly, I detour in his direction, tucking the rucksack with Worm's bloody Rolex inside in the inner-breast pocket of my trench coat. I take it upon myself to stay informed when it concerns the family. Tommy and Santino are Angelo's cousins, so if someone owes Tommy money, that means they owe Angelo money.

I round the corner and lean against the doorframe, catching Santino's attention. He's sitting on the sofa next to his mother, Kay, who is scoffing at the sap who's now indebted to the Salvatores. And for quite a bit of money, at that.

"Who's this guy you're talkin' about?" I ask, folding my arms over my chest.

Santino's only seventeen, and while he's invested in the family business, he's also a blabbermouth. Today, it's a good thing. But one day, it might get him iced.

If he even comes home from the war after he's drafted in a few months, that is.

"Name's John Parsons. He and his detective friend, Frank Williams, been comin' to the lounge for the past few months. He had the funds at first, but the dip keeps tryin' to get his money back and can't pay no more. Tommy challenged them to a game of poker last night, and John couldn't seem to help himself."

I raise a brow, surprised Angelo's cousin was gambling with Frank.

He's one of the leading homicide detectives in Seattle and is typically the one working on the cases that have resulted from the war between the Mafia families.

He's also firmly in Angelo's pocket and is very well-acquainted with the two of us, unbeknownst to John.

"Tommy gambled with the fuzz?"

Santino grins. "No one's ever called him a genius, Ronnie."

I'm tempted to bark at him for calling me Ronnie, but learning about this Parsons fella is more important than arguing with a kid about my damn name. I've smacked every male member of this family upside the head for calling me that, and every single one suffers from short-term memory loss.

I've always hated it. Reminds me of my father, who bore the same name, and even still, it hurts to think about him.

Angelo's father called me by it as a young boy, and it lived on through his son. The rest of the family follows his lead, despite my misgivings.

"John Parsons," I state, bringing his attention back to the matter at hand. "Who is he?"

Santino shrugs. "Don't know. All I know is he didn't pay Tommy a dime. Promised he'd come up with the money later, but I think we all know how that goes."

"You know anything else about him?" I question.

"Just that he owns Parsons Manor down by the Sound. He kept goin' on about it while he was draining a bottle of whiskey," Santino responds, annoyance in his tone. "Fella wouldn't shut up."

I push off the doorframe and head back toward the front door of Angelo's estate. I'll report to Angelo later.

"Hey, Ronnie, if you're gonna whack him, let me come, yeah?" he calls after me.

"Santino," Kay admonishes.

I don't bother responding. If I wanted one of Angelo's crew to handle anyone for me, I sure as hell wouldn't enlist a kid to do it.

Soon enough, he'll get plenty of experience pulling a trigger, and he's better off pointing that gun toward a Nazi than someone like John Parsons.

Santino's got bigger things to focus on than the organization. He's got a war to worry about.

March 18, 1944

Parsons Manor is unlike anything I've ever seen before. If it were in downtown Seattle, it'd stick out like a sore thumb.

With the black siding and gargoyles poised on top of the roof, it looks like it came straight out of the *Dracula* film. Houses like these just don't exist in this city, yet here I stand.

Tucking my hands in my trench coat pockets, I stroll through the front yard. An array of colorful flowers bloom in front of the black-painted porch, making the house look like a gloomy storm cloud among a bright rainbow.

It's an interesting house, and it only strengthens my curiosity about who John Parsons is and why the hell he's residing in a home like this.

My question is answered a moment later when movement in the large bay window catches my eye. A tall, curvy woman sits down in a chair directly in front of the glass. Instantly, I'm riveted by the sight of her. Red stains her full lips, and her black tresses are curled to perfection. She wears a canary-yellow dress, the sleeves drooping down the sides of her arms, the fabric clinging to her curved waist.

My heart stills, like God himself froze time as I watch her peer down at something in her lap. One side of her mouth curls upward the slightest bit. By the way she angles her head and moves her arm, she appears to be writing.

I'm entirely smitten by her, and though there's no way for me to know, I'm confident she is the mastermind behind Parsons Manor.

Hypnotized, I drift toward her, my mind vacuumed into a trance that it can't seem to find its way out of.

I'm not only riveted by her.

I'm possessed by a need to have her.

And she *must* be mine.

As if she heard my internal proclamation, her head lifts, and her gaze locks onto me. It feels like a bolt of lightning strikes through me where I stand. Her mouth parts, shock rounding her eyes at the corners, and though it appears like fear is sinking its claws into her, she's no less vexing.

I came here to learn who John Parsons is, and the only thing I know is that he comes home to the most beautiful woman alive.

And he doesn't deserve it one damn bit.

Her hand drifts over her heart, a chunky gold pen woven through her fingers.

What is she writing? And will she write about me?

I'd love nothing more than to be consumed by her words, no matter how they greet me. Whether it's through those red-stained lips or from her delicate hands. I want to know every facet of her, every centimeter of her—mind, body, and soul.

Chest tight, my movement mirrors hers, and my hand drifts over my heart where it clenches almost painfully. It takes monumental effort to draw my gaze away from hers. To take a step away, then turn and slowly retreat down her extensive gravel driveway. The trek to my car parked on the street takes several long minutes, yet I don't remember a single second of it.

She plagues my mind, infecting it like a parasite and overriding any autonomy over myself. My free will is indebted to her, and without her, I am nothing.

I shut the door to my Cadillac and can only sit there and mourn the life of John Parsons's wife.

She will never be the same, as I am not.

Her husband has unintentionally dragged her into a world where she doesn't belong. Yet it is I who will never let her leave.

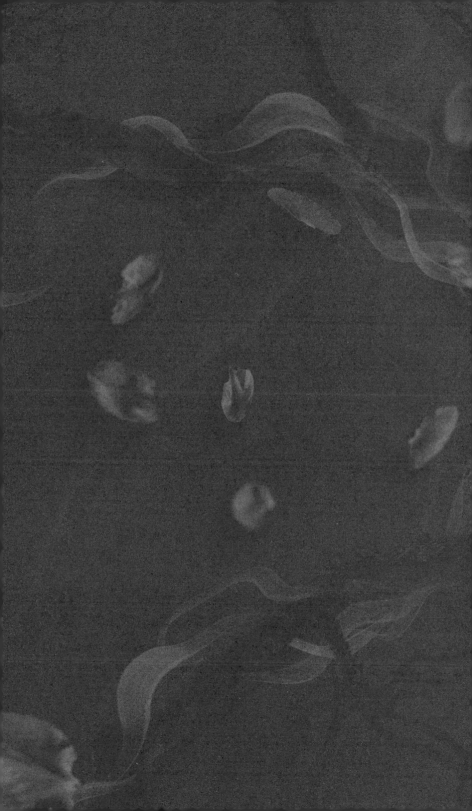

CHAPTER 2

THE RAVEN

March 19, 1944

Five men have perished in this house.

Some days, I wonder if I'll meet my own tragic end here, too.

I'm sure my husband will be the culprit. With the stress he's causing me, my heart is destined to give out.

We have no money.

And no other friends or family we can lean on.

We have nothing, and we are alone in our nothingness.

Teardrops stain the piece of paper on my lap from the debt collectors that proves just how little we have left.

It's dated from two days ago, and he never thought to tell me. I found it peeking out from a stack of opened mail on the counter, along with bank statements declaring his accounts in the negative. There was nothing unordinary about the papers, yet a little voice in my head told me to look.

And my God, part of me wishes I hadn't.

We're in danger of losing our home. There isn't enough money to pay our mortgage, let alone any of the utilities.

He spent almost everything. *Everything.*

How will we support Seraphina? Feed her, clothe her, ensure she sleeps in a warm bed? She works in a deli after school a few days a week to learn some responsibility and fund her war-tax stamps—and truthfully, to sustain her ice-cream addiction, too. But I could never ask her to pay the bills. She's only thirteen years old, for God's sake!

It's not uncommon for parents to rely on their children these days— times are hard, and war is rampant—but until now, we've been able to shelter Sera from a lot of those hardships.

And why should she have to pay for *his* mistakes?

We've always had the security from the wealth passed down in John's family, along with his successful bookkeeping firm, and it's kept us more than comfortable. I never expected that he'd do something like this to us.

He spoon-fed me lavish fantasies when he courted me, and like a fool, I ate them up. He swore he'd build me a house with my odd sense of style, and he followed through with that promise because it made me happy, even at the cost of those poor men who died building it, causing society to turn their noses up at us. But he also swore that we'd surpass his grandfather's wealth and we'd live a life of luxury beyond our dreams. He swore that one day he'd buy us a big boat and we could sail across the ocean.

So many promises, and instead . . . he went and spent it all.

My throat tightens as I recall the man who lingered outside my window yesterday. I had convinced myself he was just another lost soul, but now that I know the trouble John has gotten us into, I'm second-guessing myself.

If a man is coming onto our property, it can only mean John's done something terrible.

As frightening as it is, I wonder if he has somehow gotten mixed up with the wrong people. And now, Sera's and my life could be in danger.

Oh, John, what have you done?

"Mama? I'm hungry. Is there anything to eat?"

Sera's quiet voice draws me away from my sorrows. Hurriedly, I swipe away stray tears from my cheeks and turn to face her with a bright grin. I've been sitting in my rocking chair at the window, trading off between staring at the piece of paper in shock and staring out the window mournfully.

"Sure, baby. You want me to whip you up some lunch?"

She smiles, and a brightness radiates from beneath her freckled cheeks.

She's a beauty among the ashes that seem to collect in this damned home.

"Yeah. It tastes better when you make it."

I snort. She swears that her sandwiches never taste as good as mine, even if we use the same exact ingredients. Regardless, I've always loved doting on her. One day, she'll stop asking for my help, and I'm reluctant for when that day arrives.

Sera takes off toward the kitchen while I detour to the small washroom in the hallway. I reapply powder to my stained cheeks and refresh my ruby-red lipstick until not a single trace of my turmoil is to be seen.

Perfect.

My daughter will never know just how close her world is to crumbling down around her.

When I make my way back through the living room, I relish the beautiful checkered tiling that expands all the way into the kitchen. There, Sera sits at the island, her feet swinging as she focuses on her homework.

The sight immediately dulls the persistent ache in my chest.

Oh, what I wouldn't give to feel that childlike innocence once more. Anything but Sera.

"What are you hungry for, sweet pea?" I ask as I trek into the kitchen, my house shoes clacking against the floor.

She shrugs. "I dunno."

"How about elephant tails?" I suggest.

She pauses her homework to look up at me with a wrinkled nose. "Ew, no!"

"Panda tongue? Giraffe hooves?"

"Mom," she whines, drawing out the syllable. A silly grin paints her face, however, and I consider my mission successful.

"Okay, fine," I relent dramatically. "How about a turkey sandwich?"

"Yes, please," she says, her cheeky grin widening.

"Or . . ." I pause. "Turkey feet?"

She sighs theatrically, as thirteen-year-old girls do, and I turn to the fridge to grab the ingredients, though my smile quickly fades beneath the artificial light. How much longer will she be able to eat so freely rather than wonder when her next meal will be?

Pushing it from my mind, I paste a grin back on my face and begin prepping her sandwich. It's a requirement that I cut off the crust from each slice of bread before the turkey, cheese, and mustard go on.

"Daddy said we're getting a new car and he'll let me drive it," Sera announces casually.

I pause, the knife in my hand poised just above the bread.

"What?" I ask breathlessly, my heart having vacated my chest.

"Yeah," she chirps. "He said we're going to be super rich, and he'll buy me the Cord 812."

I blink, forcing myself to focus on slicing the bread rather than my trembling fingers. Sera knows nothing about cars, but my husband sure does, and I've heard him talk about that specific car frequently. It's one of his many dream automobiles, and now he's gone and made sure that it will *stay* a dream.

Bastard.

"Did he, now?" I question, forcing a serenity that I don't feel into my tone.

"Yup!"

I finish with both slices before I can find the breath to ask, "And when did he say this was happening?"

She shrugs for a second time. "Didn't say."

It feels as if a rock has formed in my throat, and anger slowly pollutes my bloodstream.

How *dare* he make such grandiose promises when we're on the brink of homelessness? And to Sera, of all people! I could forgive him for getting my hopes up but certainly not my little girl's.

"Well, that's something Daddy and I will have to talk about. Maybe something a little safer once you're older? How about a Dodge?"

Her nose wrinkles again. "That sounds boring. Like an old-people car. *You* should drive that jalopy."

I scoff and hand her the plate with the sandwich atop, complete with a handful of potato chips. "I'll have you know, I am still young and beautiful, little girl."

She giggles around a bite of food while I struggle to keep my smile plastered on my face.

"You are, Mama."

My heart eases a fraction, and I walk around the island to place a soft kiss on her head.

"Love you, sweet pea."

"Love you, too." Her words are garbled, but this time, I don't berate her for talking with food in her mouth.

I'm not sure how much longer she'll have that luxury.

March 19, 1944

I'm a pipe on the verge of combusting when my husband comes home, my cheeks flushed hot with anger. He's late, which used to be an unusual habit but has become more typical of him in recent times.

Since the moment Sera went to bed, I've been in my rocking chair, glaring out the window and stewing in my fury, planning all the harsh words I would dare say to him.

He's always been hot-tempered, but my wrath has proven to burn brighter a time or two.

The front door shuts behind him, and John comes sauntering toward me, several envelopes in his hand. His eyes are red, and once he's near enough, I detect a faint whiff of booze.

My husband has always been conventionally handsome, with short, light-brown hair that is as thick as it is soft and always seems to be effortlessly windswept. Unusual light-brown eyes, a square jawline, an aristocratic nose, and an incredibly charming smile. When we were teens, he had birds lining up for him, hoping for just a minute of his attention. He's always been tall, handsome, and wealthy.

Now, only two of those things are true.

"You have a letter from Daisy," he announces, dropping an envelope onto the footstool in front of me, familiar handwriting scribed over it. She and I have been best friends for nearly three decades. We write to each other often since she moved to Spokane. However, Daisy is the least of my concerns right now.

"Did you happen to promise our daughter a luxury car?" I ask, my tone dangerously sweet.

He grins and tugs at his tie, exhaustion weighing down the corners of his lips. John has always been a hardworking man, yet his spending habits have proven to work harder.

"She's nearly fourteen. Gives her somethin' to work towards," he says casually. As if he's not getting our little girl's hopes up only to let her down so cruelly.

"You want to explain how on earth we're going to afford that?"

His brow furrows. "Genevieve, what are you on about?"

"We received a letter from the debt collector. We can't afford the mortgage payments right now, let alone *food*. So why would you promise her a car?"

His face drops, guilt instantly coloring his eyes.

"Baby—"

"Don't you dare address me that way, Johnathan. When were you going to tell me?"

"There's no need to get bent out of shape, Gigi. I'm going to get it all back, I promise you," he swears, coming to crouch in front of me before taking hold of my hands. He stares up at me with a softness I see only when he requires my forgiveness.

I'm seconds away from blowing a gasket.

"Where did it go? With your inheritance and business, you've always made more than enough to support us. And yet there's nothing to show for this money spent."

He never came home with lavish gifts for Sera and me. Hasn't bought any new vehicles. No expensive jewelry or any impromptu vacations. And he so clearly hasn't paid off the house yet. It doesn't make any sense!

He works to swallow, radiating a nervous energy.

"I had a few too many poker nights with Frank," he admits.

I'm shaking my head in disbelief before he can finish. "John, you didn't," I breathe. "You gambled away our life savings!"

"Keep your voice down," he shushes, a tinge of anger in his tone. Truly, I believe he's only embarrassed.

As he should be.

"How do you expect to recover?" I ask, lowering my voice for Sera's sake.

"I—I don't know," he admits. "I could count cards or—"

I stand abruptly, tossing my journal onto the chair before I pace the checkered floor, so overwhelmed that I can no longer sit still.

I've married a dip.

"Do you realize how unbelievably dangerous that is? John, if you're caught, you could end up in the hoosegow—or worse, you could . . ." I can't even bear to finish that sentence.

He could be killed, and Sera and I would be stranded.

Worse yet, what if they came for us instead?

Maybe that man outside the window was a debt collector. But did he come from an agency, or is he a part of something more sinister?

It's not my own life I'm concerned about, but Sera's.

I can't even begin to fathom how he could put her in such a position.

He steps toward me, holding his hands out in a *calm down* gesture.

"I swear to you, no matter how I do it, I'll make everything back tenfold. Soon, our pockets will be so deep, we won't know what to do with all of it. I'm so close to getting this game down."

I'm not stupid enough to believe him.

When a gambler promises to make back everything he's squandered through more gambling, then he's well and truly lost.

But what am I supposed to do? I'm a housewife with no skills of my own. John has refused to allow me to work, preferring I take care of the house and our daughter. But Sera is older now, so if he keeps this up, I may have no choice.

For now, I am as bound to my husband as he is bound to a poker chip.

I give him my back, staring at the home that was supposed to embrace this family yet has only borne witness to sorrow. Tears well in my eyes, and helplessness takes root.

We are so much worse off than I imagined. If he had frivolous spending habits, we could sell those things and recoup our losses. But our money is tucked in the pockets of other men, and they won't be so kind about returning it.

"Gigi," he pleads, but I hold up a hand, silencing him.

"You're destroying this family, Johnathan," I choke out, the words as unstable as my heart rate. "And I have no choice but to let you."

March 22, 1944

I must be living in a nightmare.
A waking nightmare that I cannot seem to escape.
John will fix this. He has to!
If he doesn't, then what will become of Sera and me?
The family that is left between John and me is sparse, and
they do not have the means to take us in.
We'll be left in the streets!
He will fix this.
Dear God, let him fix this.

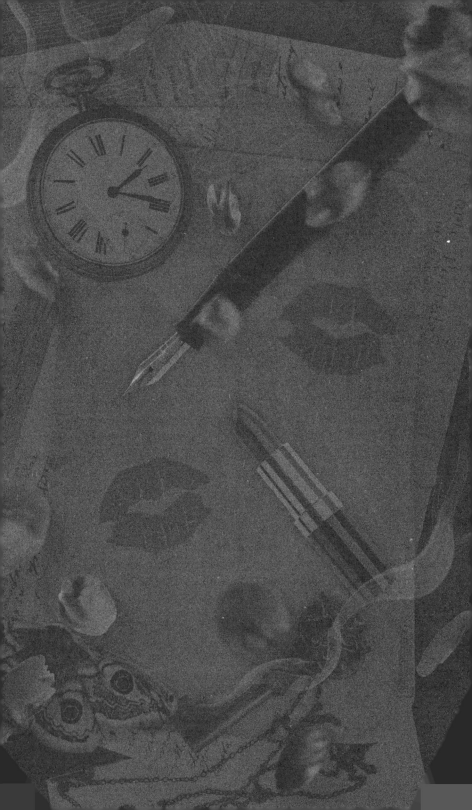

CHAPTER 3

THE RAVEN

April 4, 1944

There's a strange man outside my window.

He wears a black fedora and a trench coat, and he shields his face from me.

My hand trembles as I repeat the words in ink, forever ingrained in my journal.

This isn't the first time I've seen him, and I'm convinced he's here for John.

For two weeks now, my husband's been working on getting our money back. Each night, it's a different story. He wins some only to go belly-up.

He was out late playing poker last night, and it's likely he didn't make back enough to pay his dues. Maybe this man is here to collect on a debt he's owed. Or to hurt me.

Whatever the case, I'm terrified.

I had hoped he was no more than an apparition when I first saw him, but now I can see there is nothing ghostly about this man. He is as real as the heavy beat of my heart, and his presence as potent as the adrenaline coursing through my veins.

Yet I'm also intrigued. Even through the glass, I swear I can feel his burning stare. It's caressing my face, down the column of my throat, and over my breasts.

An undeniable burn has settled low in my stomach—something I haven't experienced in years. Not since John and I first began courting.

I'm unsure why this mysterious man is causing such a visceral reaction. Or why I'm allowing it to continue.

I should call the authorities. Call for help and plead for John to come home straightaway.

Still I do nothing—*say* nothing.

I'm home alone and terrified.

But I'm also intrigued.

April 6, 1944

"Is there something out there that I'm missing?"

Frank's sudden voice jolts me out of my daydream, startling me and nearly sending my heart flying out of my throat.

Hand over my chest, I stare up at him with widened eyes. His brow is furrowed, and his blue-green eyes are filled with concern. Despite his charming smile, he has strong features with his sharp jaw, cleft chin, and pointed nose. He has the type of face that instills fear when he gets a certain look in his eyes.

I suppose that's what makes him such a good detective.

"You startled me," I breathe.

Frank grins, then pointedly stares out of the bay window beside me. "Are you looking for something?"

My shadow.

"No one, of course. Don't be silly," I answer, chuckling nervously.

My visitor came back earlier this morning, again standing in the tree line. Just watching me, as he has been for the past couple weeks. I was too afraid to confront him, so I sat in my chair and watched him back. Hoping and praying that he didn't dare to break into my home. He left after an hour, yet my heart has refused to settle.

Frank scrutinizes me carefully while he pulls out his tobacco pipe from his coat pocket. "John tells me you've been bustin' his chops lately."

I huff, fluttering my hands over my dress only to give them something to do.

Frank Williams and John have been the best of friends since I met my husband. Frank's around nearly as much as John and knows me just as well, too.

"It seems you have enabled these new habits, haven't you?" I accuse, sending a cross look in his direction.

He takes a few moments to suck on his pipe, little ringlets of smoke releasing past his lips.

"Of course, I haven't. I go along to ensure his safety, but I don't partake."

"Why haven't you stopped him?" I snip.

He guffaws. "Have you tried to change his mind, dear? He's as stubborn as a bull."

I shake my head, so incredibly disappointed. For a long while, I was completely taken with my husband. I loved him thoroughly. And now . . . I don't know anymore.

I haven't known for years, truthfully.

"I've offered to help," Frank announces.

That draws my focus back to him, surprise flashing through me.

"Help? Help how?"

"The mortgage payment was late, and I paid it so you and Sera wouldn't be without a home," he says, flashing a suave smile my way.

Instantly, embarrassment stains my cheeks red. It's almost unheard of to pay for another man's bills. Just as quickly, I'm stricken with concern. John is in debt to his best friend, and that makes me deeply uncomfortable.

And while there is a tinge of relief that Sera and I won't be on the streets as of yet, there's a pit in my stomach, eating away at my insides.

For the first time, I'm grateful John and I didn't have a huge family like we had initially planned. My pregnancy with Sera was extremely complicated, and I nearly died giving birth to her.

I awoke in a hospital bed with my uterus removed from an emergency surgery and a healthy newborn baby. It was devastating for John and me that we would never be able to have another, but the two of us were eternally grateful for the one we did have.

Sera is more than enough for us, but there's always been a residual pain on the back side of my heart, grieving the children I'd never have.

But now? Now, I am grateful. I'm so beside myself trying to figure out how we'll support Sera, I couldn't imagine having multiple kids to worry about.

Frank crouches in front of me, the tobacco pipe tucked in his pocket again. He rests his palms on my lap. Heat sinks into my knees and deepens the cavernous pit beneath my ribs.

"I will always take care of you, Gigi. You should know that."

"That's not your duty, Frank," I snap.

"Maybe not," he concedes. "But I am happy to provide for you when your husband cannot. You and Sera are family to me, and I love you both dearly. I would never allow anything to happen to you two."

While Frank has expressed his love for us on many occasions, something about this proclamation feels different. Maybe because he only speaks of Sera and me rather than John and us as a family.

It's unsettling, to say the least. And in the back of my mind, I worry that now *I* am indebted to Frank, too.

Clearing my throat, I say, "It's greatly appreciated, but I'm sure this won't happen again." Yet we both know that's a false hope. John isn't getting any better—he's getting worse.

Deliberately, I remove his hands from my lap and stand, shuffling toward the kitchen where I can breathe.

"Gigi, you know he's in far worse debt than just a mortgage payment," he tells me. Irritation pricks at my nerves, and tension gathers in my shoulders.

"You don't think I *know* that?" I snap, whirling to face him. "He's drained all our money! Worse yet, he's been coming home sauced every night, slurring about how he's being cheated. We have nothing, Frank, and I will not allow you to continue to pay for his mistakes, either. We may have a roof over our heads for another month, but we will be in no better a position if he doesn't figure out a way to fix this."

He takes a step toward me. "I will do everything in my power to ensure that doesn't happen."

I exhale heavily and turn away once more. "Just help him kick this habit. That's all I need from you, Frank."

"I will, Gigi. I'd do anything for you." He said that already, yet I don't feel any less hopeless—or uncomfortable.

April 4, 1944

There's a strange man outside my window.
I do not know who he is or what he wants from me. But I
think he knows me. He watches me through the windows when
John's not home. He wears a fedora on his head, concealing his
face from me.
I haven't told John yet. I cannot fathom why, but something
keeps me from opening my mouth and admitting that a man is
watching me from the shadows. John wouldn't handle it well.
He'd go out with his shotgun and try to find him.
I must admit, I'm more afraid of what would happen to my
visitor should my husband succeed.
I'm very afraid of this strange man.
But my God, am I also intrigued.

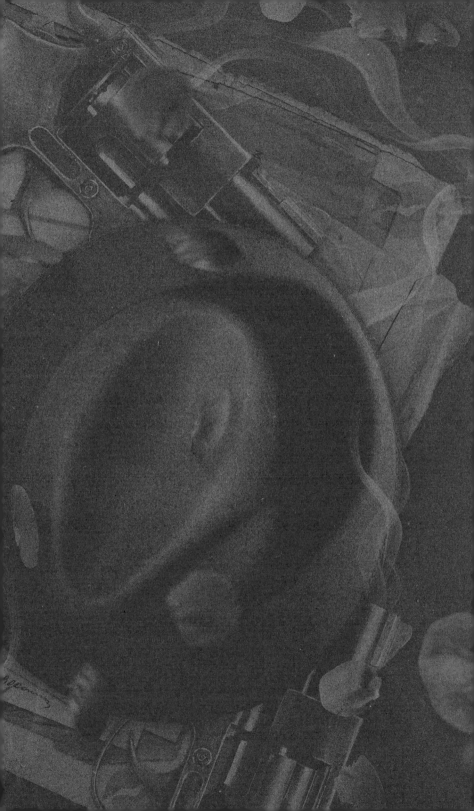

CHAPTER 4

THE PHANTOM

April 10, 1944

Genevieve Parsons knows she's being watched, yet she didn't bother to lock her door. I can't contain the smile that comes to my face.

I've been visiting her for weeks, though I've scarcely allowed her to see me. I've been staying hidden in the trees or just out of view from the window.

She's fascinating when she thinks no one is watching. Too often, I spent hours circling the manor, viewing her through windows while she cleaned, sang along to the radio, or sat in her chair writing in her journal.

She must write about me. And I'm curious to see what she has to say.

Earlier today, she was staring out the window, a mournful look on her face. It wasn't the first time I'd seen her appear sad, nor the first time I'd longed to run to her and make her forget about the husband I'm sure is ailing her. I could make her forget if I was inside her.

My feet carried me to her as if I was in a trance. My body was no longer mine to control, but hers. She sat in her rocking chair and turned to look out the window, and it was like feeling the sun warming my face for the first time in years after being trapped in a dark dungeon.

I watched with rapt fascination as her eyes landed on me and rounded at the corners. Fear flashed through them, yet *I* felt something entirely different.

Hunger.

All I felt was hunger.

Her gaze continuously drifted back toward me as she attempted to ignore me, to favor her journal rather than holding my stare. She was frightened, and she was trying to hide from me.

I fought with myself, tempted to walk through this very door and claim her as mine. But it was too soon. I needed to wait until her curiosity overrode her fright.

Maybe . . . that's already begun to happen, and her curiosity is winning.

Did she leave the door unlocked just for me?

It's not uncommon for normal civilians to leave their doors unlocked. Despite the rampant crime in Seattle, robberies are almost unheard of—unless they're actively related to the crime syndicate.

It's unfortunate Genevieve has found herself at the center of a dangerous man's desires. I don't feel guilty enough not to step through the front door and softly close it behind me.

It's the first time I've been inside Parsons Manor, and the interior is even odder than the exterior.

Where the hell did she get her taste from?

It's incredibly dark in here, but even with my limited eyesight, I'm able to glean a few details. A sparkling chandelier hangs above my head, dripping crystals from warped steel.

The black-and-white-checkered floor is prominent in the darkness, along with the black grand staircase directly ahead.

Silently, I trek further into the home, finding the living room to the left of the stairs. My gaze instantly finds the large bay window on my far left. There is Genevieve's rocking chair, with a stool placed right in front of it. It's where she sits while she pens in her journal. It's where I've seen her those few times I've caught her just watching the rain or staring almost longingly at the dark woods that surround her house.

My footsteps are light as I walk over to the chair, running my fingertips along the soft red velvet. Then I lean down and inhale, catching a faint whiff of her perfume. I pick up subtle accords of cinnamon, amber, oakmoss, sandalwood, and a touch of plum.

A scent made just for my Genevieve. It suits her perfectly.

Moving on, I note a black stone fireplace in the center of the wall before me, where red velvet couches surround it. Next to the fireplace is a stand with a radio atop, and I can imagine Genevieve and her daughter dancing next to it, laughing and singing along.

I feel a small pang in my chest, knowing I don't have the privilege of joining them. I'm destined to watch from afar, outside the bay window. It's a life I'll accept for now, though it doesn't enrage me any less to know that John has the pleasure of filling that role.

The kitchen is directly ahead opposite the bay window. I'm tempted to make my way through toward the back of the house where their glass room is. I've only seen it from the outside, but considering all three walls and the ceiling are made of glass, it wasn't difficult to inspect the inside of the room.

I'm sure it's beautiful there when the stars are out, but I'm too eager to see my Genevieve.

I'm unsure of which bedroom is hers, but I imagine it won't be far from her daughter's. From my research on the Parsons, I've learned quite a bit about them, including little Sera.

If I have it my way, someday in the future, John will be gone, and Sera will know me as a secondary father. I would never attempt to replace John, but I hope to find a way into her heart and will love her as Genevieve does. But that'll take time.

I can be patient.

The wooden steps hardly creak beneath my weight thanks to years of practice keeping light on my feet. The air is colder up here, and it's nearly pitch-black. I patiently wait to be able to make out the edges of the wall so as not to stumble into them.

The first bedroom is empty, so I move on to the next one on the left side of the hallway.

I'm careful as I open the door and find Sera curled up in a ball, softly snoring. Leaving her be, I shut the door and move on to locate Genevieve's room.

As I tread down the hallway, an ice-cold chill prickles at the back of my neck, stopping me in my tracks. Goose bumps scatter across my flesh, sending a tremor down my spine.

Slowly, I turn my head over my shoulder, finding nothing behind me.

Yet I feel a presence as surely as if blood runs through its veins.

During my research into the Parsons, I came across an article recounting a fire that took five men's lives while building the manor.

These lands claimed those souls, and I've seen shadows and angry faces a few times when hiding within the tree line.

They don't scare me, though.

I've faced far worse souls than those of a few construction workers.

Genevieve and John's bedroom is on the right side of the hall, far enough from Sera to give them a sense of privacy but close enough to hear if she's ever in distress.

The door quietly creaks as I open it, the sound of John's snores arising as I enter. Their room is decorated as dark as the rest of the house, and if it weren't for the balcony doors on the wall opposite me, I would be sightless. However, the thin curtains allow moonlight to peek through, offering me a view of the four-poster bed to my left.

John snorts, his body jolting from whatever dream is playing behind his eyelids. He's on the side of the bed closest to me, and the sight of his sleeping form prompts an array of murderous thoughts.

Without thinking, I slide my revolver from the back of my trousers, though I don't take aim. I just hold it while I fantasize about pressing the cool barrel to his forehead and pulling the trigger. The following *pop* would be as satisfying as watching the blood ooze from his skull.

The urge is so demanding, I force myself to walk around to Genevieve's side, farthest from the door.

At least John got that much right.

She sleeps on her side, her hands held together as if she's praying and tucked beneath her cheek. Her hair is curled into rollers, a satin scarf wrapped around them.

It's the first time I've seen her lips bare of red stain. I imagine it's a rare sight—one that John doesn't deserve. I get the inkling that her red lips are her armor, and I'd love nothing more than to be the one to strip it away and behold her at her most vulnerable. To see her face as bare as her body, lying on her back with her legs spread wide for me, her beautiful eyes sparkling up at me as she waits for me to worship her.

My cock hardens at the thought, pressing painfully against my trousers.

One day, I will convince her to grant me that honor. And when that day comes, she will never have screamed louder.

While I still grip the gun in one hand, I bring my other fist to my mouth, biting down on the soft flesh as the fantasy takes flight. The different positions I could arrange that beautiful body in. The sounds that would spill from her lips. I'd leave no part of her untouched, whether it's my hands or my tongue doing the exploring.

Fuck.

It takes control I didn't know I possessed to take a step back.

The carnal impulse to take her here and now is becoming difficult to suppress. I'd make her pathetic husband watch, unable to stop me from making his wife come undone in a way that he will *never* accomplish.

Inhaling sharply, I tuck my gun back into my waistband and head toward the door, my movements wooden and robotic.

It's physically painful for me to walk away from her, but I know that I must.

I'm a bad man, but I won't be her monster.

No.

I want to be her savior.

April 11, 1944

It's late morning, and I'm leaning against a thick trunk right on the outskirt of the tree line, watching Genevieve watch me. I puff on a cigar, a luxury I rarely allow myself.

I have distinct memories of my father smoking like a chimney—a habit my mother claimed he started when he was only ten years old. Many times, he came home on leave from the Great War, and I remember how he'd be hacking up a lung while sitting on the couch doing absolutely nothing, unable to breathe around the tar in his lungs.

I couldn't imagine how miserable he was during the battles, having to fight for his life while trying not to cough.

However, I still enjoy an occasional smoke when I need to take the edge off. Booze is a vice I refuse to indulge in when my job requires that I be alert. All it takes is one night getting sauced for a rival family to take advantage.

They won't put me in a grave so easily.

Genevieve glances at me again, evoking a smile on my lips, despite myself.

She nibbles on her red-painted lips, continuously tucking her perfectly curled black strands behind her ear. A nervous habit, it seems. From what I can see, she's wearing a pretty pale-pink floral dress.

Just for me, baby?

Crunching gravel beneath tires draws my attention away, prompting me to take a step back into the shadow of the trees.

Moments later, a milk truck is cruising up her driveway. The curved front end reads *Seattle Dairy*. The driver's side is doorless, allowing the worker to get in and out quickly. The back end of the truck is completely open with a flat bed and a metal canopy over it to protect the glass containers of milk piled beneath.

Genevieve catches sight of him, too, and immediately leaves her post. A few moments later, she opens the front door with a wide smile and a wave. The milkman steps out of the truck in his usual all-white uniform—and *Christ, can his clothing be any tighter?*

He grabs a basket from the side of the truck, returning her wave.

I step forward, recognizing him the moment I get a better look at the face beneath his white cap. Ernie, I think his name is. He's one of very few young men that were exempted from the draft for having a job deemed essential. He delivers to Angelo's estate, and too often, I've heard Angelo's sister, Lillian, gushing over him. She's completely taken with him, and it's a wonder Angelo hasn't shot the kid dead just to end his suffering from hearing her yap about him.

And now he's approaching *my* woman—who's *home alone.*

It's no goddamn secret that lonely wives tend to invite milkmen into their homes for a bit of fun. And now that I recall, Lillian has mentioned that this knucklehead in particular has accepted a few of those invitations. She had complained about it because he's evidently too scared to accept *her* invitation, being the sister to a mob boss.

Without thinking, I slide my gun from my trousers as he steps up onto Genevieve's porch. My chest burns with jealousy, hating that he has all her attention. If she dared to invite him . . . it'd be an incredibly cockeyed decision. Ernie would be dead before he could take a single step, and then Genevieve would have a terrible mess to clean up afterward.

She's a charming woman, yet I notice the tension lining Ernie's shoulders and his wooden movements. He glances around nervously as he grabs two empty bottles from the insulated box on her porch, exchanging them for fresh milk from his metal basket.

When he straightens, she's handing him the payment, her mouth moving as she says something to him. My eyes narrow as I count each second their skin touches.

But he moves away quickly, taking several apprehensive steps away from her as if he can sense my wrath.

Oddly, he doesn't seem to respond to her. He flits his restless stare around the house instead.

He's incredibly nervous, and the more I study him as Genevieve continues to attempt a conversation, the more I realize he's jittery and eager to leave.

Ernie abruptly turns and scurries off the porch right in the middle of Genevieve's talking. It's incredibly insulting, but I'm too relieved that he's leaving to find a need to correct that behavior.

He's in his truck and whipping it around within seconds, the glass milk bottles rattling as he zips out of the driveway, leaving gravel dust in his wake.

Genevieve stands at the doorway, wearing a perplexed expression.

Huh.

Guess the milkman doesn't like Parsons Manor.

April 11, 1944

I wrote a letter to Daisy today. I told her the truth about John and his gambling. Expressed how utterly heartbroken I am over my husband's actions.

I didn't hold back with her, and a large part of me dreads her response. Partly because I know what it will be. It's the same thing she has said many times throughout the years we've been friends.

"You settled for him."

I also told her that I miss when we were young girls, always up to no good and the best of friends. Back then, our biggest stress was homework and quizzes. And while Daisy didn't have the best homelife like me, we were able to escape our realities with each other.

Daisy is still my best friend, and though she lives a few hours away now, I tell her everything.

Except about my phantom.

It's the first time I've kept a secret from her, and I feel awful about it. Not only because I feel like I'm lying to her for the first time, but rather, if this man ends up hurting me, I will have made it easy for him to get away with it.

I'm such a fool.

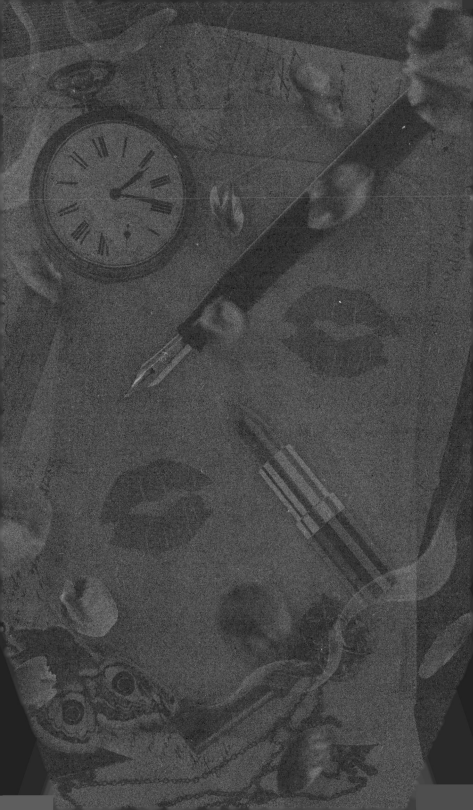

CHAPTER 5

THE RAVEN

April 12, 1944

The red lipstick glides across my lips with ease, though my hand quivers, causing me to smudge it above my Cupid's bow.

"You fool," I whisper beneath my breath, hurrying to grab a tissue and wipe the mistake from my skin. Once more, my trembling hand bears little grace, and I wipe too much away. Frustrated, I slap my hands on the counter, leaning heavily on them as I pinch my eyes shut and try to just . . . breathe, for God's sake.

What are you doing, Gigi?

My phantom has been visiting again; just yesterday, he was standing outside the window.

Watching me, as he seems content to do.

John left for work, his breath still reeking of booze as he walked out the front door, and Sera has gone to school.

Though the man has appeared in my window only a few times now, he comes during the day, hidden in the tree line where shadows conceal his face.

Today feels different. Like something more than his lurking beyond my window will happen.

And for reasons I refuse to consider, I've done my makeup heavier today and am wearing my best day dress.

For the better part of the morning, I avoid my own thoughts. At least the ones that are screaming at me, asking me what on earth I'm doing.

I have no answer.

Hours tick by while I go through my routine of chores. Washing our clothes before hanging them up on the clothesline behind the manor, dusting, dishes, picking up messes, and prepping for dinner. All the while, there isn't a single sight of him.

Later, I sit on my rocking chair, staring out the freshly cleaned window, waiting for my shadow to materialize.

Yet he doesn't. And my disappointment grows with each passing minute.

Sighing, I finally give up and relent to my flustered conscience, berating myself for being so silly. Waiting for a strange man to show up outside my window as if his actions haven't been concerning. As if *my* actions aren't concerning.

Trudging over to the kitchen island, I slump onto the barstool where bank notices litter the countertop. Rather than agonizing over my phantom, I stupidly focus on the papers that show my husband's betrayals.

I'm angry with myself, John, and the entire world.

My mood is foul when I hear the slight creak of the front door, but my brain instantly accepts it as my daughter coming home from school.

I don't even bother to look at the clock to confirm, and instead call out, "Afternoon, sweet pea. How was school?"

There's no answer, and that's when awareness comes barreling back to me, my eyes snapping to the clock above the stove. It's only eleven in the morning—Sera wouldn't be home yet. Nor would John.

My muscles tighten as quiet footsteps approach me from behind, the sound slow, heavy, and deliberate.

My breath catches as my spine snaps straight, but I'm too frightened to turn around.

Is it him?

My phantom.

The pitiful muscle in my chest ceases to work, and I can no longer draw oxygen into my lungs. Terror encases my being in solid ice.

Has he come to hurt me? To make John pay with my life?

Who will find me?

Please, God, don't let it be Sera.

A form appears in my periphery, my stare immediately focusing on him as he silently makes his way around the island.

His scent envelops me first. It's intoxicating, and my frazzled brain takes a moment to process the notes. Sandalwood, oranges, and a hint of tobacco.

Just as suddenly, he's before me—every feature in plain sight.

He's breathtaking. And so very tall, donning all-black attire with his fedora, long trench coat, button-up shirt, trousers, and dress shoes. It should be a drab outfit, but he looks expensive thanks to the glinting gold ring adorning his pinky finger. Even smells expensive.

The man stares down at me with piercing pale-blue eyes nestled beneath thick, dark brows—a contrast to his olive skin. Though something is off with the left one. Instead of a black pupil, it's completely blue, giving his eye an almost translucent effect.

He's blind in that eye, and my curiosity piques as to how it happened.

Regardless, it seems to only heighten his beauty. His black lashes are long, giving the illusion that he has kohl lining his eyelids.

The alluring man studies me carefully, just as I study him.

Never in my thirty-four years has a man made my breath stutter. But this man . . . he commands the very lungs beneath my bones.

My gaze traces over his nose—a small crook in it from a prior break—down to his full lips that are framed by a five-o'clock shadow. Though the small grazing of hairs doesn't dare hide the sharpness of his jawline.

He doesn't speak, nor do I. I'm frozen completely solid, and I fear only his burning stare has the capability to melt the ice from my bones.

I exhale, the breath stuttering from my throat.

Chest heaving, I still don't move a muscle as he slowly circles around the island. Within moments, he's next to me. Heat radiates from his body in waves, warming my skin, yet goose bumps rise on my flesh, and I can't help but shiver.

"What's your name?" I ask breathlessly.

He doesn't speak.

Instead, he lifts his hand and gently brushes a crooked finger against my cheek. I gasp, my skin coming alive beneath his electric touch. It takes monumental effort to keep still.

He circles around me, dragging his finger along my skin, moving it down to the back of my neck and sending chills down my spine. I glance at him, now standing on the other side of me, and note the breathtaking smirk tilting his lips.

Then he moves away, his touch disappearing, and his footsteps begin to retreat. I gather enough courage to tip my head over my shoulder, staring at his back with my mouth agape.

Almost as suddenly as he appeared, he's walking out the front door and leaving me in utter silence.

"What just happened?" I whisper to myself.

My fingers brush across my cheek where he had set me on fire just moments ago.

There's no physical evidence he was ever here.

Yet I feel his presence so strongly, he may as well have left his soul behind.

And my God, I fear how badly I hope he stays.

April 12, 1944

My red-painted lips press against the paper in my journal just as John, with his mussed hair and red eyes, stumbles through the bedroom door. The first few buttons of his white shirt are undone, and his tie is sloppily pulled away from his neck. He's hammered.

Again.

"I'm tellin' ya, Gigi. Hitler ain't gonna win this war, I just know it," he slurs, tugging at his tie until the cloth breaks free. He trips over his toes and catches himself on the nightstand, causing a few items to topple to the ground.

"My God, John, how much have you had to drink?" I whisper-shout, setting my journal on my nightstand.

He waves his hand dismissively. "Not much. Just a few drinks with Frank at the bar," he answers, though half the words are unintelligible.

"'Not much'?" I echo in disbelief. "You're going to break something!"

He sits heavily on the bed, and that causes me to jump out from under the quilt and storm around to his side. I grab his arm and tug. "You're getting your filthy clothes all over the sheets! I just cleaned these," I reprimand, my frustration mounting as he pulls away from my grip to take off his work shoes only to fail miserably, nearly toppling face-first toward the floor.

I catch him in time and once more try to pull him off the bed, which proves difficult when he's hardly capable of bearing his own weight.

"Gigi, I'm fine," he mumbles, finally standing upright.

"You know better than to sit on the bed in your outside clothes. Especially when you've just come from a bar!"

I don't know why I'm focusing so much on something so insignificant rather than the fact that we don't have money for him to spend on booze. He's come home like this more nights than not, and every time, I find out he's gambled and lost more of our money that we don't have.

Again.

Tears well in my eyes as I drag him to the washroom. I keep my eyes downcast as I lean him against the sink counter and begin unbuttoning the rest of his shirt.

"Why you got your red lipstick on s'late?" he mumbles, his thumb swiping over my lip and smudging the color down my chin. I huff and jerk my face away from his touch.

"I just finished writing in my journal. I got to it later than usual today—I've been cleaning the house for the better part," I snip, though my words shake from my mounting anger.

"Look at me, sweetheart," he coos, pinching my chin between his thumb and forefinger and forcing my gaze up to his.

I stare at him, searching for the man I fell in love with. For the man who swept me off my feet, vowed to my parents that he'd always take care of me, and who loved me so much, he built this house for me.

But the person in front of me now—I don't recognize him anymore.

He's more of a stranger than the man outside my window.

Disappointed, I remove my chin from his grasp and slip his button-up down his broad shoulders. Only then do I notice the bruises marring his chest.

"Dear God, John! What happened?" I ask, brushing my fingertips over the purple and blue mottling his pale skin.

He turns, forcing me to stumble away as he unbuckles his belt. His back isn't much better off, and dread sinks down my throat and drips to the pit of my stomach.

"Just a few people at the bar that run their mouths too much," he mutters.

"John, please tell me this isn't from the people you've gambled—"

"Drop it, Genevieve," he snaps, turning his head just enough to allow me to see his side profile. Anger furrows his brow, and his stare is sharper now. Less glazed.

I shake my head, the tears returning tenfold. A few spill over to my cheeks, and I quickly brush them away as my husband finishes undressing.

Before he can see me break down, I turn away and rush back to the bedroom. My heart has climbed into my throat, constricting in the tight space and making it feel as if it takes effort just to beat.

By the time he makes it to bed, I've cleaned the red off my lips and slipped beneath the covers, my back facing him. Without a word, I switch off the bedside lamp, leaving us in darkness.

"I love you, Gigi."

I don't respond.

He's breaking my heart, and the only thing I can feel for him is resentment.

I close my eyes and picture a different face to fall asleep to.

One that doesn't belong to my husband.

April 12, 1944

He came back again. I dare say I would be disappointed if he
didn't. John left for work, and Seraphina went off to school.
The minute the house emptied, I waited by the window.
Not my proudest moment, I must admit.
This time, he walked into the manor. I froze when he did,
terrified of what he would do but also anticipating his next move.
When he revealed the entirety of his face to me, without shadows
concealing his features, my breath caught.
He's beautiful. Piercing blue eyes. A strong jawline.
And big. So very big.
He approached me, still refusing to speak. He caressed my face.
So gently. He circled around me, letting his fingers drift across
my skin.
I shivered beneath his touch, and he smiled. His smile made my
heart stop in my chest.
And then he left. Walked out without a word. I almost pleaded
for him to come back, but I stopped myself.
He'll be back.

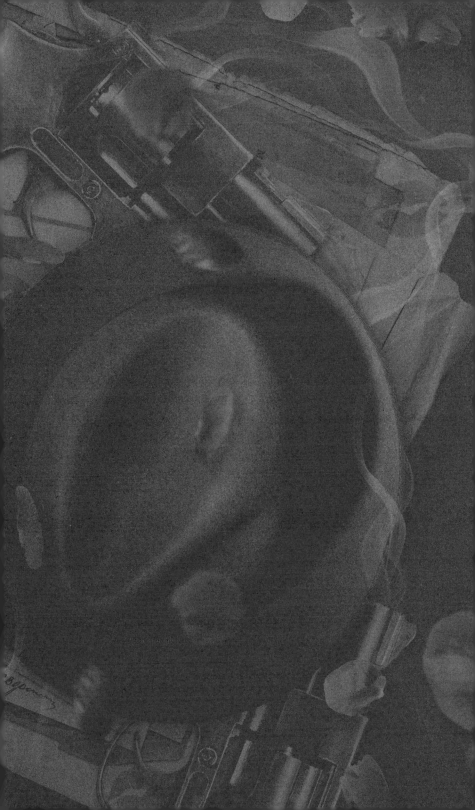

CHAPTER 6

THE PHANTOM

April 28, 1944

I f there's one thing I've learned about Genevieve Parsons, it's that she is as devoted to writing in her journal as she is to her husband.

I have no plans to come between her and her penmanship, but the latter—that, I would love nothing more than to change.

Rain descends from the heavens steadily, blurring my view of her through the bay window. Yet I know every detail of her face—features I've grown intimate with over the weeks. The softness that she reserves for her daughter. Every crease around her mouth and eyes when her husband comes home drunk. The fire that ignites in her bright-blue eyes, or the way her soft lips part when she catches sight of me.

If it were up to Angelo, she would be collateral for her husband's debts.

A means to an end.

Yet I fear she's meant to end me.

John managed to pay off his debt to Tommy, but then just last week, he dug himself into another hole. Now, he owes Tommy a grand and hasn't been able to claw his way out of it yet.

So yesterday, Paulie showed up at John's business, reminding him of his debt to the Salvatores, which John promised to pay. He asked for up to three months, which Angelo has granted him.

If he knows what's good for him, he will pay Tommy back sooner.

I slide my hands into the deep pockets of my trench coat and slowly approach the front door. My hat shields me from the worst of the storm, droplets pouring from the rim and pattering off the leather of my shoes.

If Genevieve is my end, then I open the door to death with no hesitation.

The warmth from the fireplace is instant as I enter the foyer. Above me, the chandelier's crystals twinkle in the soft light emitting from the sconces hanging on the dark walls. Cold rain puddles on the checkered floors, leaving a trail behind me as I head toward the living room to my left.

As soon as I round the corner, I'm faced with Genevieve standing before her chair, the piece of furniture rocking behind her.

Chest heaving, she stares at me wildly, as if she's an untamed animal that can't decide if it wants to devour me or run away.

I can't imagine that I stare at her any differently.

"If you wanted to hurt me, you would have by now," she breathes, almost as a placation to her own fearful thoughts.

She's wrong.

I do want to hurt her.

I'd love nothing more than to see her bare ass reddened by my hand. Or the faintest of bruises around her neck where my fingers grip as I drive into her. And those beautiful eyes filled with tears, pleading for me not to go any deeper down her throat.

Husbands don't hurt their wives the way I want to hurt her. They save those darker desires for their salacious nights in brothels, where those actions are considered disrespectful but acceptable.

Men are supposed to be gentle with the women they love. Take care of their fragile bodies and treat them like fine china.

I'm confident John has already loved her in such a way, and here she is—so very unsatisfied. If she weren't, she'd never stare at me so seductively.

There's nothing gentle about the way I plan to love Genevieve Parsons.

With slow, deliberate steps, I approach her. Her breath quickens as I near, yet she doesn't move. Doesn't run from me.

My hand twitches, desperate to touch her.

Even when I'm a mere foot away, she stays.

"Why won't you speak to me?" she asks, her voice a soft whine.

Because she's not ready.

She's not ready to hear what I plan to do with her—*to* her. Most of all, she's not ready to hear that I won't be letting her go.

Not ever.

The thought of it has my hand twitching again, this time for the gun tucked in the back of my trousers, ready to unleash my wrath on anyone who stands in my way of keeping Genevieve.

Just like every other time I've visited her, I lift one finger to her soft, reddened cheek. It's the only contact I allow myself. A small reprieve to my yearning—yet not nearly enough to abate it.

I want so much more, but her daughter will be home from school soon. I retreat and quickly leave, back out the front door, before I do something stupid like stay.

April 30, 1944

"The FBI pinched Manny Baldelli's son, Gabriele," Marco Viscuso announces, leaning back in his chair and locking his fingers across his stomach. He's the don of the Viscuso family, and beside him is his underboss and son, Gianni, and their *capo*, Luca.

The Viscusos have a good standing relationship with the Salvatores, having operated beneath Angelo's command for decades. As the godfather of Seattle, all families are beholden to him.

The Viscusos are loan sharks and are ruthless in ensuring they're the only other family in Seattle that has the authority to lend money— besides the Salvatores, of course. But Angelo has always been more interested in the trafficking business.

Marco stares at Angelo and his underboss and brother, Alfonso, with clear expectation. *What are you going to do to handle this?*

Alfonso gives him nothing in return.

He's always been a reserved man, and despite his quiet nature and limited conversational skills, he's intelligent and astute. He's a year younger than Angelo, but you'd think they were twins. Both with jet-black hair, aside from grays invading up through their sideburns. Aquiline noses, tan skin, and dark, bottomless eyes. The two of them grew up with birds dripping from their arms, and it's no surprise they married beautiful women.

"I heard about Gabriele," Alfonso responds shortly.

Marco stares at him for a beat, waiting for him to expand. When Alfonso stays silent, puffing on a cigar, Marco turns his gaze to Angelo.

"He a rat?" I ask calmly, wishing I had my own cigar with me right about now. There's a buzzing beneath my skin, and I haven't been able to place the cause. It's a nagging feeling, like there's something you've forgotten and you can't recall what.

We've gathered at a restaurant, Caserta's, on the outskirts of the city. It's a remote location that resides in neutral territory. Many mob families come here to dine, and there are strict rules in place that no one is to fight.

The owner, Orazio Caserta, is the son of a congressman and offers his restaurant as a haven for all families, regardless of their loyalties or positions of power. Their family has had ties to the Mafia even in Italy, and it's a relationship they continue to maintain. They only ask for two things: mutual respect and peace when in their territory.

It's a rule that even Angelo wouldn't dare cross.

We are all very aware that Orazio holds an extraordinary position, and if any of us were to break his rules, his father could have us in cuffs and in solitary confinement in a matter of days. No trial. No hope of freedom. Only a promise to slowly rot away in the dark for the rest of our miserable lives.

But that's not what truly keeps us all in line.

Orazio has made examples out of many and has built quite a barbaric reputation—one that mob bosses tell their young children stories about at night.

My fingers drum against the cherrywood table in a rhythmic pattern, and my knee bounces as I cast my gaze over the restaurant for the millionth time.

Orazio designed Caserta's to transport us back to Sicily. Stucco cream walls, vaulted ceilings with raw beams, rounded stone doorways, dark woods, paintings of grapes hung on the walls, and plant life mingles throughout the booths and tables.

Fedora Mingarelli croons "Un'ora sola ti vorrei" in the background, and the volume of chatter is at a quiet murmur. There are a few other families dining today, but no one that is cause for concern at the moment.

Upon entering, the doorman frisked us to ensure we brought no weapons onto the premises—another strict rule to access the restaurant.

It's calm. Peaceful.

Yet it still feels like something is . . . *off*.

"Ain't all Baldellis rats?" Marco retorts, scoffing.

"Last time a Baldelli got pinched, he was singin' like a canary," Luca pipes in, lighting a cigarette, inhaling deeply, and peering at me through the smoke billowing over his face.

"We have reason to believe that Gabriele could cause trouble for us should he run his mouth," Marco continues, his finger beginning to tap restlessly against his hand. "My son, Alessandro, was quite taken with one of Manny's daughters. He swears he didn't reveal any information about our operations to her or her brother, but my son is young and uses his cock more than his brain. Before Gabriele was pinched, he was heard talkin' to others about private matters with my family. Matters he would have known nothing about had my son kept his mouth shut."

Angelo arches a brow and takes a large swig of his Macallan scotch, hissing at the burn and smacking his lips. Still he says nothing.

"We've pledged our loyalty to you, Angelo. I was there for every one of your sons' birthdays. I was there when Antonio—"

"I'm aware of your attendance throughout my sons' lives, Marco," Angelo cuts in, an edge to his tone.

Antonio is Angelo's firstborn son, and he's currently fighting in the war alongside his brother and the second oldest, Alessio. The younger two, Aquino and Aretino, are seventeen and sixteen, respectively, and are on the brink of being drafted should this war continue for years yet.

That his two eldest sons are fighting in a brutal war has been a sore spot for Angelo since the day they were deployed two and a half years ago. And the knowledge that he may have to see off two more has driven him to the bottle on many occasions.

Angelo is many things, but no one could ever claim he isn't a damn good father.

"Speak plainly, Marco," Angelo clips impatiently.

"I'm requesting your blessin' to put a contract out on Gabriele before he can rat to the fuzz," the don says. "I understand this decision may come back to you, so I want it on the record."

I study Marco closely, noticing how his stare shifts toward the doorway every so often, as if he's waiting for someone to appear. I turn to look, noting that the entire wall is glass.

I return my focus to Marco just as he's glancing away from me. His left eye twitches as I stare at him. I may only have one working eye, but I'm not blind to the stench of apprehension leaking from Marco's pores and his obvious nervous tic.

Angelo taps his pointer finger against his glass contemplatively, takes a slow sip, sets it on the table, then taps it again.

"Gabriele is Manny's son. Should he be whacked, that could put my own sons in more danger," Angelo states.

"I understand—"

"I don't think you do, Marco," Angelo drawls, leaning back in his chair and staring down the don. "Clearly you didn't raise your son to understand the implications of not only sleeping with the daughter of a rival family but sharing business operations. Which leads me to believe that Alessandro does not see you as an authority figure to respect. That makes me question your authority, too, Marco."

Marco's lips thin into a firm line, and he casts another quick glance toward the door. Again, I follow his line of sight and find nothing.

"I assure you, Angelo, I have drilled into Alessandro's head the consequences—"

"If you want to drill consequences into his head, do so with a bullet," I cut in calmly.

Marco chokes, staring at me with bewilderment. Luca and Gianni glance at each other, apprehension beginning to line their shoulders. Gianni is Alessandro's older brother, and by the rage flashing across his eyes, he doesn't appreciate my suggestion.

As Angelo's consigliere, I'm in a unique position to counsel him. He also entrusts me to step in, offering suggestions or solutions on his behalf. And while this particular suggestion is cruel, it's not one that will be expected to be acted upon.

Which is exactly why I've said it.

"Your son has become a problem. If he suffers the consequences, I will allow you to ice Gabriele," Angelo says, reading my mind as he always does.

It's an ultimatum Marco won't take. Angelo gave him an impossible decision rather than an outright refusal as a lesson.

You can't have an out-of-control son and then cover his mistakes by putting other families at risk. If Marco wants to fix his problem, remove the actual problem.

If Gabriele's clipped, Manny *will* retaliate against Angelo and come after his sons. This risk costs far more than trouble for Marco's business operations.

"I understand, Angelo," Marco says finally, bowing his head.

Angelo waves his hand, signaling the Viscusos to leave, an order they waste no time in heeding.

Angelo and Alfonso are silent long after the Viscusos are gone, yet that feeling persists.

"Angelo," I say, staring out the window, watching as cars pass by on the street.

"Hmm?"

The Macallan is pricey. Knocking it out of Angelo's hand would be a great offense. But expensive scotch will never be worth more than his life. I slap his hand, sending the scotch careening off the table. Before Angelo has time to process what I've done, I'm out of my chair.

"Down!" I shout, watching in slow motion as a black car stops outside of Caserta's and the barrel of a tommy gun appears from the passenger window.

I'm tackling Angelo to the ground a second later just as dozens of bullets crash through the glass windows. Chaos erupts, and within seconds, everyone frequenting the restaurant is on their stomachs and crawling to find cover. I roll Angelo beneath the table, lying on top of him to shield him from the spray of bullets as an enforcer unleashes a magazine into the building.

Dinnerware shatters, thousands of glass shards raining over us. Food and drinks splatter to the tiled floor while cutlery, pictures, and lampshades come crashing down. It feels as if it lasts hours but could only have been a minute or two before the magazine's emptied.

Then . . . a squeal of tires and a deafening silence, save for "Tango del mare" by Oscar Carboni singing from the speakers.

Heart pounding, I peer down to find Angelo on his back, staring up at me with a feral grin on his face. Holding my gaze, he croons along with Oscar, though a wild look glimmers in his eyes.

Sighing, I roll off him and onto my back, quickly checking to ensure Alfonso is alive. He catches my stare, rage simmering in his dark eyes, but otherwise appears unharmed. Angelo's voice draws my attention back to him, and I watch my friend sing, his voice growing in volume even as patrons begin to check each other for injuries while a few women softly cry in the back corner.

I chuckle when he directs his gaze to me, his hands animated as he bellows the words.

Then I join in, the two of us belting out the lyrics while the restaurant falls silent once more.

Some of the patrons are merely spooked, and some of them are dead.

CHAPTER 7

THE RAVEN

May 2, 1944

"Mama, is Daddy okay?" Sera's sweet voice draws my attention away from the faucet and the hot water cascading over my hands as I scrub at a dish that's been clean for the last five minutes.

Is he okay?

Am I?

Our poor daughter has known nothing but stability for her entire life. Seeing her parents slowly crumble must be confusing to her.

We're failing her.

John is slowly descending deeper into the pits of his addiction to alcohol. His addiction to gambling has already taken hold of him, and now the draw of poker chips is no less alluring than a beautiful woman's crooked finger.

All the while, Sera lives blissfully on, convinced that she comes home to a happy family every day. Or, at least, she used to. She used to not have a worry in the world.

It breaks my heart knowing that may no longer be the case.

"Yes, baby, of course he is," I lie, finally setting the dish on the towel beside the sink. My hands are bright pink, and there's a lingering sting as I shut off the water and unplug the stopper, an obnoxious sound arising as the dirty water drains.

"He smells like whiskey when he comes home now."

I close my eyes, so very disappointed that she knows that.

"I know. He's been indulging a bit lately, hasn't he?" I say, staring at the sudsy water slowly swirling down the drain, feeling like it's a perfect representation of my life. Since when did it become comparable to dirty water filtering out of a sink?

"I hope he doesn't for my birthday party," she mutters.

I frown, feeling utterly helpless. Her fourteenth birthday is this Friday, but we're having a party Saturday. During the day, a few of her girlfriends and other classmates will meet at an arcade for cake and a few games. With the sugar rations, we won't be able to provide many sweets, but all the moms are hoping to scrounge up enough to satisfy the little heathens.

Later that night, we'll celebrate—just the three of us.

And I don't know that John will leave the booze alone. He'll have hell to pay if he doesn't, but lately, my wrath isn't enough to stop him.

I would hope not disappointing his daughter would be convincing enough, but I can't be certain about that anymore, either.

"Sweetheart, I will do everything in my power to make sure your daddy behaves," I assure.

I hate making false promises, so I don't dare swear to her that he will. But I'll certainly protect her however I can.

"Do you think it's because he doesn't love me anymore?"

The moment the last word leaves her mouth, my heart instantly cracks into pieces.

"Oh, baby, of course not!" I assure, turning to face her. She's sitting on a stool at the kitchen island, drawing random doodles in her notebook. I rush over to her and pull her into my embrace while placing a kiss on top of her head. "Your daddy loves you so much, as do I. Never think otherwise."

She nods, the movement shaky. She doesn't cry, but I can feel from the slight tremble rattling her bones that she's emotional. I can't imagine how long she's been thinking her father's drinking is her fault, and that only forms more fissures in my fragile heart. She doesn't deserve to feel like that. Ever.

"How about when Daddy comes home, I talk to him, and we plan a date night for the three of us? Maybe a drive-in. Or we could go out for ice cream?" I suggest, already feeling a pinch of worry.

We still have no money, and the last thing I should suggest is to spend more. But I'll scrounge up every last penny if it puts a smile on her sweet face. I'll figure it out. I always do.

"I'd love that," she whispers.

I pepper a few more kisses over the top of her head and release her. She's at that age where my hugs have time limits now. Before I return to the sink, I catch sight of a few of her drawings.

My heart drops when I notice she drew a figure of a man wearing a long trench coat and a fedora.

"Honey, who is that man you drew?" I ask lightly, pointing at the sketch. I quickly cross my arms, tucking my trembling hands beneath my armpits.

She shrugs. "I don't know."

Children and their cryptic, unhelpful answers when you need them most . . .

"Have you seen him before?"

She shrugs again. "There's been a couple times I thought I saw him outside our window, but when I looked again, he wasn't there."

Whatever is left of my heart is now scattered into a million different pieces—none of them where they belong.

I clear my throat. "You tell me if you see him again, yeah?"

"I guess, but he's not real, Mama," she insists, rolling her eyes.

Oh, how I wish that were true.

May 3, 1944

Parsons Manor is haunted—has been since the moment I moved in. Those poor souls that lost their lives here are angry. They always have been.

Some days, I worry that I'll end up here with them.

Because despite how vengeful the spirits are, I love this house. So much so, I feel it's become a part of me. When I'm angry, the temperature in the house drops as cold as the ice that clings to my words.

"You were supposed to help with his problem."

Frank stands beside me while I rock in my chair, staring out the bay window, my gaze locked onto his reflection in the glass. Or rather, what's behind him.

There's someone standing behind him—some*thing*.

It appears to be around seven feet tall, and while its form is entirely black, its sharp claws and red eyes are clear.

Whoever he was when he was alive is no longer who he is now.

It's no longer human.

Nor does it want Frank in this house.

The sight should bother me, but I've long grown used to the phantoms in this manor.

Must be why I'm so reckless with the one who continues to materialize before me long enough to whisper his finger across my flesh before disappearing again.

I look away from the sinister being and refocus on Frank's reflection.

I don't bother to tell him he's not alone.

Frank sighs. "Gigi, I've been trying. You know how stubborn he can be."

I do know that.

"I also know that we've barely scraped by these last couple of months. John recouped some of what he lost, just enough to pay a few bills. But we're still on the brink of losing everything, Frank. And his drinking . . ."

Frank takes a menacing step toward me, though his ire is reserved for his best friend. "Has he hurt you?"

I scoff. "Don't be ridiculous."

However, the nervous energy spilling from my pores is potent enough to taste. My fingers flutter over my white-and-blue-floral dress, twisting the thin cotton material until wrinkles form. I spent an hour ironing clothes this morning, including this dress.

I force myself to stop abusing the fabric and settle for staring out the window again.

The monster is no longer in the reflection, and I let out a sigh of relief at that. Sometimes they like to scratch and push, and I'd hate to explain to Frank that an invisible entity is responsible.

It may make John's drinking habit appear *reasonable*.

"Gigi," he says with a sigh. "I told you . . . If you need help, I'm here for you. Whatever you need, anything at all, just tell me. Even if it's comfort, I can help with that, too."

I shake my head, speechless and uncomfortable. John may as well have stuck his fist down my throat to grab hold of my heart and crush it. I can't speak around it, can't stop him from shattering the muscle that I always thought was his to take care of.

I'm just . . . so tired.

Tears well in my eyes, distorting Frank's reflection until my vision is as blurry as a window during a thunderstorm.

All the turbulent emotions inside me rise until they're bubbling out, and before I know it, the dam releases.

"He came home so drunk last night, he didn't even recognize me," I choke out past a sob.

I sense Frank's charging toward me, so I hold up a hand, stopping him in his tracks. The last thing I need is comfort.

At least . . . not from him.

"He had spit-up on his shirt, and when I was unbuttoning it to help him remove it, he laughed and asked me to promise not to tell his wife." A tear spills down my cheek, and I quickly wipe it away. "He wanted . . ." I shake my head, unable to finish. Unable to tell his best friend that he pinned me to the bed and fucked me, fully convinced I was a random floozy.

When he was finished, I slapped him sober.

I've never been the type of woman to let a man treat me so awfully, and I certainly won't start for my husband.

He had no idea what he had done when he awoke this morning.

Not until I told him, at least. He apologized profusely, claiming that his actions were not his own and that he deserved to be slapped for it.

Like he had every day for the last sixteen years, he tried to place a soft goodbye kiss on my lips, but for the first time, I turned my cheek to him.

Wherever my forgiveness is, it's not with him.

"Anyway," I continue, sniffling and wiping away a few more stray tears. "I don't expect you to fix his mistakes. I just want my husband back. I want my daughter's father back. If you can make that happen, that's the only thing I want from you."

The temperature in the room seems to drop, and for a moment, I'm convinced the monster has returned.

I face Frank, only to find him glaring at the floor, his knuckles bleached white from how tightly he curls his fingers into his palms. After a few beats, he turns his fiery stare up to mine.

Frowning, I open my mouth, prepared to ask him what's wrong, but he bites out his response first. "As you wish, Gigi."

Then he's turning and storming away, the front door slamming shut behind him moments later. I startle, a hand drifting over my racing heart.

What has gotten into all these men?

I can't keep up any longer, and I'm beginning to favor the ghosts that haunt these halls.

At least *they* are predictable.

May 3, 1944

I don't know if I've ever been so hurt.

My mother has called me many names in my life. Spit many insults at me. Degraded me in ways that have stuck with me for decades.

None of that compares to what John did to me last night.

In our years together, our lovemaking has always been gentle. Soft. The two of us hidden under the covers, nearly silent, as to not wake our daughter down the hall.

Last night, he ravaged me.

And it hurt.

Had he been in his right mind, had he even known who I was, I might have loved it. The aggressiveness, the untamed wildness to it, and the loud grunts coming from his throat that I don't think I have ever heard before.

Except he didn't know who I was. He didn't take care of me, and ensure I was ready for him. He didn't care about my well-being. He didn't care that, in his mind, I was another woman.

It hurt.

It still hurts.

CHAPTER 8

THE RAVEN

May 16, 1944

"What has gotten into you, Gigi?" John asks me, clearly affronted by the way he glowers at me while tugging at his tie, loosening the black-and-red-striped fabric.

He stares at me as if I'm a stranger.

He just finished his supper and is undressing before our armoire. Usually, I eat alongside him and Sera, but I excused myself, claiming that I didn't feel well, and left my husband and daughter alone at the dinner table.

Something I've only done when I was truly ill—too weak to put on my red lipstick.

I crawled into bed in my nightgown and cracked open my leather-bound book of Edgar Allan Poe poems. However, the evidence that I'm not as unwell as I'd like him to believe is smeared across my lips now.

I stare at the pages, the words to "The Raven" blurring in my unfocused vision.

I'd always been hopelessly called to horror and mystery novels as a young girl, obsessing over Edgar, Mary Shelley, H. P. Lovecraft, and many others. They are the reason I became enraptured with the gothic style. My mother hated that I read them, but she finally gave in when I became a much more agreeable child with one of their books in my hand.

But even Edgar can't save me from my husband tonight.

"Is it because I forgot your birthday yesterday? I told you I'm sorry about that, and we'll celebrate soon."

Unlike yesterday, he didn't come home drunk tonight, so his perception is sharper than it has been lately. He must see the secrets I'm storing inside beginning to leak through my pores.

"No. It's nothing," I deny, giving him an incredulous stare.

Though it did hurt that I turned thirty-five and he didn't say a word once he finally came home. Sera took the day off school yesterday, and we spent the day together dancing to the radio, baking cookies, playing board games, and then camping out in the glass room.

John didn't come home until nearly ten at night and was completely sauced when he did. While our daughter and I celebrated my birthday, he stayed out drinking and gambling all night, and frankly, I was okay with that. I'd take his absence over his inebriated presence any day.

The only birthday that mattered to me was Sera's, anyway. Thankfully, that day flew by without a hitch. John was a little sauced, but he did nothing to embarrass Sera or me, so I refrained from lecturing him about it.

"I just feel a little under the weather today."

Lies.

I *never* used to lie to my husband. To anyone, for that matter. My mother would've whipped me silly had I ever dared tell a lie to her. Telling the truth has been ingrained in me since I was a child.

And now, look at me.

This morning, he woke me up with an apology and a peck on the forehead. Fresh carnations awaited on the kitchen island, along with a new dress.

Then he was off to work again while Sera left for school. He promised he'd come home on time, which he did. But his playing poker and getting drunk on my birthday wasn't the only reason I felt unsettled today.

No. Earlier, the strange man entered my home again. I've lost count of how many times he's visited now. Many days, he stays outside, watching me from afar. Other days . . . he likes to see me up close.

Admittedly, I've long since grown desperate to know his name. So, I begged him to tell me, even offered to get on my knees if he'd only whisper it in my ear. And when that didn't work, I offered him a kiss. Even a touch, of my breasts or . . . or between my legs.

He smiled, yet my scandalous offerings were to no avail.

He brushed his fingers along my cheek, tucking a black curl behind my ear and leaving me a shivering mess in the wake of his electric touch.

The things I was willing to do just to hear his name . . .

Guilt eats at me, tearing apart my weary soul. The shame I feel is so heavy, and there are many moments where I gaze at my husband and ask myself how I could ever even think to stray.

It's been two months now, and still I keep my visitor a secret from my husband. Why? I'm not sure I'll ever know.

I love my husband. I've loved him for years. Except, I don't know if I'm *in* love with him anymore. Or if I ever was.

John continues to stare at me, suspicion inked into his irises. "Is there anything you want to talk about?"

The truth is on the tip of my tongue, teasing the air between us.

But then he grabs a whiskey bottle left stranded on the dresser from a previous night, unscrews the cap, and takes a long swig while he waits for my answer.

The truth dies, and I swallow it back down, the words burning a path down my throat as if I had been the one to drink the whiskey.

"No. There's nothing to say," I whisper.

Who he is now—I no longer recognize him.

And how could I tell my darkest secret to a complete stranger?

May 25, 1944

He's back.

And I'm certain it'll go precisely the same way it did all the other days. I'll ask him who he is. How he knows me. What he wants with me. And I'll receive no response in return.

Just . . . silence! It's infuriating that he's been stalking me for over two months and doesn't have the decency to even tell me why.

Yet each day, I hope he returns anyway. I'm terrified, yet the traitorous butterflies fluttering deep in the pits of my stomach have no concern for whom they erupt.

I should squash them for revealing the thoughts I try so hard to deny. To run from.

This man excites me in a way I've never felt before.

I've no idea where my mind has gone, but it certainly isn't in my skull any longer.

Once again, the strange man enters my home in silence. This time, I'm standing at the island, facing his direction as he approaches. He's unnaturally light on his feet—something that is telling of the type of man he is.

He's a phantom.

I could disappear without a trace.

And I'd deserve it, wouldn't I? So freely watching a stranger walk into my home as if he owns the place. And I'm allowing it as if I'm not a married woman with a daughter.

If he were to decide killing me is in his best interest, I'd only receive pity in response.

A helpless, idiotic woman she was, they'd say.

"What's your name?" I ask, attempting to insert even a morsel of authority in my voice.

He only smiles—a smile that is equally unsettling and disarming.

I narrow my eyes, growing frustrated with his silence. If I'm going to be so stupid, I should at least know the name of the man who I'm sacrificing my intelligence for.

"Tell me, or I'll have the police find out for me when I call them. Surely you can't hide who you are from them, can you?" I threaten, though my voice wobbles.

Nothing. Not a single word!

Growling, I whip around and angrily slide out the largest knife from the butcher block on the counter. Then I'm charging toward him and pressing my chest against his before I know it. I hold the tip of the knife to his throat, thinning my eyes into slits.

For a moment, his scent overwhelms me, and my mouth instantly waters from the sandalwood and oranges emanating from him. Just a hint of tobacco, too, and if I weren't so angry, I'd find an excuse to inhale him deeper.

"I demand you tell me. Or I'll slice your throat open without remorse. The authorities will understand, I'm sure," I snip, refocusing on his infuriatingly handsome face. "My husband's best friend is a detective. He'll believe me."

The corners of his lips tilt up, and fury erupts in my chest. "Why are you smiling?" I shout, stomping my heeled foot onto the checkered-tile floor. "Nothing about this is funny!"

Breathing heavily, I glare at him.

I've tried everything. And still—nothing!

"You don't want me," I surmise breathlessly. "So, what do you want?"

He shakes his head in disagreement, and when his lips part, I cease to breathe.

"I want you so badly, it hurts to breathe without you near," he whispers softly, finally—*finally*—gracing me with his voice.

It's so very deep. So rough, and alluring. Like waves crashing into treacherous boulders beneath a cliff. Both incredibly dangerous forces, yet where one is rugged, the other is beautiful. And together, they create something mesmerizing.

I work to swallow, paralysis rendering me speechless.

All this time, I've been pleading for him to speak. Now that he has, I'm at a loss for what to do.

"W-why?" I force out finally, the word coming out as a pathetic squeak.

Unconcerned with the knife pressed to his throat, he brushes my bottom lip with his thumb, staining it with crimson lipstick. Fire laces through my nerves, sparking brighter when he smears the residue over my chin. It seems crude, yet my eyes flutter, overwhelmed with how sensual it feels.

"Because you possess my lungs, as you do my heart, Genevieve. And I intend to take yours for myself," he answers, his voice deepening impossibly further.

His other hand closes around mine, where I hold the blade to his throat. He doesn't remove it from his skin but rather presses it in deeper. I gasp, resisting, but he doesn't allow it.

"I will bleed for you, *mia rosa*, but I must require you to bleed for me, too," he warns.

"Stop it," I breathe. "I don't want to hurt you."

He releases my hand, allowing me to pull the blade away from his skin. There's a small scratch and a tiny bead of blood forming atop. I've given myself worse paper cuts.

"How sweet," he murmurs darkly. "You would've fulfilled many of my desires if you had."

Drawing my gaze back up to his, we stare at each other silently. The tension between us is thick, and I find it difficult to breathe with him so close.

Especially because I feel the burn of his eyes caressing my face, down my neck, and over my breasts . . . The fire within them is as potent as if he were holding a lighter to my skin.

I work to swallow, my throat bobbing and drawing his attention there.

Can he see my pulse thrumming beneath the delicate flesh? With the way his pupil dilates and his tongue darts out to wet his bottom lip, it would appear so.

"What's your name?" I ask again breathlessly.

"Ronaldo."

"Do you want to hurt me, Ronaldo?"

"Never," he answers. "I only want to cherish you, Genevieve."

"How do you know my name?"

"I know everything about you. Just as I know you will love me, too."

That answer arrests the oxygen in my lungs. I'm struggling to find the words to respond to such a bold declaration when he smiles.

"Will you kiss me?" he asks quietly, gravel lining his throat.

I should slap him for asking such a thing from me.

Yet my gaze drifts down to his lips, which are slightly parted, awaiting my touch. I've already offered before, but . . . that was out of desperation.

Kissing him will only ensure he returns. I shouldn't lead him to believe that this is anything other than a crime. Or that I'm anything other than a helpless victim.

I don't feel like a victim, though.

I feel . . . powerful. Like I possess everything this handsome stranger could ever want, and it's up to me to decide if I give it to him.

I quite like how it feels.

"What's your last name?" I ask thoughtfully. "So I know who to report to the police should you grow too bold."

Mirth dances in his strange eyes. "Capello," he answers easily. "Ronaldo Capello."

I hum. "One kiss, Mr. Capello. Then you leave," I respond, my tone low. I hardly recognize my voice, as if a vixen has possessed me.

He doesn't move, allowing me to have control.

I press the knife to his throat again, a silent warning that while I may not want to, I *will* hurt him if he dares take more than I offer. The corner of his mouth ticks, seemingly pleased with my promise.

With my breath stuttering from my lungs, I take a single step into him, my breasts brushing against his chest. Surely he'll feel how brutally my heart beats against his. He'll feel how deeply I tremble at his nearness and how I'm on the verge of collapsing at his feet from how weak my knees have grown.

These reactions—they're nothing compared to how my body behaves the moment my lips connect with his.

Despite how heavily it rains outside, there's no thunder, which cannot exist without lightning. No wonder it's nowhere to be seen. I've somehow swallowed it the moment my lips touched Ronaldo's, and the electrical currents are ravaging my insides.

Time ceases to exist outside of the way he moves his mouth over mine, yet he's pulling away all too soon. I follow him, stepping into him closer, but he doesn't allow me another moment of his forbidden kiss.

He retreats, and it feels as if he's taking all the oxygen in my lungs with him. Instinctively, my fingers brush over my lips, both in awe of the way they tingle and entirely shocked by what just transpired.

A hint of a smirk graces Ronaldo's lips, then he's turning and walking out of the front door without another word, my knife still poised in the air where he had just been.

Dropping my hand, I stare sightlessly at the place he was standing only moments ago, questioning if I made the entire thing up.

I'm losing my mind.

I must be mad to kiss a complete stranger in the home my husband built for me.

I blink, now realizing my vision has blurred. A single tear slips down my cheek, only one thought running on a cycle through my head.

What have I done?

May 25, 1944

My phantom spoke to me today. For the first time since he
started coming around.

I raged at him, demanding he tell me his name, even going as far
as to hold a knife to his throat. I still can't believe I did that,
but that's what he seems to do to me.

Make me crazy.

He finally gave in, and I was shocked when he did.

His voice is so deep . . . so alluring. Once he spoke, I had hoped
he'd never stop.

I asked him why he kept coming around, watching me.

He confessed his desire for me. His need to have me. I asked for
his name, and he gave it.

Ronaldo.

An interesting name, but it suited him perfectly.

He didn't stay much longer after that. But he did ask for a kiss.
I was hesitant, but in the end, I kissed him.

I'm ashamed to admit I hadn't even considered John at that
moment. All I could think about was what his lips would feel like
on my own.

My imagination did not do it justice. When he kissed me, I flew
into the stars.

I don't think I've come back down yet.

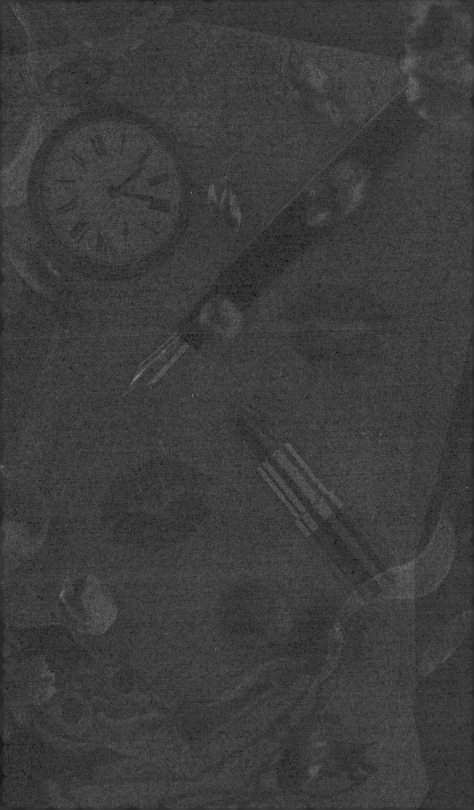

CHAPTER 9

THE RAVEN

June 7, 1944

I watch the moment the clock's hands turn from 8:59 to 9:00. I've been sitting in our bed, staring at the timepiece hanging on the wall opposite me for the past hour. Sera is already in bed, and John was due to arrive home from work four hours ago.

These days, it's the new normal.

Before, a hot meal would await him at the table, which he'd eat eagerly while listening to Sera tell us about her day at school or the deli. After dinner, we'd gather around the radio and dance to tunes. John taught Sera the jitterbug, and I would sing along, the three of us laughing until our cheeks ached.

Some nights, we'd bring blankets to the glass room. There, we would stare up at the sky and search for all the constellations.

Now, it's just Sera and me, occupying ourselves. I still dance and sing with her, but there's a noticeable absence that curves Sera's shoulders inward. She doesn't laugh as loud or smile as wide. And oftentimes, I catch her staring at the front door, wondering when her daddy is coming home.

I've tried my best to shield her from his drinking, but there have been many occasions where I failed, and she would smell the cheap whiskey on his breath and watch him make a fool of himself as he stumbled and tripped around the house.

I hate that she's witnessing our marriage fall apart. More so, I hate that her relationship with her father is also beginning to crumble.

I've long since written in my journal for the night, staining my rage in ink. So, I grab a Virginia Woolf novel, *To the Lighthouse*, from my nightstand, hoping to preoccupy my mind while I wait.

Twenty more minutes tick by before I hear the distinct slam of the front door. Instantly, my spine snaps straight, and I toss the book back onto my nightstand. I hadn't absorbed a single word of it.

My heart is thumping, the rage that's been simmering deep in my chest now coming to a boil.

A few moments later, John stumbles through the door, tripping over absolutely nothing, causing him to glare at the floor like it personally set out to make a fool of him. When he sets his sights on me, a sloppy smile takes over his face.

"What are you doing up so late?" he asks. He flicks a gaze at the clock, then narrows his eyes, as if that's going to make everything stop spinning.

"Don't you have to be up in a few hours to get Sera ready for school?

That's very irresponsible of you, Gigi," he blathers on.

"It's only nine, John. And if you weren't so drunk, you'd remember her last day of school was yesterday. She ended the year at the top of her class, remember?"

"Oh."

Oh? The infuriating man forgot about his daughter's accomplishment, and all he has to say is *oh*.

"You were supposed to take her out for ice cream today to celebrate," I remind him stonily. "She cried because she thought you were hurt."

He waves a dismissive hand in the air. "I'll tell her I'm sorry and take her out tomorrow instead. We got all summer."

My throat constricts with fury, and it takes three deep breaths before I cull my rage enough to speak at a reasonable volume.

I clear my throat. "Okay, then. Have you sent the check in for our mortgage and utilities today?"

He casts me an annoyed glare. "Yes, Gigi. I said I would, and so that's what I did. Why are you always nagging me?"

I bite my tongue before something malicious comes out of my mouth. He's clearly sauced, and I don't want to start a fight with him in this state.

"I'm just making sure you remembered since you've been so stressed," I respond woodenly.

"Well, now I'm even more stressed! I got paid today, and my entire damn check went to bills. Barely enough left for a pack of beer." He mutters the last sentence, and I'm so damn annoyed by it that it's impossible to curb my reaction.

I roll my eyes, and within a second, he's storming over to me and getting in my face before I can utter a word. Like a flip of a switch, he went from normal to a raging man.

"Don't you roll your eyes at me. I am your husband, and you will show me respect," he hisses, spittle wetting my face.

I see red, and my hands tremble from the fury working its way through my system.

John has *never* talked to me like that.

It takes effort to remain still rather than lashing out. My palm itches to connect with his face. Until he began drinking, I'd never lain hands on him. Although I never had a reason to before.

"You're drunk, Johnathan. Where have you been?" I ask flatly, forcing calmness in my tone. My nails dig into the flesh of my palms, an attempt to abate the shaking.

He straightens, staring down at me. "You know where I've been," he mutters, turning away from me. "You have no idea what it's like to be me. I go to work and bust my ass all day while you sit at home and write in that—that *stupid* journal! What do you even do to deserve to live in this big house, Gigi? Wasn't it enough that we decorated it like some godforsaken horror film? You get to just live in luxury, and when I finally find something to blow off some steam, I'm not allowed!"

By the time he finishes his tirade, his chest is heaving, and I'm struck speechless. Slowly, I get out of the bed, seething at him.

"You told me you didn't want me to get a job," I bite out. "I offered to join the workforce now that so many are fighting in this war, and you refused to let me! You said I needed to be home with Sera, and you were happy to take care of our needs."

"Do you know how embarrassing it'd be for me to send my wife off to work? The men at the firm would laugh at me!"

"Then *what do you want from me?*" I almost shout, losing the precarious hold I had on my temper but mindful of our daughter enough to quiet my volume.

He's silent for a beat, then he's getting in my face again. This time, I make no promises to myself not to slap him stupid.

"I want you to do your wifely duties," he spits.

Before I can ask what exactly he means by that, he's fisting my hair tightly at the back of my head and forcing my face into the bed. I struggle against him, my nails clawing at his hand as panic overrides any rational thinking.

"No, no, no, stop, John!" I whisper-shout.

Even intoxicated, he's so much stronger than I am. I bite back a scream, conscious that Sera is sleeping down the hallway, and the last thing I want is for her to walk in on this. It would devastate me to have her see her father like this.

"John, stop!" I bark, still attempting to keep my volume down while also hoping my voice gets through to him.

It doesn't.

He's lifting my nightgown and pushing it up past my hips. He tears down my knickers, exposing me to him.

"John," I snap louder, but again, he doesn't listen.

"Please, just stop," I whisper, the words coming out as a helpless squeak.

Still he doesn't listen.

I force myself to still completely, my muscles locking tight. There's no use in fighting, and I refuse to wake Sera up. The best thing to do is just let it happen. The sooner I let him finish, the sooner he gets away from me.

Tears well up in my eyes and spill over as he quickly removes his belt and unfastens his trousers. He breathes heavily as I feel him push inside me, the pain blinding for a moment.

He grunts, keeping my hair fisted in his grip as he moves. With each thrust, his groans grow louder. I squeeze my eyes shut, praying that Sera stays asleep.

Did he bother to lock our door? No, he's too far gone.

Anytime we've been intimate before, we were always so careful to keep our noise level below a whisper. She won't understand what's happening if she sees this. She *can't* see this.

Inhaling deeply, I arch my back and squeeze my legs tighter, evoking a sharp moan from him. His pace quickens, and my heart thuds heavily, silently urging him on.

One more thrust and he stills, another sharp grunt leaving his lips. Once he's finished, he pulls away, and I make quick work of scrambling off the bed to pull up my underwear and fix my nightdress.

John tucks himself away, a satisfied gleam in his glazed eyes.

"See? That's what a husband should come home to every night. I work hard, Gigi. It's the least you could do."

I swallow down my retort and instead hurry out of the room. Unsurprisingly, he doesn't stop me. He got what he wanted, and I'm sure it'll be a matter of five seconds before he passes out.

I check on Sera first, creaking the door open to see her form huddled beneath the blankets, sleeping soundly. My eyes close, the relief almost dizzying. Overcome with it, I lean against the doorframe and just watch her for a moment, a few more tears slipping down my cheek.

If this is my life, it's one I'll readily accept for her. If she sleeps as peacefully as she does now, it's worth it. All of this with John . . . it's worth it.

Inhaling deeply, I leave her to her dreams and head to the washroom. Moonlight spears through the window, offering just enough visibility to use the toilet and quickly clean myself up. When I'm finished, I stand at the sink, staring at myself in the mirror. I can't see much of my features, but I make out enough to notice how glossy my eyes are and the tearstains tracking down my cheeks.

I turn the faucet on just enough for a small trickle of water to come out, and I splatter it on my face, wiping away any evidence that I was upset.

After patting my face dry, I straighten again, only to bite back a scream for the second time tonight.

There's a man standing behind me, directly in front of the window, only his silhouette visible. I hadn't noticed when I was washing my face, but the temperature in the room has dropped, chilling the air substantially.

I'm paralyzed, unable to move save for my heart thundering in my chest. Typically, I ignore them. I've found that the more I acknowledge them, the more they seek my attention. I'm not sure if the events tonight have me more rattled than usual, but I can't seem to pull myself away from the mirror and calmly leave.

Instead, I can only stand frozen, silently panicking.

A few beats later, the man begins to approach, sending my heart flying up into my throat. My trembling becomes violent, yet still my feet refuse to unglue from the floor.

It comes closer and closer until I feel its ice-cold breath whispering across my nape. It's *right* behind me now.

My mind screams at me to get out, my survival instincts thrashing against their unmovable prison, desperately trying to get me to just *move*.

A deep growl emanates from its chest, and apparently, that's the trigger I needed to finally move. Instantly, I dart to my left toward the door and scramble out of the washroom without looking back.

Stomach filled with adrenaline and panic, I run down the hallway and burst into my bedroom, almost completely forgetting about who I left inside.

I softly shut the door behind me and plant myself against it as I coax my breathing into a normal rhythm again. It takes a few minutes, but soon, I calm myself enough for my heart to return to a steady pace. It's not the first time a spirit has gotten that close, but it has been a little while. And of course, it tested that boundary when I was at my most vulnerable.

Men.

My disdain for them even surpasses the physical realm.

I take another deep breath and focus on my husband, my upper lip instantly curling with revulsion.

As suspected, John is passed out on the bed, snoring loudly. And of course, he's still in his work clothes, which in itself is abhorrent.

Though I suppose I shouldn't be surprised to be sleeping next to filth.

My husband has proven himself to be exactly that after tonight.

June 7, 1944

I think I hate my husband.

What a terrible thing for me to write. To even think.

Yet, staring at the words now, I cannot find even a morsel of regret.
How could he do this to Sera and me? How could he build a beautiful
life with me, create an even more beautiful child, and then destroy us
so callously?

I'm heartbroken.

Not only for myself, but for our daughter, too. He had made a
promise to take her out for ice cream after dinner to celebrate her
ending the school year at the top of her class. He never showed, and
Sera broke into tears, concerned that something terrible had
happened to her father.

And that . . . that made me so angry. Our sweet daughter didn't
think for one second that her father had forgotten about her. The
only thing that made sense in her head was that he had gotten in
some sort of accident.

I knew the truth, but how could I tell her? How could I wittingly
break her heart?

So I lied. I assured her that her father was okay and that he must
have gotten held up late by an important client. She understands her
daddy works hard, and while disappointed, I know that she will
forgive him.

But I won't.

I think I hate my husband.

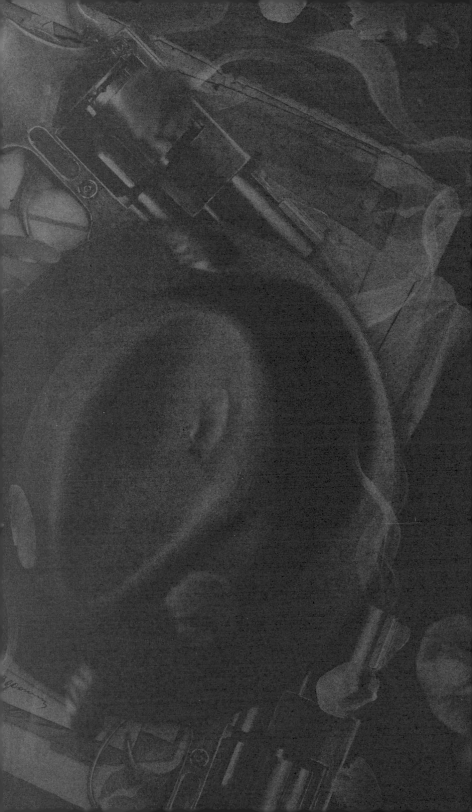

CHAPTER 10

THE PHANTOM

June 8, 1944

O f all the days I've walked into Parsons Manor, I've never entered without being greeted by sparkling blue eyes.

For the past two weeks, I've visited her every day while Sera and John were away, spending hours with her until it was time for her family to come home. And as each day passed, I've watched her timidness melt away as she grew accustomed to my presence. Trusting, even.

I've been careful with her, focusing on baring ourselves for one another emotionally rather than physically. I've been honest about needing to keep my job a secret for now, and she's respected it. However,

I did assure her I'm not visiting her because of John's debts. At least, not anymore.

Otherwise, we've stripped ourselves raw and have shared secrets and dreams that neither of us has confessed to another soul. She's told me everything about herself, from her strict upbringing at the hands of her religious mother and the neglect of her absent father to her sightings of the ghosts that haunt Parsons Manor and how they both frighten and excite her. My obsession for her has deepened to love, and I care little about how short of a time I've known her. I only care that I spend the rest of my life with her.

Today, I stop short, taking in the view of Genevieve sitting in her rocking chair, staring out the window sightlessly, hands crossed in her lap; her journal is nowhere to be seen. It's late morning. The sunshine glows on her face, yet even beneath the bright rays she radiates darkness.

Concern pinches my brow, and I slowly approach her, cautious of startling her out of her musings.

"Mia rosa?" I ask softly.

After a few seconds, she drags her gaze to mine. Her stare is empty, and though her black hair is curled to perfection and her lips are painted red, she looks nothing like my Genevieve.

I close the distance between us, adrenaline and worry unfurling in the pit of my stomach. My heart races as I sit on the stool in front of her and grab hold of her hand, frowning when I feel how cold it is.

"What's happened?" I ask, struggling to keep my voice calm.

Instantly, her bottom lip trembles, and tears spring to her eyes. There's no thought to my actions, only instinct. I stand and scoop her from the chair and carry her over to the couch. Setting her on the plush velvet, I coerce her to lie down before lying next to her, pulling her into my embrace. She's stiff but doesn't resist, and she lays her head on my shoulder as she tucks her feet beneath her.

"My love, please tell me what's happened," I plead, tucking a curl behind her ear.

A soft sob ruptures from her throat, prompting her to slap a hand over her mouth to contain it. She shakes her head as if she's disappointed in herself and trembles in my hold while she works to calm down. All the while, I remind myself that I can't kill someone if I don't know who they are yet.

It does little to ease the murderous rage building inside of me or the need to get up and wrap my bare hands around someone's throat as I watch the life drain from their eyes.

"I-I'm fine," she chokes out finally.

I crook a finger beneath her wobbling chin and gently lift her watery gaze to mine.

"Tell me the truth," I demand gently.

She sniffles, then hiccups. Before she can cover her mouth again in embarrassment, I grab hold of her hand and squeeze.

Sighing, she closes her eyes. "John," she whispers, her words cracking with unshed tears. The explosion of my fury is instant, and it takes everything in me to keep myself planted on the cushion. "He came home sauced again last night."

Inhaling deeply, I take a few seconds to compose myself before I ask, "Did he hurt you, *mia rosa*?"

Her response is delayed, but she ultimately nods. Another deep breath, though blackness licks at the edges of the little vision I have left.

"Will you tell me what he's done?"

"Ronaldo, I don't . . . I don't want you to hurt him."

If she's fearful for his life, then he's done something that deserves retribution. And that . . . That has a rage so black polluting my insides, my organs feel like they're wilting and rotting beneath it.

"Genevieve." The word is stern though not sharp. I refuse to force her if she truly doesn't want to share, but if she chooses not to, I will have to ask John myself.

She sighs. "He . . . he just demanded a marital duty from me, and I told him no, but he didn't listen so—"

I stand so abruptly, she gasps. I hold up my pointer finger at her, silently asking for a moment.

My vision is completely snuffed. The average human is capable of a wide range of emotions, yet I can't seem to feel a single one outside the urge for violence. There's a beast I keep contained deep inside me. It's a side of me I scarcely let free. And for the first time in *years*, I'm on the verge of letting it loose.

John Parsons is a dead man.

There are many men who were raised to believe that they have ownership of their wives' bodies. And there are many women who are raised being told to give that autonomy away. And they do—simply because it's expected of them.

But that is *not* how I was raised. According to my mother, my father didn't stand for the mistreatment of women, and neither do I.

For John to—

I close my eyes and try to breathe.

For John to force himself on Genevieve is one of the worst things a man can do to a woman. He violated her. He stripped her of her humanity and took something from her she was not willing to give.

"Ronaldo." The whisper is soft, and I hate that she feels the need to placate *me*.

It takes a few more moments for my limited vision to return. When it does, I sit beside her and pull her back into my embrace.

"I'm sorry, my love," I rasp, placing a gentle kiss on her forehead. "I lost my mind."

She peers up at me with sadness, her thick black lashes heavy with tears and clumped into little spikes. Though the redness in the whites of her eyes brightens her blue irises into a startling shade. Her smile is somber as she asks, "Have you found it?"

I shake my head. "Not since the first moment I saw you," I confess quietly, brushing the pad of my thumb over her red bottom lip. "I don't understand how anyone could ever hurt you, Genevieve."

She raises a hand, gently brushing her fingers over my chin, my stubble scraping against her fingertips.

"You hurt people, don't you, Ronaldo?" she asks. Her tone isn't accusing but curious.

"Yes," I admit, unable to lie to her.

"Will you refrain from hurting John for me?"

Again, I close my eyes, searching for my next breath. How can I deny her when I know it would break her heart?

You can't.

I know.

"Why? Tell me why."

"Because he's the father of my child," she responds softly. "And as much as it pains me to look at him, I don't wish to see him dead. We've been married for so long, and while these past few months have opened my eyes to how truly unhappy I've been in our marriage, it would devastate my daughter if she lost him, and that hurts worse. That hurts so much worse than anything he could ever do to me. I know it's hard to understand, but even if not for me, please do it for Sera. She's the only reason that truly matters."

I've never met a mother as selfless as her.

My mother lost herself after my father died. She held on for years, but by the time she passed, I no longer recognized her.

I didn't hate her for loving him so much, but I resented her for loving him more than me.

While I may never know what it's like to have a child of my own, I do understand that kind of love. And it's exactly that love that has me conceding. I dip my chin in acquiescence.

"Promise me," she whispers. "Promise me you will never play a hand in his death."

One day, I will tell her just how close her husband has come to death, though not by my hands. He only just paid back Tommy, plus interest, but I imagine he will be back at that table in no time, digging himself into yet another hole.

The muscle in my jaw pulses, but I force myself to speak the words. "I promise, *mia rosa*."

Her fingers brush over my cheek again, almost in reverence.

"Distract me. Tell me something about you I don't know," she pleads softly.

It takes a few moments of sifting through memories, trying to find something of substance before I recall the scar on my hand.

I hold it up for her, showing her the thin, white line spearing across the top of my palm.

"I got this from saving a baby raccoon when I was fifteen," I tell her. Her eyes widen, interest sparking in her gaze. "He was caught in a chain-link fence and screaming at the top of his lungs. He was struggling and hurting himself. Poor thing freaked out when he saw me coming."

"Did he bite you?" she asks.

"Thankfully, no. The metal was digging into his sides, and I was trying to keep him from hurting himself more when I was trying to get him out. Got really cut up in the process and earned me this gash." Her fingers trace over it gently. "But once he was free, he just stood there and stared at me."

"Really? He didn't run off?"

"Quite the opposite. He followed me around everywhere I went after that, and he even let me clean his wounds from the fence. I named him Links."

She stares up at me with wonder. "You had a pet raccoon."

I grin. "I suppose I did. He was my friend and lived a long life."

Her bottom lip trembles, but she quickly drops her gaze, likely wanting to refocus her attention before she cries again. "And the ring? Where did it come from?"

"My mother gifted it to my father on their first wedding anniversary. After he passed, she gave it to me. It was too big for me at first, but once I grew into it, I put it on and haven't taken it off since."

"That's so sweet," she whispers. "You're good at holding on to things."

"I am," I agree. "Just as I will always hold on to you, *mia rosa*."

She lifts her watery blue gaze to mine again. "Why do you call me that? *Mia rosa?*" she asks softly.

I grab her hand briefly, placing a kiss atop it before letting her continue whispering her fingers across my skin. There are no words to describe how heartwarming it is knowing she has gone through something horrific yet still seeks my touch.

"My mother told me a story about the time my father asked her out on their first date. He was in love with her and chased after her wherever she went. She said he'd asked her on dates a thousand times before, and every time she would ask him why. He would give these shallow reasons, like her beauty or her smile and so on. So, she said no. Then, one day, he came to her with a single rose in his hands, the thorns plucked from the stem. He handed it to her and asked her on a date. When she asked why, he admitted that he was dirt poor and stole that rose from his neighbor's garden. The owner caught him and shot at him for trespassing. Clearly, he got away unscathed except for his bleeding hand. The thorns had pricked him, and he couldn't fathom giving my mother a rose when it could hurt her. So, he sheared them from the stem and ran straight to her. He told her that despite his nearly dying, he'd do it again. That he'd put himself through hell just to see her smile. That he would take all her pain so she would suffer none."

By the time I'm finished, I look down to find Genevieve staring up at me with tear-filled eyes.

"She said yes, right? She didn't make him try again?"

I grin. "How could she say no?"

She smiles. "If you are anything like your father, then I imagine she couldn't."

I swipe away a curl from her face, reveling in the feel of her soft skin against mine.

"I call you my rose because for you, I would take all your pain so you would suffer none," I tell her softly. "I would go through hell for you. Die for you. Do anything you asked. I love you, *mia rosa*. More than you will ever know."

She smiles, albeit shakily, a single tear slipping down her cheek. "Can you sing, Ronaldo?"

I'm surprised by her question, but I know that despite what I would do for her, she *is* suffering. So, if singing eases that, I would do whatever she asked. After a few beats, I say, "A little."

"Can you sing something for me? I promise I'll return the favor one day."

I could never deny her.

I settle deeper into the couch, the two of us getting comfortable. She lays her head on my chest, and I croon in her ear the words to "T'ho vista piangere" by Alfredo Clerici.

The sad song lulls her to sleep, but I may never find another moment of rest until John Parsons ceases to breathe.

And since I'm beholden to my promise to Genevieve, I suppose the only thing for me to do is spend every waking hour loving her the way she deserves.

June 8, 1944

I think I love Ronaldo.

Another terrible thing for me to write as a married woman. Yet I still do not feel any regret for my words.

Before Ronaldo arrived, I was in an unimaginable amount of pain after what John did to me last night. Truthfully, I was still trying to wrap my head around it. To somehow justify his actions in my head to make it hurt less. I'm his wife, and he didn't do anything I haven't allowed him to do before. Yet those reminders didn't make me feel any less empty. Nor did it rid me of the utter negativity polluting my mind and soul. It made me want to crawl outside my skin. And for the first time in my life, I truly did not want to be alive, if only to stop feeling that way.

If I had slipped off into nothingness, I would have welcomed it.

Until Ronaldo walked in.

While these feelings did not magically disappear, I did find a little morsel of light in the darkness plaguing my mind.

When he cradled me to his chest and told me about the beautiful love story between his parents, it settled my aching heart a little.

And then, when he looked down upon me, even more beautiful words spilling from his lips, it started to sing.

I couldn't help but ask him to sing, too. I wanted to know if his voice would harmonize with the melody in my heart.

It did.

CHAPTER 11

THE RAVEN

July 7, 1944

My heart is racing, and I'm not entirely sure why yet.
Lies. You know exactly why.
It's been years since I've felt this nervous. The butterflies in my stomach and I are old friends, and the last time they visited was my first date with John. I thought I laid them to rest after that, but it appears they've come back with a vengeance.

I've reapplied my red lipstick twice already, and it's hardly been an hour since Sera left for school. She's taking a few summer classes so she can graduate early. Other days, she's either working at the deli or spending time with her best friend, Martha, and her family.

Martha is the oldest child and had to drop out of school this past year to care for her younger siblings while her parents work. They're not very wealthy, so Sera has taken it upon herself to pick up more hours at the deli so she can help their family.

When she first told me, I bawled like a baby in awe of how she's grown up to be so selfless.

Unlike her mother.

However, I did ask her to conserve most of her earnings, preaching about the importance of saving money. I didn't tell her I'm terrified she'll need that money if John puts us on the streets.

Sighing, I force myself to keep my tongue in my mouth this time. I'm paranoid that my lipstick smudged on my teeth, so I keep licking them.

I'm acting like a fool. A lovestruck fool.

Ever since Ronaldo found out what John did to me, he's been diligent in visiting me during the week over the past month. We've spent most days getting to know one another—sharing our childhoods and stories from our youth. And aside from a few stolen kisses and his holding me in his arms, he's kept his hands to himself. At first, I was thankful, far too shaken to even desire a man's touch. But now, I crave it. I want *him* to replace that terrible memory.

Luckily, John hasn't forced himself on me since, but he has lost his temper and acted aggressively a few times, throwing things in fits of drunken rage. One night, he punched a hole in the wall, which he promptly fixed that weekend.

He's out of control, but there is one facet I have control of, and that's Ronaldo's affection.

I want to know what being loved—*truly* loved—by Ronaldo feels like. And I want him to know what it's like to be truly loved by *me*.

And I intend for us to find out today.

I place a hand on my forehead, shaking my head at myself. With my free hand, I lean heavily on the kitchen island. I'm getting myself all worked up, and it may be for nothing. There's no guarantee he'll even show up tod—

The front door opens, then clicks shut behind me. My heart stalls in my chest, and my muscles tighten. A chill scatters down my spine, causing it to snap straight.

My back is to the living room where he slowly approaches. I can't see him, but my God, I can feel him.

How does one breathe when the one who possesses their lungs is standing behind them?

It takes a few moments to work up the nerve to turn around and face him. Another breath gets caught in my throat. After all this time, I still haven't gotten used to how tall he is—how imposing of a man he is.

He only wears a black button-up, matching trousers, and a fedora today, but his piercing stare has me completely arrested.

My God, I'm still not accustomed to how devastatingly beautiful he is.

"Ronaldo," I breathe, his name rolling off my tongue like it's a language I've been practicing for years.

One corner of his mouth quirks up, suspending further oxygen from reaching my lungs. This man . . . he will be the death of me. It's as certain as the moon rising.

"Mia rosa," he greets, his deep, volcanic voice as smooth as lava yet as rough as the rock that inhabits it.

My hand drifts to my throat, where my pulse thrums heavily. I feel the skin there reddening, my body heating under his blazing stare.

The echo of his footsteps radiates in each heartbeat as he nears. By the time he's standing within an inch from me, my chest is heaving, and

I'm inhaling his delectable scent.

"You look like you have something on your mind," he drawls casually.

"I love you." The words burst out of me like water from a broken pipe. That wasn't entirely what I meant to say, but I couldn't keep it bottled inside anymore.

Several emotions flit across his gaze. Surprise, elation, then absolute hunger.

"I hope you weren't hoping for a romantic moment," I babble. "Because that was entirely unromantic of me. I'm a little ashamed that—"

"If I could, I'd lower to a knee on this checkered floor and ask for your hand. It would be entirely unromantic of me, but it wouldn't stop me, either."

I bite my lip, and it's like all my happiness has filled up a balloon inside me. It's floating up toward my throat, expanding my chest until I fear it's going to pop.

"Love cannot define what I feel for you. But I will settle for it with my words and show you what I truly feel with my actions," he says quietly.

He crooks a finger and glides it across my cheekbone, awakening a lightning storm in the air and sending the currents scattering across my skin.

"You look absolutely divine today, my love," he purrs. My eyes flutter from his electric touch, and goose bumps rise as he slides his hand to my nape, cupping it firmly.

"How divine?" I whisper breathlessly.

"Enough to feast on," he rasps. But then he draws away, and my heart surges. I grab his arm before he can retreat, catching him by surprise.

"Then prove it," I demand shakily before fastening my bottom lip between my teeth. God, I'm nervous. So nervous. Though I'm sure of what I want.

He studies me closely, scrutinizing every detail on my face before focusing on my lip trapped between my teeth. It's unnerving, especially when his expression is so carefully smoothed into marble. What is he thinking?

He must think me ridiculous.

"You want me to eat you, *mia rosa*?"

I flush hot, my cheeks burning. "Well, n-not *actually*. I—I didn't mean—" I huff, frustrated with my stuttering. "I want you to touch me, Ronaldo. Please."

His hand returns to the nape of my neck while I move the two of mine to his chest. His heart thumps heavily, the only indication that he's more affected than he lets on.

With his other hand, he toys with the button at the collar of my silky white blouse. "These clothes look exquisite on you, Genevieve."

My mouth dries, and it takes an effort to swallow. His saying my name like that—it has a breathtaking effect on me. My core throbs and I squeeze my thighs tight.

His fingers drift up to a gold raven pendant dangling below the hollow of my throat. I found it in a boutique years ago. It reminded me of my favorite Edgar Allan Poe poem, and while it's a simple piece, it's always been my favorite.

Now, he toys with the small bird, sending goose bumps scattering across my flesh.

"Your clothes would look so much better on the floor, though, don't you think?"

"On the floor?" I repeat dumbly, the question coming out as a pathetic squeak. My cheeks burn in response, mortified that this man has barely touched me and I'm acting like a fool.

He hums his approval, dropping the necklace and staring at me with a reverence I haven't seen in . . . well, ever. How does one look from him have me questioning my entire life until this point? Were John and I ever truly in love? Or were we two kids that latched on to the first relationship we found?

I had kissed many before John, but I had taken none of them seriously. John and I were each other's first for nearly everything. First date, first relationship, first lover. And I never looked back—never thought to.

For a long time, I had convinced myself that was ideal. Neither of us needed to explore because we loved each other. Now, our marriage is falling apart, and I'm unable to blame the man before me. The destruction began well before Ronaldo came around, but he might just be the one to knock over the last pillar that's keeping John and me standing.

John has done terrible things, yet I cannot say with confidence that he's ever stepped out on our marriage. Aside from that night when he mistook me for another woman, I haven't seen any other indication that he's strayed.

I've never smelled the perfume of another woman on his clothes or seen red lips imprinted on his shirt collar that didn't come from my kiss. He's hardly looked at another woman in the years we've been together. If the booze has led him to an affair, I've seen no evidence of it.

And so what if he hasn't? What if, despite all his sins, he's stayed faithful? Does it even matter when he could be hiding so much more from me?

In some ways, John has ruined me. Tainted me and covered me in stains that will never wash away. For the rest of my days, I will remember the ways he's defiled not only my body but also my trust.

If John has taught me anything, it's that I don't really know him at all.

I don't even know *myself* anymore.

And truthfully, I kind of blame him for that, too.

But look at what you are doing. You're betraying him, too.

And in the worst way.

I've condemned him for so much, yet I'm no better, am I?

I'm not without sadness for the fact that I'm losing my husband to a whiskey bottle and a game. Rather than being consumed by my red lips, it's the red poker chips that captivate him. He drank me in only to spit me out and replace me with a swig of dark, bitter liquor. And when he came back for me, he slammed into me like an empty liquor bottle on a table, demanding something from me I didn't have to give.

A spark of anger ignites at the reminder that my husband has violated me in ways no man has the right to. Any shame that was circulating through my system dissolves beneath the weight of my husband's transgressions.

He shouldn't be the only one allowed to sin.

"Would you like to see?" I ask, staring up at Ronaldo through my lashes. "I think this blouse would be a fine addition to the checkered pattern."

I'm still nervous, but I've always been a confident woman. And something tells me Ronaldo would appreciate that about me.

I grab hold of where his fingers are twirling a button, reveling in the roughness of his hand. He stills beneath my touch, watching me closely as I gently push him aside and pop the button free.

I'm not sure what reaction I was expecting, but it wasn't for him to step away from me completely. I frown, embarrassment and shame punching me in the chest.

"Sit down there," he directs, pointing toward the dining room table. Utterly confused, my mouth flops.

"Did I do something wr—"

"No, *mia rosa*, you could never." His tone is deeper now, and my lips part when I notice the rather large bulge in his trousers.

Oh . . .

When I draw my gaze back up to his, he tilts up his chin and rolls his tongue in his cheek, staring down at me with a wicked look, daring me to test him. *You have five seconds before I . . .*

Excitement replaces any ugly feelings I had moments before, and I pivot on my feet and do as he says. My hands tremble, though I couldn't blame my erratic nerves on anything but anticipation. Especially as his footsteps echo from behind me, approaching me as slowly as he always does. Like a predator stalking his prey, keeping himself hidden until the second he pounces.

He pauses directly behind me, the back of the chair separating us. Another shiver racks my body when his fingers brush across my shoulder, when he slowly gathers my loose curls and lays them down the middle of my back.

Then his lips caress the shell of my ear, evoking another tremor. "A queen has more important duties than undressing herself. Let me take care of that for you."

If I didn't know any better, I'd think the devil was on my shoulder, whispering to me in such a wicked way.

My thighs clench, wetness gathering between them.

I hold my breath as he reaches around and releases the second button on my blouse. Slowly, he unbuttons each one, ensuring the tips of his fingers brush against my flesh with every movement. All the while, I resist the urge to squirm beneath him.

When the last button is free, he guides the soft material off my shoulders so I can free my arms from the sleeves. The brassiere I wear is the most flattering I own, with strips of lace over the silk ensured to ensnare a man's gaze.

Ronaldo's fingers trace over the lace, and though the material separates him from my bare flesh, it feels as if nothing is between us anyway.

Toying with the zipper on the side of my emerald-green slacks, he comments lowly, "I don't see very many women wearing these."

"I saw them in a boutique and thought they looked interesting," I explain, the slightest tremor in my voice. With the war going on, many military and workforce women wear slacks for necessity and comfort. Now, they're slowly becoming popular in society and popping up more often in boutiques. They're scarce due to the material shortages, which is why I couldn't resist purchasing them. "I like to try new things."

Something that should be obvious, given our current circumstances.

"I think these would complement the tiling, too," he drawls, the glide of the zipper quiet beneath my thumping heart. The cotton material parts and droops, revealing my matching lace-and-silk girdle leading down to the straps securing my stockings in place.

Typically, I wouldn't wear them with slacks, but I had hoped he would undress me today, and I wanted to wear something that would make him lose his mind.

A deep hum rumbles in his throat, his approval like fine red wine— intoxicating, and a taste I'd never tire of.

"Lift up for me, love," he orders gently, his voice lined with gravel. I obey without question, allowing him to slide my slacks down until they drop to my feet and I kick free of them.

"Ravishing," he breathes. "Nothing could compare to the likes of you, my love. You are the most beautiful flower and the rarest gem, more breathtaking than any of earth's wonders."

He speaks to me more beautifully than anyone ever has before. My throat closes, utterly speechless over his proclamations.

Reaching over me, he dives his hands between my thighs and brazenly spreads them. I gasp, and my cheeks burn hot when I see the evidence of my arousal so boldly on display. My panties are soaked, and the visible wet spot extends down my thighs, glistening under his stare.

Embarrassed, I attempt to snap my legs shut, but he resists and only spreads my thighs wider.

"I— Oh my . . . Ronaldo, this is . . ." I can't get a single coherent thought out of my mouth. I'm mortified that he's seeing just how he affects me. I've never had a reaction like this before. Never soaked through my undergarments like this. It looks like I soiled myself, for God's sake.

"You've made a mess," he purrs, sounding delighted.

"That's not . . . I didn't—"

"I know, my love. Your cunt is weeping for me."

I bite my lip, a throb emanating from between my legs from his vulgar language. I've never heard a man speak like that to me. But my God, do I like it. And it *is* weeping—and crying out for him, too.

"Will you touch me there?" I ask boldly, needing to feel him almost as much as I need to breathe.

He hums again, a response that's neither a confirmation nor a denial. His fingers drift over the strip of bare flesh between my girdle and bra, sending electric shocks scattering across my body.

"I think I'm too curious," he murmurs finally, his hands drifting over various areas, his touch sensual yet evading everywhere I need him to be.

"About what?"

"How far you would go to feel me inside you," he answers darkly. "And if, by the time I give in, you could drown me with your cunt."

He cups my face and tilts my chin up until I'm staring at him from upside down.

Leaning closer, he brushes his lips across mine, teasing me until I grow impatient and capture them in a fervent kiss. His tongue greets mine for a second before he retreats, leaving me desperate for more.

"When you become the ocean, I will gladly sink into you, *mia rosa.*"

Then he pulls away, and before I can process what's happening, the front door shuts behind him, leaving me alone.

And so very empty.

July 7, 1944

Ronaldo likes to tease.
Only an hour after I sent Seraphina off to school, he came to
visit. After what I went through with John, I wanted to let go of
that and replace those awful memories with new ones. So I told
him to touch me. I begged for it.
He resisted at first, but it didn't take long for him to concede.
He told me to sit in my dining room chair.
I followed his orders eagerly. He unbuttoned my blouse. Then my
slacks. He pulled them down and left me in nothing but my
undergarments.
His fingers whispered against my flesh. And he said beautiful
things to me as he did. Dirty things, too.
He smiled when he saw the desperation in my eyes.
Yet he still denied me. He never touched me where I wanted him
to. Where I needed him to. His fingers taunted me. And then he
left.
It took everything in me not to beg for him to come back. One of
these days, I won't be able to control myself any longer.

CHAPTER 12

THE RAVEN

August 14, 1944

I've learned a lot about Ronaldo over the past couple of months. And while there are certain things he hasn't confided in me—such as his job—I've asked him just about everything else.

Except if he likes sweets.

I pull the baking sheet from the oven and set it on the stovetop, staring at the chocolate chip cookies as if they're centipedes—something he confessed he's terrified of that might chase him away.

They're just cookies, for God's sake.

But what if he hates them? What if he hates chocolate? I should've made sugar cookies.

I'm lost in thought, running through scenario after scenario, solidifying that baking for this man was a colossal mistake.

Ever since he undressed me in the kitchen a month ago, we've been spending a lot of our days growing more accustomed to one another's touch. Mostly kissing and heavy petting, as his refusal to take things further is persistent. Even still, my lips have been too darn preoccupied to ask him a simple question.

Do you like cookies?

I'm so lost in thought that when a heavy weight lands on my shoulder, I belt out a scream that damn near shatters my coffee mug.

Whipping around, I find Ronaldo standing behind me, his brows nearly in his hairline in a mildly amused expression. Meanwhile, I'm standing frozen solid, stricken by his sudden appearance. I can't breathe around my thunderous heart lodged in my throat.

In fact, I'm fully convinced I'm experiencing a heart attack.

His smile grows, and it's enough to coerce my body to breathe.

"Have those cookies insulted you, my love?"

I deflate, shooting him a disgruntled look.

"*No.* As a matter of fact, they did not. Not that it's any of *your* business what warfare I engage in with sugary food," I snip haughtily, though my words lack heat. If anything, I'm entirely mortified.

The mirth twinkling in his gaze is distracting, however, and I can't help but fall into some type of trance. He told me many stories about his days in the military. About the shrapnel that flew into his eye after a comrade standing beside him shot off his gun, unaware of the obstruction in the barrel. He said it caused the gun to explode and send shrapnel flying into both their faces. It completely blinded his comrade, but thankfully, he was spared the worst of it.

He was incredibly lucky that the shard was tiny enough that he didn't lose the eye completely, but the damage was still permanent. The light milky-blue color that has corroded his pupil isn't too much lighter than his iris, and it gives him such a peculiar look.

Oddly enough, I find it incredibly attractive. Something I also confessed to him.

"Baby."

He sounds amused. The single word pulls me out of the trance, and my cheeks instantly flush hot.

You're just intent on making a damn fool of yourself today.

"I— What?"

I blink, and he's chuckling, the sound as pleasing to my ears as a Frank Sinatra song.

"The cookies," he reminds. "Are they for me?" He flicks his eyes toward them, and I follow his line of sight, having completely forgotten about them.

"Yes?" I answer, though it sounds more like a question. Clearing my throat, I try again. "Do you like cookies?"

His grin is less teasing and warmer this time. "I love them."

Relief rockets through me, and rather than continuing to stare at him like a goof, I spring into action. It takes two minutes to plate the fresh cookies and hand them to him, a wobbly smile on my face.

"I feel a little silly baking for you," I admit sheepishly. "It's hard to cook for you without John's noticing missing food or random leftovers, but these will go undetected."

I cringe, hating to bring up my husband. It's not necessarily a sore subject between us, but we often avoid talking about him. It hasn't slipped my attention that every time I say John's name, Ronaldo's eyes darken and flash with fury. For obvious reasons, he's never been thrilled about my having a husband. But after John hurt me, that contempt has transformed into murderous rage.

He's careful to control the reaction, the emotion flicking through his gaze with speed. But I hate making him feel it at all.

He leans forward and places a soft kiss on my mouth. Then he pulls away just a few centimeters, enough for him to whisper against my lips, "I've always loved cookies. Maybe because I enjoy eating things that are sweet and melt on my tongue."

His voice is so incredibly deep, and his tone is devilish. A shiver crawls down my spine, the salacious implication of his words not lost on me. It takes a few tries before I manage to swallow the rock in my throat.

"They're all yours to eat," I choke out.

"Only mine?" he asks, stepping closer until his body molds into mine, my eyes ensnared by his.

"Yes." The word comes out as a squeak, and my cheeks burn, both from his proximity and my lack of control.

"Good," he rasps. "I'm starving, *mia rosa.*"

Then the space in front of me is suddenly empty, and I'm staring at his back as he carries the plate of sweets to the island. He doesn't just walk away from me—he *saunters.*

I narrow my eyes, a surge of determination and annoyance burning through any resistance I had for this man.

"You *keep* walking away," I snap.

He pauses, turning his head over his shoulder to peer at me.

"Are you going to stop me, my love?"

"Why do you keep making me chase you?" I parry.

He stays quiet as he sets the plate on the island countertop, then approaches me again. He stops a foot away, deliberately not touching me this time.

"Because I don't know that I'd handle it well if you ran away," he responds simply.

I frown, not sure I understand what he means.

"I would follow you anywhere, Genevieve. If you were standing at the edge of the earth and wanted to fall, I would only stop you long enough to take hold of your hand so I could go with you. There isn't a life where I wouldn't be your phantom, or a death where I wouldn't be your reaper."

He places his hand flat on my chest, keeping me at arm's length.

"If you tried to run away from me, I don't think I'd let you. I would do . . . *anything* to make you stay. And there are moments where I feel . . . Where there are things that I want to do to you that might cause you to run. And I'm afraid of that, so I walk away first."

I grab his wrist and remove it from my chest, then step into him, inhaling his intoxicating scent.

"What makes you think I'd run?" I ask, my voice hardly above a whisper. "How do you know I wouldn't beg for the things you want to do to me?"

His upper lip curls into a snarl, and he glances away from me just as his gaze darkens with feral desire. He's trying to collect himself, likely before he loses control.

Yet that reaction alone has me unraveling at the seams, and I am no more in control than he pretends to be.

"Genevieve," he bites out, still refusing to meet my stare. I press myself into him, molding every inch of our bodies together. His eyes close, inhaling deeply as my lips whisper across his neck.

"You think you'll scare me—that you'll make me scream. Yet screaming for you is exactly what I would love to do, Ronaldo."

He snaps, and before I can take my next breath, his hands are clutching either side of my jaw and he's crashing his mouth onto mine.

There's no process of losing my mind to this man. It's there and gone in an instant. I return the kiss with just as much passion, my hands tearing at his shirt, buttons scattering to the checkered tile.

Once the tattered fabric drops to the floor, he lifts me in his arms, and I hook my legs around his waist as he carries me to one of the red velvet couches in the living room.

I'm on my back as he settles over me, trailing his lips down my jaw before sinking his teeth into the delicate flesh beneath my ear.

I arch into him, a moan unleashing from my throat.

"Ronaldo," I plead, needing more. Needing all of him.

He rips himself away to stare down at me, the two of us panting heavily, our breaths shaky and frenzied.

"We will take things slow," he orders. I'm shaking my head before he finishes, nearly blind with lust. If this man dares walk away again, I will—

"I will give you what you need, Genevieve. I won't leave you wanting," he vows. He lowers his head to place a gentle kiss on the swell of my breast, right above the neckline of my dress. "But today will be all about you."

I'm selfish and want everything, but I'm desperate enough to accept anything from him, even if it's small.

"Uh-huh," I eke out, roving my hands over every part of him I can reach. His chest, his shoulders, down his arms—I want to feel all of him.

He sits up, pulling me up with him. Confused, I watch as he sits down on the couch and spreads his legs. He taps his lap, a devilish grin playing on his lips.

"Come sit on my lap, pretty girl. Let me take care of you."

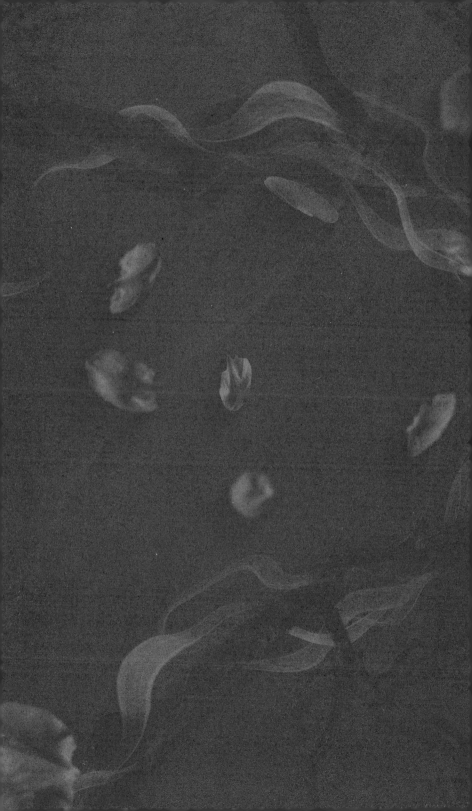

CHAPTER 13

THE RAVEN

August 14, 1944

My heart is beating in my throat as I climb onto his lap, facing him. I bite my lip, feeling his hard length pressing into my core. He feels so much bigger than I'm used to. Yet he doesn't seem interested in satisfying his own needs.

Another thing I'm not used to.

"Have you ever touched yourself?" he asks, his hands sliding up my thighs, eliciting a full-body shiver. Breathing heavily, I shake my head.

His hands pause at the junction between my thigh and pelvis.

"Baby, tell me you've at least had an orgasm before," he says, his tone nearly a plea.

"I—I don't know. How would I know if I have?"

His blue eye darkens to a color similar to the Sound at the bottom of the cliff. A dark, stormy color that exhibits clear displeasure.

"You would know, my love," he answers, a mischievous curl to his lips.

Now, I wish I had thought to touch myself. My mother never taught me anything about intimacy, and I never learned much from John, either, other than how to fall pregnant.

Sex has always felt . . . nice. But there wasn't anything about it that made me feel inclined to seek that pleasure on my own.

The glimmer in Ronaldo's eye suggests he's almost anticipating the absolute devastation coming my way, and I wonder if I have been robbing myself of something far greater than what John has always made me feel.

His hands glide closer to my core, and a buzz forms beneath my skin as if a million little bees have found their way inside me.

I gasp as soon as I feel the pressure of his finger press against me, a little zing igniting from where he touches.

A single touch, and he's already surpassed John.

My lip finds itself between my teeth again, and I'm embarrassed to admit how wet I've become. I'm not accustomed to these reactions he brings out of me.

"Your cunt is soaked," he rasps, swiping his thumb over me. Even with a thin barrier between his flesh on mine, it has a visceral effect on my body. I'm two seconds away from grinding against him just to see how much better this could get. "Is that normal for you?"

"No," I say, the word shaky and breathless. "Should it be?"

"Only for me," he responds darkly.

He moves my underwear aside, and I'm unprepared for the jolt that rockets through me or how utterly satisfying his touch is. A shudder works through me as he explores, swiping down my center until the tip of his finger prods at my opening.

The sounds that arise should be shameful, yet sitting atop him with my legs spread open and his hand hidden beneath my dress makes me feel powerful. Instead of hiding from him, I want to display myself for only his viewing pleasure.

And rather than have him wielding my body to his every whim, I'm keen to turn it against him. Have *him* simpering while he pleasures me.

A sharp moan releases from my throat when he drives a digit inside of me. He groans, watching me carefully as I shudder around him.

Holding his gaze, I reach up and slide one sleeve of my dress down my arm, then the other. I'm thankful I went with a light, breezy outfit today, making it easy for the top half to droop down my waist.

Ronaldo pauses, his stare sharpening and bursting into flames.

The reaction gives me all the confidence I need to reach behind me and unclip my bra, freeing my breasts.

I roll my hips against his hand and peer at him through half-lidded eyes, injecting every bit of sensuality into my demeanor as I ask, "Why'd you stop?"

His mouth parts as I glide my hands over my breasts, moaning as I grind against him again.

A deep growl unleashes from his throat, and he's surging forward, capturing one of the hardened peaks between his teeth. I throw my head back as his hand resumes and adds a second finger, pumping them in and out of me with vigor.

I was right.

I completely robbed myself of pleasure unlike anything I've ever known. And I certainly won't be making that mistake twice.

Ronaldo sucks harshly on my nipple, eliciting pinpricks of pain followed by steep bliss. Then his thumb presses against a sensitive part of me, and I'm unable to refrain from moaning loudly.

He pulls away, popping my nipple from his mouth. "This is your clit, baby," he explains, taking a moment to nip at my breast. "And if you rub it just like this, you'll make yourself come easily."

I couldn't answer him if I tried.

One of my hands dives into his hair, gripping the strands tightly while the other clutches onto his shoulder. I whimper, my hips moving by their own volition. I wouldn't care if he were to stop moving, I'd do the rest myself. At this moment, he's a tool, and I will use him as such.

However, he only works me harder, his fingers moving over and in me expertly and with a skill that I don't know I could replicate.

My stomach tightens, a knot forming as the euphoria rises with each passing second. It grows, and grows, and grows until I cannot fathom how this isn't an orgasm—how it could possibly feel any better than this.

"Do you like the way I make your cunt feel, *mia rosa*?" he asks, his voice as rough as gravel and deeper than the Sound beyond the cliff. Another sharp nip to my breast, and I'm moaning again.

"Uh-huh," I moan, my eyes fluttering and my chest heaving.

"Let me hear you say it," he demands. "Tell me how good I make you feel."

"G-god, Ronaldo," I whine. How could he possibly expect me to utter another word, let alone a full sentence? His teeth sink into my sensitive nipple, causing me to jolt against him, the pain flaring brighter this time. It was a warning bite, yet it backfired and only heightened my pleasure.

I thought I didn't need him to make me come, yet I *want* him to. I want him to lose his mind as I say dirty things to him—words I've never spoken in my life. I want him to be so overtaken with need for me, he can think of nothing else.

I want this man to bow at my feet and serve me.

His pale-blue eye locks with mine, causing my core to clench around him from the pure animalistic lust swirling in his gaze. His left eye may be lacking in eyesight, but it does not lack in showing how greatly he desires me.

"You make my cunt feel so good, Ronaldo," I purr, cupping the underside of my breasts and lifting them closer to his wet mouth. "And it's all yours to do whatever you want with."

The pupil in his right eye dilates, consuming the blue of his iris until it's nearly entirely black. They remind me of yin and yang, and it's a riveting sight to behold. Even more so knowing that I drew that reaction out of him.

"You think I need your permission to play with this pretty pussy whenever I please?" he asks, binding his free arm around my back, entrapping me in his embrace. "I would dare to do so with your husband right next to us, forced to watch while I lick you and fuck you. And neither of you could do a damn thing about it."

I had thought he sounded like the devil before. But that was nothing compared to now. His voice is unrecognizable—his eyes, too. He stares at me as if I'm a measly mouse caught beneath his paw and he hasn't eaten in ages.

"You think so? What if I fought you, pleaded for you to stop?" I challenge breathlessly, struggling to keep my eyes from crossing.

He groans, nearly crowing at the thought of me fighting him. "It would only be a shame if you didn't cry, too," he responds wickedly. "Those tears would be as delectable as your pussy."

His words are awful, and at first, I wonder if he's trying to scare me, especially given what John did to me. But despite the pleasure turning my brain to mush, I soon understand what he's doing. He's testing me, presenting me with a fantasy in which I'd enjoy my power being stripped away. A fantasy that will still keep me up at night, but only because I'm aroused by the thought of it.

My skin flushes hotter, and my core pulses around him, driving me closer to the edge. An image sparks in my mind of John and me both tied to our bed. Except I'm completely nude with my legs spread wide, and Ronaldo is between them while his cock pumps in and out of me. My husband is forced to watch, and I'm undeniably enjoying everything my phantom is doing to me.

I can't breathe, and blackness is beginning to lick at the edges of my vision, threatening to consume me as entirely as the man beneath me.

I'll let it, too, just as I'm helpless to stop Ronaldo from doing the same.

"Ronaldo, I think I—" I'm lost for what to say and how to describe this foreign feeling. There's pressure on my bladder, and it almost feels as if I'm going to soil myself. "I don't know what's happening," I whimper, my thighs trembling violently as the ecstasy climbs to a sharp point.

"Relax, *mia rosa*," he soothes. "Your body knows what to do, so just let it happen."

I cry helplessly, overwhelmed with the pleasure, and a little nervous about how my body is going to react.

"That's it, baby. You're doing such a good job. Let me see how pretty you look when you come all over my fingers."

"Oh my— Ronaldo, I—"

"Be a good girl and fucking come for me, Genevieve. Don't make me ask you again," he snarls, his tone dropping wickedly.

My head kicks back, and I'm careening over the edge with a violent scream. Though it's no less devastating than the explosion that rocks through me. And I lose my ever-loving mind to it.

Faintly, I feel my body seizing above him, shamelessly grinding into his hand as my fingers claw at his skull and tear at his hair. Unintelligible sounds pour from my lips because I'm either unable to form words or hear a damn thing.

My body is completely possessed, and I no longer control any part of it. Not the way it moves or the noises it makes. I'm a slave to the euphoria, and all I can do is succumb to it.

His fingers continue to work me, only prolonging my climax until I quite literally am unable to breathe.

I think I'm okay with dying in his arms.

My God, is it a good way to go.

I'm not sure how much time passes before I'm finally given a reprieve. The orgasm wanes, and all awareness comes rushing back in. I'm cradling his head and draped over him, and his face is tucked into the crook of my neck while I mindlessly ride his fingers.

"You're so goddamn pretty when you come. *Fuck*, Genevieve. Keep fucking my fingers. Your pussy is squeezing them so tight." He bites out the words, his voice impossibly deep and scarcely penetrating the cloud engulfing my mind.

Moans and cries spill from my throat, slowly tapering into breathless whimpers as it becomes impossible to suck in a breath of air.

Even as I come down, the aftershocks take over, causing me to quiver and jolt against him. My head swims, and my lungs burn from being deprived of oxygen for so long.

All the while, Ronaldo continues to croon encouragements in my ear. "Such a good girl. I'm so fucking proud of you, baby."

Butterflies writhe and thrash senselessly in my stomach from his words, and if my brain wasn't so fried, I'd give more of a reaction other than a twitch and a blubbering sound.

Eventually, I deflate, utterly spent. Gently, Ronaldo removes his hand and readjusts my underwear. It's only then I realize that wetness is quite literally dripping down my thighs. I lean back slowly, almost afraid to look down.

I do, anyway, and my mouth drops from the sight. Not only are my thighs and underwear soaked but Ronaldo's entire lap and stomach are . . . he's drenched! His hand is— *Oh my God*, there's a small pool of my arousal in his palm.

Flabbergasted, I'm rendered speechless as he lifts his cupped palm to his open mouth and tips it, the liquid dripping into his mouth. His eyes roll as if he's found a pond in the middle of a desert and has only his hands to drink it down.

"Ronaldo!" I screech, finally finding my voice.

He grins, his lips and chin glistening. It's the most erotic sight I've ever been privy to, and I'm confounded as to how to react.

So I gape at him as he slowly and thoroughly licks his fingers clean.

"You've lost your mind," I whisper.

That only widens the satisfied smirk crawling up his face, and I'm tempted to smack it. The man has every right to feel good about himself, but that doesn't mean he has to gloat about it.

"Since the moment I saw you, *mia rosa*."

August 14, 1944

Shame is what I'm supposed to feel. I feel none of that.

Maybe except for allowing my husband to go years without making me feel what Ronaldo did today. My God, I didn't know the human body was capable of feeling something so glorious.

And I am a little miffed that it took thirty-five years for me to feel it just once. Especially because John has experienced it all this time. The bastard.

But how will I ever stop now?

After dinner, Sera went off to do her schoolwork and John sat in the living room, drinking a beer and listening to the radio. So I sneaked off to the bedroom and touched myself for the first time. I wanted to experience that feeling again, and I couldn't contain myself.

It wasn't as intense as when Ronaldo touched me, but the euphoria was still very much present. Admittedly, it took me a few minutes to figure out what I liked. My mind slipped away, and all I could think about was my phantom. The raw hunger on his face as he touched me today, the filthy words that spilled from his mouth. My fingers took over after that and moved on instinct.

It was incredible. And oddly enough, all I want to do is tell Ronaldo about it. See the flames in his gaze as I recant every moment of what I did to myself. Already I want to do it again, but worse yet, I want Ronaldo to do it again.

I fear he has created an insatiable monster, and now he must live with the consequences.

A mad woman, he has made me.

But if this is madness, I don't ever want to be sane.

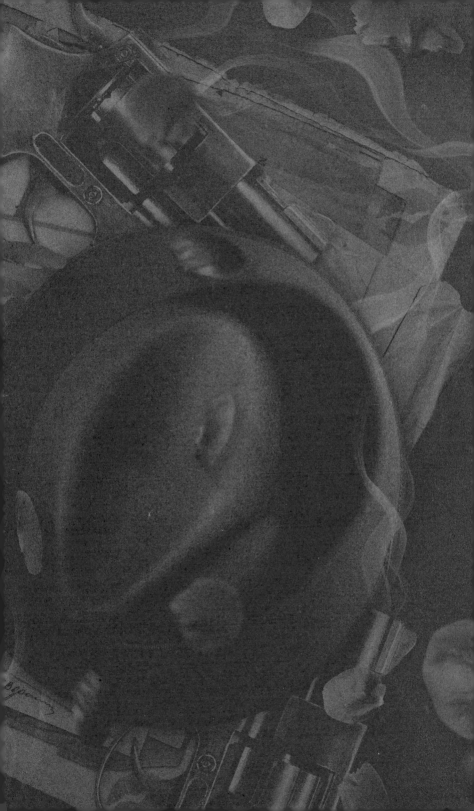

CHAPTER 14

THE PHANTOM

August 21, 1944

There's a reason even the godfather of Seattle respects Orazio Caserta's rules.

He's always been a ruthless son of a bitch. Despite his affinity for peace in his restaurant, he is very much capable of destruction.

Truthfully, I never thought I'd see the day where anyone disrespected his rules, but part of me is glad I lived to see it.

The photographs splayed out on Angelo's desk would have a weaker stomach purging. Evidence of Orazio's work on Manny Baldelli's oldest child, Nico, and Marco Viscuso himself.

Turns out, when we had dinner with the Viscusos at Caserta's, Marco had already pledged his loyalty to Manny in exchange for his son, Gabriele, to keep his mouth shut to the fuzz about Marco's operations. But for Manny to accept his pledge, he had one requirement of Marco.

Whack Angelo.

That day at Caserta's, Marco made one last effort to gain Angelo's approval to ice Gabriele, but Angelo refused and unknowingly sealed his fate.

So, although it was Marco's men who pulled the trigger that day, it was Manny who put out the contract.

Orazio took that as a great insult and punished *both* families for daring to cross him at his restaurant.

"Kid just turned eighteen and was gettin' ready to be shipped off to war," Angelo says, slapping yet another photograph onto his ornate wooden desk before Alfonso and me.

Such ugly images to lay upon such grand furniture.

Angelo has always had expensive taste. Rococo ornamentation engulfs the office in intricate golden designs that crawl up the white walls to a plafond ceiling. Built-in golden shelves span the wall behind his desk, save for an alcove in the center where a copycat painting of the *Mona Lisa* hangs. Miniature statues and old books inherited through his family fill the shelves, and Roman mythology paintings make up several art pieces and murals around the room, completed by a diamond-pattern tile floor, each piece a different shade of brown.

Angelo Salvatore is a devout Catholic man, which is why he turns away his religious statues when it's time for his cocaine fix.

"Seems that would have been a mercy," Alfonso drawls, inhaling his cigarette as he stares at the images with detachment.

It would have.

Orazio's father, Paris, loves horses, so much so that he owns two derby-winning stallions. He bets on them, too, and so far, he hasn't gone home empty-handed.

Growing up, Orazio was a jockey in some of those races and became very well-acquainted with the beasts. Paris used to call him the horse whisperer for his knack for taming them and getting them to do exactly as he asked.

A skill that seems to have stuck with him, seeing as how he got four horses to rip Nico and Marco into pieces.

"Orazio made it clear it wasn't a quick death," Angelo says, chuckling. "Apparently, the horses didn't run. They *walked*. Slowly rippin' off the limbs from their bodies."

I cock a brow, aimlessly rubbing my thumb across my bottom lip as I stare at the photos. The men's torsos are in the middle, and each of their limbs is placed several feet from where they're supposed to be. I don't need to see the photographs in color to know that barely a speck of the grass beneath them is still green.

Somehow, that's not the worst part. No, the worst part is the tourniquets wrapped around each of their remaining stubs, cutting off the blood flow and subsequently keeping them alive for longer.

"Did he say how long they were alive after?" I ask, focusing on Angelo. Yet the sight of Nico and Marco each ripped into five pieces is one that will forever be burned into my memory.

"Little under two hours."

"Jesus," I mutter beneath my breath. "Marco deserved that fate. But Nico?"

"Don't feel too bad," Angelo drawls. "Manny raised Nico to think that whatever he wanted, he got. That included girls."

My thumb pauses on my lip. "He raped them?"

"Manny had complained on many occasions about payin' a few parents hush money to keep their daughters' traps shut."

I nod slowly while Alfonso mutters, "Those are just the ones who accepted it. The parents that didn't? Their daughters were silenced."

Rage burns in my chest, and my finger twitches with the need to unload a few bullets in Manny's goddamn head. "So, Marco and Nico were whacked," I state plainly, needing to push the conversation along before I give into my urges and go looking for Manny this goddamn second. "You put a contract out on Manny the moment you heard he was behind the hit, and no one has gotten close enough to get the job done. We've gotten ourselves into several shoot-outs over the past few months. And now that Orazio got one over on his kid, he will consider them even. You want me to clip him?"

Angelo glowers, but I know he's reserved all his wrath for Manny.

"An enforcer from the Russo family clocked Manny at a rental on the outskirts of town two hours ago," Alfonso supplies woodenly.

The Russos are a good family, and they've stayed loyal to us throughout this war Manny began. If they're sure of Manny's presence, then I believe it.

"I want him dead, Ronnie," Angelo bites through gritted teeth.

"Are you askin' me or tellin' me?"

Angelo shoots back his whiskey, hissing through his teeth. When he sets the crystal glass down, he meets my stare.

"I'm tellin' ya."

I stub out my cigar, smoke billowing between us, but it does nothing to hide the murderous delight shining within Angelo's and my eyes.

"Then I'll take care of it."

August 22, 1944

Manny Baldelli's snores could wake the dead.

I don't know how his wife sleeps next to him, but she lies just as still as he does.

Wouldn't surprise me if she's merely a corpse he keeps next to him. He's always been off his rocker, and it's not something I'd put past him.

The bedroom they're staying in is on the bottom floor, with one wall entirely a window, giving me a perfect shot of him. He and his wife, Carmen, sleep on a four-poster bed, Manny closest to the window and his wife barely visible behind his large body.

Normally, a wanted man would never think to leave himself so exposed. But Manny has always had more ego than brains, and he believes he's in a hidden location surrounded by several guards, which gives him a false sense of security.

Unfortunately for him, those guards are all dead.

I took out each one quietly when the others were out of view. A simple rope around the neck prevented them from making any noise while I choked the life out of them.

A mere appetizer to the entrée.

There's a buzz beneath my skin, demanding more blood on my hands. More souls to release into the ether. Nothing will satisfy me more than watching the life drain from Manny Baldelli's eyes.

My tommy gun is strapped on my back, so I quietly remove it and take aim, uncaring if I hit the possibly alive wife or not. She's collateral damage and nothing more.

And then I unload, the unmistakable sound of dozens of bullets firing through glass, shattering it and startling Manny and his wife awake, their eyes nearly popping from their skulls.

The two of them roll toward the other side of the bed and out of shot, though I don't let up on spraying metal, even as I kick at broken glass, making enough room in the window for me to step through.

Just as I enter the room, the magazine runs empty. Instantly, I slip the tommy gun to my back and pull out my pistol, taking aim just as Manny jumps to his feet, his own gun aimed my way.

Glass shards catch on my clothing, a few pieces slicing through flesh. But I hardly feel it.

I'm quicker and shoot the second he's within sight.

My bullet hits him directly in the chest, though he manages to squeeze off a shot of his own that comes within millimeters of my face.

I don't even blink.

The following silence is almost deafening save for Carmen's soft cries. I'm unable to discern if they're from pain or terror or maybe both, but she is the least of my concerns.

Carefully, I approach them. Many have gotten themselves killed thinking they completed a hit, only for their target to still have enough breath to fire off one last fatal shot, determined not to meet hell's gates alone.

Manny lies on his back, his eyes closed and chest unmoving while Carmen cradles his head in her lap. Her response to my presence is delayed, but the moment she notices me, she curls herself over him, renewed cries spilling from her lips. She doesn't appear to be hit anywhere, though I can't say I would consider her lucky.

"Please," she whimpers.

I raise my gun and fire off another shot in Manny's chest. His body automatically jerks as the bullet sluices through his muscles and organs, and it evokes a sharp scream from Carmen's throat. Her trembling hands cover her ears, and she begins to rock back and forth, her husband's head still cradled in her lap.

Carmen Baldelli is no saint.

She's known for beating her staff to death over simple mistakes, and the ones she doesn't kill, she makes them wish she had.

Carmen has enough innocent blood on her hands to warrant a single bullet through the brain.

So that's what I give her.

Her cries silence, and so does the buzz beneath my skin as I finish taking lives for the night.

I roll my neck, releasing the tension that has gathered in my muscles since the moment I left Angelo's estate.

Then I slide my gun into the back of my trousers and head back out of the broken window, feeling lighter than I've felt in months.

Tucking my hands in my pockets, I whistle a Frank Sinatra tune as I stroll toward my car, thinking of nothing more than seeing Genevieve Parsons again.

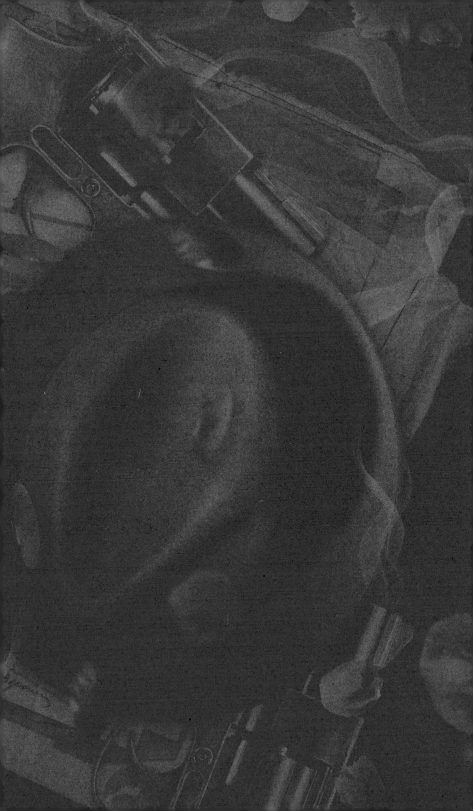

CHAPTER 15

THE PHANTOM

September 10, 1944

"**Y**ou know I don't take kindly to not bein' paid what I'm owed, don'tcha, Paulie?"

The rage simmering in Angelo Salvatore's brown eyes has always had a profound effect. It should be photographed, destined to become a cursed image. If you meet that black stare, you're doomed to a terrible fate.

"Of course, boss," Paulie responds mechanically. He stands to my left, solid on his feet, despite being on the receiving end of a vicious glare.

I sit before Angelo's desk, keeping my stare pinned just above his head where Mona Lisa is hanging. Alfonso sits to my right, puffing on a cigar and staring at the painting as well, appearing uninterested.

However, I know he's hanging onto every word spoken.

"This Johnathan Parsons, he can't seem to get his act together, can he? He owes us money, he pays it back, then finds himself in debt again. This is, what, the third time he gambled with Tommy and put himself in the hole?" Angelo looks to me for confirmation.

I tighten my lips and nod.

John has had to pay off the Salvatores twice before, plus interest. Just barely, he managed to scrape by from the money he makes from his business. But just last month, John got drunk and insisted on playing again, intent on making Tommy owe him money instead.

He lost miserably, and this time, he owes Tommy an amount of money he may never be able to pay back.

"Ronnie, how much is he in the hole for this time?" Angelo asks, twirling a pure-gold box cutter between his fingers, which are adorned in rubies, sapphires, and emeralds, all housed in the same expensive metal.

If anyone dared to gift him silver, he'd likely shoot them in the face.

My friend has expensive tastes.

"He's down about fifteen large," I answer.

Angelo pauses, the box cutter glinting in the overhead light. We lock stares, and the slightest snarl curls his upper lip. Then he's swinging the blade toward Paulie. "Take care of it. Immediately."

I move my gaze to above his head once more while Paulie asks, "Any particular method, boss?"

He waves a dismissive hand and sets down his box cutter with the other. "Don't burn him yet. He's got a wife and kid at home. Take the broad hostage until he pays his dues."

My teeth clench, and decades of practice keep my fists from curling.

John Parsons has overstepped, and it's not uncommon to threaten family members to get someone in line. And while being a don doesn't come without violence, I trust Angelo to treat Genevieve Parsons well.

However, I simply will not tolerate my boss kidnapping my girl. Not unless I want to sign a death warrant and put a bullet through his skull.

"I expect his payment soon," Angelo finishes, grabbing a cigar from the tin on his desk along with his cigar cutter. He holds up the tool. "Or I'll be choppin' off the tips of *your* wife's fingers with this."

Paulie doesn't react. He's only twenty-five years old, but he's a damn-good enforcer, and ruthless too.

While he wasn't born into the family, he's worked for the Salvatores for years and became a made man at the ripe age of eighteen. When he was twenty-two, he was drafted into the military and fought in WWII until last year. He was too close to a mine when it detonated, resulting in his losing an arm and eventually being honorably discharged. He wears a prosthetic, but Paulie's missing limb is not a weakness.

The kid is very dangerous, and thanks to the unimaginable horrors in the war, he is experienced in the art of masking emotions. Not much fazes him.

"Of course, boss," he answers mildly.

I'm lucky enough not to have a family like Paulie or some of the other men that work for the Salvatore family.

When I was eight, my father died in battle during WWI at only twenty-six years old. Devastated, my mother wasted away in a bottle until she died when I was twenty. I never had siblings, and neither did my parents.

The only family I had was Angelo himself. He's four years older, but we played in the same streets as kids, the two of us bonding over our Sicilian roots and parents that forced us to grow up far quicker than we should've. His father was the don of the Salvatore family and raised him in this life. As his best friend, I grew up in the family business alongside him.

Angelo served in the military as soon as he turned eighteen, and by the time he completed his service, I was being sworn in. I was only twenty-one when I lost vision in my left eye to a piece of shrapnel, rendering me unfit to serve. After they honorably discharged me, I came home to Angelo being the don of the Salvatore family, married to Carmella, and a father to a kid with a second on the way. He brought me in immediately, naming me his consigliere.

The Salvatores are all I've had since my father passed.

Otherwise, I'm alone.

Something that Angelo has tried to correct, consistently berating me for ending the Capello bloodline with me. But I've made peace with that.

He wants me to marry and have kids of my own. Or as I see it, marry and produce collateral for rival families to use against me. Angelo named me the godfather of all four of his sons, and that was enough for me. I helped raise those boys as if they were my own. I wanted nothing more than that.

Since the moment I realized I was going to be a made man, I chose to be alone. The only life anyone can threaten is my own, and sometimes, that's not enough to scare a man whose insides are slowly rotting away. I have no death wish, but some days, I have no will to live, either.

Now, one little bird is going to ruin that for me.

Not only is Genevieve my sole reason for living but she's also the piece of shrapnel that I can't seem to remove. She's a weakness, and one day, she just might be the death of me.

Angelo waves a hand and mutters, "Out of my face, Paulie. And I don't want to see you again until you return with the money John Parsons owes me and a smile on that ugly mug."

The enforcer is out of Angelo's office in two seconds, leaving the three of us alone.

Alfonso speaks first. "John was playing against a Baldelli two nights ago, I hear. Managed to swindle him out of a grand, then lost it to Moe last night. Word is that Baldelli feels Moe reached in his pockets and stole the money himself. This John guy is causin' more trouble than he's worth."

"He's worth the cost of the bullet that I'll lodge in his skull, the deadbeat," Angelo retorts.

"Then what of his family?" I cut in. "His child?"

Angelo is a family man, and this is a cold way to remind him that John is not alone in life. His threat to Paulie's wife is a threat he'll make good on, but not one he'll enjoy. Leaving a woman and a child alone without a man to provide for them is not something he'd get a kick out of, either.

"What would you have me do, Ronnie?" Angelo asks, annoyance in his tone as he splays out his hands to his sides. "The man clearly doesn't give a damn about his family—and that alone is a reason to pop him."

"All I ask is you give him a chance," I reason. "A dead man can't pay you back, and his wife and kid don't deserve more trouble."

Angelo grunts, then puffs on his cigar, looking thoughtfully at the Proserpine painting on the opposite wall. He paid an obscene amount of money for it, and I'm convinced he holds it in as high a regard as his own wife.

"I may be a godly man, Ronnie, but I am not a patient one. His wife better pray he loves her enough to get his act together."

I've never been a godly man, yet I pray he does, too.

CHAPTER 16

THE RAVEN

September 10, 1944

Three days.

It's been *three days* since I've seen Ronaldo, and I'm at my wits' end waiting for him to appear again.

Since I can remember, lying in bed with John felt like a duty as his wife rather than an activity I craved. I always thought that was normal, though. I never knew different. I never knew there could be so much passion between two people. With John, sex was never unpleasant, but it didn't satisfy me the way it seemed to satisfy him. Every time he released inside me, I always wondered what he was experiencing. His trembling body and quiet grunts spoke of a pleasure far beyond what I felt.

Now, intimacy with him *would* be unpleasant. I haven't allowed him to touch me since Ronaldo started coming around. And especially not after that awful June night. I still have nightmares about it, and he knows that, too. But sometimes, I worry my refusal will cause him to snap again. He's attempted to reconcile multiple times, speaking of having needs. Before, I wouldn't have understood that need. Now, I know exactly what he means. Yet I can't find it in me to care.

The only needs I do care about are mine . . . and Ronaldo's.

Worse yet, the stupid man leaves me hanging!

How does he expect me to go on like this? How could he subject me to his electric touch and passionate kisses yet leaving me starving for more? He's given me pleasure beyond what should be natural, but I can't help but crave *more*.

For the first time in my life, I feel this cavernous emptiness between my thighs begging to be filled, and only by him. He said he wants to take his time with me. Make sure that I'm truly ready, despite the numerous times I've insisted I am.

It's driving me wild.

I'm already a terrible wife, but as of late, I'm a madwoman, too.

"Genevieve!"

The sudden outburst of my name has a scream bursting from my throat. Panic and adrenaline zip through my system at a deadly rate.

John stands before me, glaring down at me with annoyance.

"You scared me half to death," I gasp, clutching my aching chest.

For the past hour, I've been staring out the bay window while Sera reads on the couch. I must have gotten lost in thought.

"I've called your name three times now. What has you so distracted lately? Shouldn't you be paying attention to your family?" he gripes, anchoring his hands on his hips.

The insult burrows beneath my skin, but I don't give him the satisfaction of knowing that. I look over to the couch, where Sera watches us with an apprehensive glimmer in her eyes.

She rarely sees us fight, though lately, that's been slowly changing. She's borne witness to the many times John and I have snapped at each other or glared through tense silences that stretched too long.

I hate it. I hate it so much.

And as hard as it is, I try to shield her from it as much as possible.

"I'm sorry, sweetie. I had an awful nightmare last night and got little sleep. I'm afraid it's made me a little spacey today." Though I paste on an apologetic smile, my stare is sharp, and my underlying meaning is clear. He knows exactly which nightmare I'm referring to.

If he wants to cast stones at me, then I will show him I have a mean throw, too.

His spine straightens, and his chin lifts so he can stare down his nose at me with disapproval. Rage simmers in his gaze, but if there's one thing that I can be sure of, it's that he doesn't like Sera witnessing our destruction, either.

"Of course, *dear*." He spits the word out like it's a rotten fruit. "*All* is forgiven."

I narrow my eyes, though I keep my smile firmly in place.

"Good," I chirp, breaking the tension and standing from my chair. I park my hands on my hips in an excited manner. "Sera, how about a game of Monopoly?"

"*Or . . . ,*" John cuts in, and it takes monumental effort not to glare. "Why don't you ride your bike downtown to the ice-cream shop and pick us up a few pints? When you get back, we can play."

The bastard. Offering ice cream to Sera is not only a clever way to get her out of the house but one that is guaranteed to work. Our daughter has a sweet tooth, and she will never say no to—

"I'd love to!" Sera exclaims, jumping up from the couch, her book long forgotten.

I sigh and drop my arms to my sides in defeat. Sera bounds up to her father, splaying out her open palm with a jovial grin stretching wide across her face. Her cinnamon-brown eyes sparkle when John drops a few dimes in her hand.

"You know our favorite flavors, don't you?" John asks.

"Yep!" she chirps, then skips off toward the foyer, hurriedly putting on her shoes and raincoat before running out the door.

The ensuing silence is heavier than rainfall during a storm.

John faces me, and all the resentment between us spills out onto the checkered floor from our stares, our body language, and the curls of our upper lips.

I'm tempted to ask him if we can even afford that ice cream, but I already know the answer. *We can't.*

John will pay our bills, and within a month, we will fall behind again, only to repeat the cycle and keep me in a constant state of worry about if we're going to lose the house or not.

I set my journal on the footstool before me, drawing his attention to it.

"What do you write in that journal that's so much more important than paying attention to your family?" he asks, though it sounds more like an accusation.

I narrow my eyes, fury bubbling in my chest from his condescending attitude.

"The gall of you," I hiss. "As if you haven't favored a bottle of booze over us countless nights."

His teeth clench, the muscle in his jaw pulsing. "What are you writing about, Genevieve?" he asks again, ignoring my barb.

"My boring, uneventful life," I bite out. "Why does it matter? I've written in a journal every single day for the past sixteen years we've been together."

He stares at the diary resting on the footstool in front of my chair, and my heart sinks. He lunges for it, but I snatch it up before he can make it a step.

"How dare you!" I shout, my heart racing while adrenaline and panic release into my system.

"Give it to me now," he barks, holding out his hand. "You've been acting suspicious as of late, and as your husband, it is my right to know why."

"Suspicious?" I screech. "My days are no different than they've always been." The lie singes my tongue, but I don't dare let it show.

"I just want to know what you're writing," he assures, attempting to correct his voice to a soothing, placating tone.

"This is the one thing I have for myself, Johnathan. The *one thing* that is mine and only mine. And you want to invade that because of what? Because you're more drunk than you are sane and suddenly think it is *I* who has things to hide? You've been hiding truths from me for months! And you have the gall to accuse me?"

I take a step toward him, holding the journal to my chest.

"If you dare read this, I will never forgive you. Any hope of our having a marriage beyond a piece of paper forcing us together will crumble away. I will cease to love you, to care for you, to hold any part of you dear. This diary is *all* I have, and you will not take that away from me. Do you understand me?"

He's furious. It's visible by the way he fumes silently, clenching his fists until they bleach white as he glowers at me with resentment.

Deep down, he can sense that I'm no longer in love with him, and while he may not realize it yet, he knows there's something wrong with me beyond being upset over his transgressions. I'm certain he doesn't know why I've strayed, but I'm sure there's a niggling feeling in the back of his head warning him of my own betrayal.

And I'm robbing him of the peace of mind that would accompany assuaging that feeling.

I do feel guilty for that, truly. But I also know that if he were to find out, not only would Sera suffer more than she already has but also I might not survive it.

Considering his drinking . . . and how hatefully he stares at me now.

I don't trust him not to hurt me.

He seems to deflate, though his gaze is still full of disappointment and anger. "You've changed, Gigi. I don't even recognize you anymore," he whispers, giving me a once-over as if I'm an otherworldly being.

"I'm the result of your betrayal," I respond calmly. His brows jump in surprise, then lower in anger.

"How long will you make me suffer for a mistake?"

"*A* mistake? *A. Mistake?* Try several mistakes, John!" I shout, baffled by his nerve. I hold up a hand and count off each point. "You gambled away our entire life savings. You nearly made us homeless—our *daughter* homeless. You come home drunk nearly every night. You slept with me once thinking I was another woman. And then last time, you forced yourself on me!"

By the time I'm finished, I'm heaving with rage. "Not to mention all the times you've disrespected me and treated me like I'm below you. I thought you were better than that, Johnathan. You always said we were equals."

"Well, we're not!" he roars, causing me to wince. His face reddens, and he takes a menacing step toward me. "We're not equals, Genevieve. I am the husband who goes to work five days a week for ten hours straight. You have *no* idea what I deal with there—the amount of stress I'm under. Not to mention the war going on. I have friends fighting right now, and I've no idea if I'm ever going to see them again! *Then* I come home, and I have to be a husband and a father. I have to make you two happy, buy whatever you two ask for, hear about your days, and make sure the both of you feel loved."

I stare at him, utterly flabbergasted that he could diminish me so deeply. "I do so much—"

"Ah, yes!" he exclaims sarcastically. "You clean an already clean house, and you cook! It's wonderful, Gigi, truly. Until it's the weekend, and I have to maintain the yard and fix a leaky faucet or hang another stupid picture on the wall. All the while, you sit in that *goddamn* chair, writing in your stupid journal and staring out at the trees!"

His chest heaves, the last of his words echoing throughout the house.

Fuming, I step toward him, my bottom lip trembling. "You have such a terrible life, don't you? Your business is *thriving*, Johnathan. You're *successful*. You were bringing home more money than you've seen in your life, doing a job that you love. And you're right, there *is* a war going on—one that you don't have to fight in. You sit in your cushy chair in a skyscraper office with a beautiful view. Does it get a little stressful sometimes? Sure, but that's just called life, my dear. It's sure as hell a lot better than getting shot at, though, huh?"

I take another step, butting my chest against his.

"If you ever wanted to spend a night sober, you *could* come home to a hot meal waiting for you on the table and a beautiful wife. A wife that spent the last two hours helping her daughter with homework or soothing her because she has a mean schoolmate, all the while teaching her values and skills and nourishing her developing young mind. Before that, I spend my hours washing your filthy underwear, cleaning the house, grocery shopping, and ensuring there isn't a *single* chore for you to do when you get home. I'm so glad you're used to seeing a clean house,

John, but that's not because you and Sera don't make messes. It's because I'm constantly picking up after the two of you before you even notice!"

He opens his mouth to respond, but I hold up a finger. "I'm not finished! Before you started drinking, you would come home after a long day of work and sit at the table to eat, and the only thing we asked you to do was *listen*. To have a conversation with us. To spend time with us. Is that really so much work? And I *never* ask you for anything except necessities for our daughter. You shove money in my hands because you expect me to look beautiful for you every day. The last time you came home to find me without a stitch of makeup and a pretty dress, you asked me why I stopped putting effort into my appearance. You said there's no point in having a beautiful wife if I'm not going to look like one."

"I didn't say that!" he denies vehemently, but the truth is in his shameful stare.

"You did!" I shout. "You said you love to look at me, and that's why God gave me a pretty face and a smokin' hot body. For *your* viewing pleasure. So, I do it, John. I get all dolled up just for you. And when we go to bed, you turn *off* the lights, fuck me until *you're* satisfied, then roll over and go to bed! And oh-ho, *please* tell me the last time you fixed a single thing around this house. I ask you to spend a couple hours mowing the lawn while I garden, then you spend the rest of the day in your skivvies, drinking a beer. So, yes, John, your life is just so darn awful that it's only fair you go off and gamble away all that hard-earned money until your family has no roof over their heads, drink until you don't recognize your wife, and terrify your daughter with your drunken ramblings. So, you know what? If I want to spend an hour writing in my journal every day and staring out at the goddamn trees, *then I will*!"

I'm the one panting now, my cheeks flushed from having to defend myself to my own damn husband. His eyes close in defeat, and he turns away, hand on his hip while the other swipes over his mouth in contemplation. It's silent for a few moments while the two of us reconcile with the fact that our marriage will never be what it used to be.

"You're right, John," I say quietly. "I have changed. And so have you."

When he turns toward me again, heartbreak reflects in the downturn of his lips and the sadness in his eyes. And it hurts seeing him like this, especially when he's not the only one who's betrayed our marriage.

And that's just it. We're destroying each other.

The cold, hard truth is that he won't stop gambling and drinking.

And I won't stop my love affair.

"I won't allow you to divorce me, Gigi. Not with Sera," he states plainly.

I bristle. While there's no malice in his tone, it feels as if he's locked a cuff around each of our wrists, chaining us together. My instinct is to rage against those confines, but I know I can't.

Truthfully, I already knew that was my fate. It's frowned upon for a woman to leave a marriage, even more so when she's a mother. The courts would refuse me the divorce, anyway. Not unless Sera and I were in grave danger, and even then it would be a battle that would cost us more than it may be worth. And despite the ways John has hurt me, he's always treated Sera like a princess. Regardless of his recent missteps with her, their relationship is strong. It would be a lie to claim otherwise.

But would John's selfishness tear apart this family like my selfishness could? It would destroy Sera if she found out about my affair. And while I've fallen in love with Ronaldo, I will do *anything* for my daughter. Even if it means I cannot love freely.

I nod, though I couldn't muster a smile if I tried. A year ago, I would've rushed to him and cupped his cheeks between my palms while vowing we could get through anything together. I would've sworn that he was the love of my life, and that I would stand by him through it all.

Those promises escape me now.

"I love you, Genevieve. Do you love me?" he asks softly.

"I love you," I whisper.

Yet it's as hollow as the look in his eyes.

Turns out, neither of us will stop lying, either.

September 10, 1944

I haven't seen Ronaldo in three days.
Three days of wondering where he is. If something happened to
him. My thoughts spiraled.
John and I got into a fight. He says I've changed. That I'm no
longer the woman he fell in love with. I'm distant now. When he
wants to have sex, I'm not interested. It's his own fault for that,
and he knows it, too. There's still so much guilt in his eyes, yet
I can't find it in me to forgive him.
I've begun to feel like my marriage is wrong and dirty.
I've begun to feel like I'm cheating, but not on my husband. It
feels like I'm cheating on my phantom.
There wasn't much I could say to assure my husband I still love
him other than those three words. They've begun to feel empty
when I say them.
Based on the vacant look in his eyes, those three words have
begun to feel hollow to him, too. I'm losing my husband.
Slowly but surely.
And I'm ashamed to admit that I don't mind that too much.

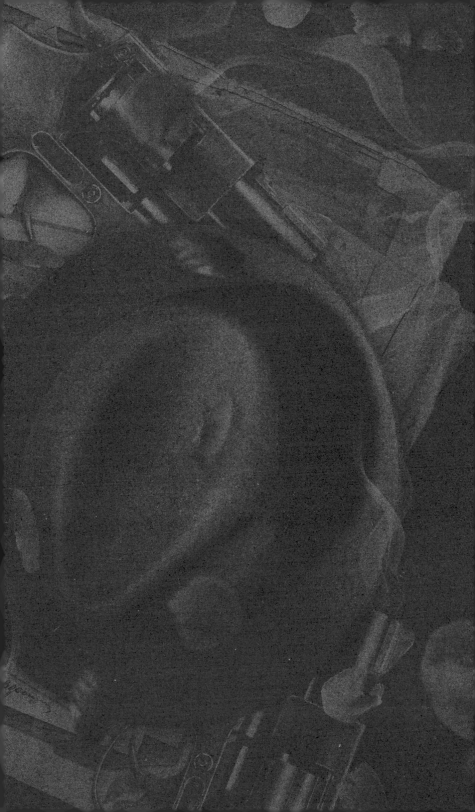

CHAPTER 17

THE PHANTOM

September 11, 1944

If Angelo knew I was here, I'd be swallowing his fist.

I couldn't convince myself to walk away if I tried, though.

I'm standing outside Parsons Manor, hiding in the shadows just beyond the tree line in front of the house.

Paulie is also hiding in the woods, though he's about ten feet ahead of me. Stalking *my* woman.

He's only following orders. If he weren't, it wouldn't be Angelo's fist flying down his throat, but a bullet.

While Paulie wouldn't dare kill Genevieve, there's no guarantee he wouldn't rough her up.

And anyone who inflicts pain on *mia rosa* will die. Simple as that.

I don't want to ice one of Angelo's best enforcers, so it's vital I make sure he doesn't get that far.

Beyond the tree line, Genevieve's daughter hurries out the front door and to the car, a rucksack hanging on her arm.

"Daddy, hurry up! We're going to be late!" she calls out impatiently.

John appears in the open doorway. "Bye, honey. Love you!" he shouts into the house. Genevieve must respond, because he closes the door behind him and makes his way to the car, quickening his speed when Sera shouts at him again to hurry.

Paulie waits for several minutes after they leave, ensuring that the car isn't returning for a forgotten item or some other reason that could take him by surprise.

Then he takes his first step out from behind the tree. I waste no time mirroring him, keeping my steps light as I quickly approach him from the rear.

He hears a twig snap too late. My arm is hooked around his throat before he can process my presence. "It's me, Paulie. It's me," I rush out just as he prepares to maneuver out of my hold.

He stills. "Ronnie? What the hell is wrong with you?" he bites out. I release him, allowing him to turn toward me with a baffled expression. "The hell you doin' here, Ron? You clockin' me?" he asks, now appearing wary, glancing around as if there's a target on his head.

I tap his cheek roughly, then point at him. "Watch what you call me, Paulie."

He rubs his cheek where I slapped him, giving me a disgruntled look. *"Ronaldo,"* he mutters.

Being the consigliere, I'm treated with the same respect as a don. Paulie knows better than to ever lay hands on me—not unless he wants to go swimming with the fishes.

"Plans have changed. We're to leave Genevieve Parsons be," I tell him, glancing behind him to ensure we're still out here alone.

Paulie narrows his eyes, staring at me suspiciously. Growing impatient, I grip him by the shoulder and pull him after me, forcing him to walk with me back toward the street.

He knows as well as I do that Angelo wouldn't give an order only to turn around and retract it within twenty-four hours. Especially when it's clear John has not handled his debts.

"You're here off the record, ain't ya?" he questions.

I clench my teeth, and when I don't respond right away, he gets irate. "Come on, Ronni—*Ronaldo*—you know he ain't gonna just bust my chops and send me on my way. It's gonna be my head—"

"Angelo will not punish you for my decisions. I'll make sure of that."

It'll be *my* head, but I have over two decades of friendship with Angelo, which offers me some layer of protection from his wrath. But I'm not completely immune. Angelo is the head of a powerful family, and I can only disrespect his orders so much before I become a problem.

I'm taking a huge risk sticking my nose where it doesn't belong, but it's worth it—*Genevieve* is worth it.

"You have a plan?" Paulie flicks another wary look my way, cementing that I'm doing something incredibly stupid, his words silent but clear: *I hope you know what you're doing.*

I don't.

But I do have an idea that may save my skin.

After scoping out Parsons Manor and stumbling upon Genevieve, I continued to look into John. At first, he was the man who owed Angelo Salvatore thousands of dollars. Now, he's the man who's married to my girl.

Eventually, I located John's place of work, discovering that he owns a bookkeeping firm in downtown Seattle. He does very well for himself, and he acquired a large inheritance, which explains how he could afford to build a home like Parsons Manor.

Now, he's broke and deeply indebted to the biggest crime family in Seattle.

It was dumb luck that John works in a field that could be valuable to the Salvatores.

The only thing I need to do is convince Angelo to see that.

Otherwise, John and I are *both* dead men, leaving Genevieve alone. A bird like that won't stay single for long, and no one—*no one*—will ever love her the way I do.

September 11, 1944

Angelo has connections everywhere. Many professionals are on his payroll, including the police force, politicians, and more CEOs than I can count.

One of those people is a powerful banker, Lenny Giordani.

He's currently staring at me like I've grown a second head. If I weren't a composed man, I'd smash my fist into his face hard enough for the design of my ring to imprint on the inside of his cheek.

"Let me get this right: You want to pay off the remainder of John Parsons's mortgage? Do you realize how much money that is?" Lenny asks, staring at me incredulously.

"What gave you the impression I was an idiot?" I growl.

"Four thousand dollars, Ronaldo," he repeats for the *third* time.

"I'm half-blind, Lenny, not half-deaf," I snap, growing impatient.

Angelo pays me more than enough to cover the cost, and Lenny knows that. It's not a matter of being able to afford it; it's a matter of why I'd spend that type of money on someone like John.

Lenny finally takes the hint and drops his gaze to the check lying on his desk already written out for the remaining amount owed on Parsons Manor. "You must really love this house," he mutters.

Only the one who inhabits it.

I keep that dangerous thought to myself. I know better than to reveal my weakness. It's bad enough Paulie knows, and I dread the day Angelo finds out.

The fewer people who know about Genevieve, the better. It's *safer*. For both of us.

Sighing, Lenny picks up the check and shakes his head.

"All right, I'll get it squared away."

"Thank you," I clip, standing from the chair seated in front of his desk. Then I toss a few bills onto the cherrywood, covering my fee for his services.

Without a backward glance, I leave his office, feeling a small weight lift from my shoulders. Parsons Manor is paid off, and I've already settled John's past-due balances on the utility bills he neglected to pay.

As far as legitimate companies are concerned, he's paid up.

As far as *I'm* concerned, he owes me now.

And it's his wife I intend to collect.

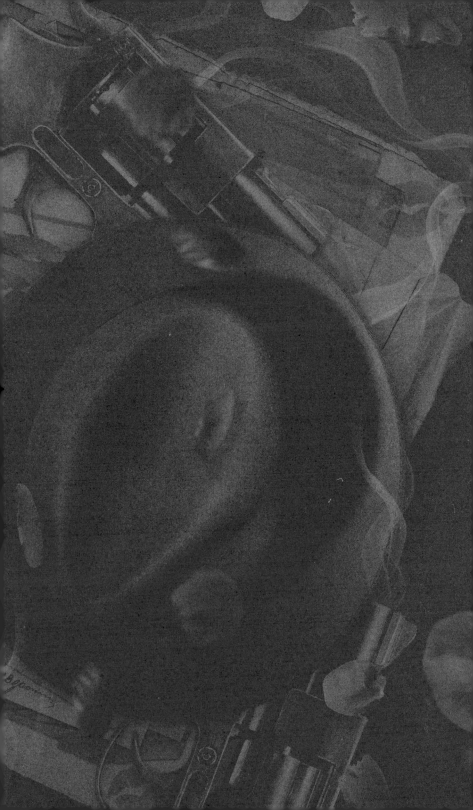

CHAPTER 18

THE PHANTOM

September 12, 1944

The fourth time Angelo's fist flies into the side of my face, I dig my blunt nails into my palms, just barely restraining myself from returning the favor.

Alfonso would shoot me dead before I could make it halfway, so I accept the hit.

Blood fills my mouth, and I'm forced to swallow it down rather than spit it on the floor at Angelo's feet. If I'm not already on the verge of eating a bullet, that would certainly have me biting one down.

"You betrayed my trust!" Angelo seethes, snarling in my bruised face. "You interfered with my order, and now the swine owes me even *more* money!"

I've failed my boss.

And it was intentional.

Allowing Paulie to take Genevieve hostage was impossible. The thought of another man laying hands on her had me seeing red. And I know that I would've put Paulie down before allowing him to set one goddamn foot in her house.

And how would she have reacted if he did break into her home, intent on kidnapping her? Would she have held a knife to his throat like she did to mine?

I think I'd kill Paulie for that alone—for having the privilege of experiencing Genevieve in such a way. When she held that knife to me, all I could think about was letting her slice through me if it meant getting closer to her.

I wanted to hurt her, all right, but her screams would have been in ecstasy rather than pain.

All I want that woman to do is love me like I love her.

I want it to be all-consuming. To be so goddamn deep, a lobotomy couldn't even carve me out of her head.

"This is *your* fault," Angelo hisses, stabbing a finger into my chest.

"Yes, boss," I agree, working to keep my tone even. It takes a special type of man to take a hit without retaliating. I've worked hard to become that type, but I will gladly unravel the moment he threatens Genevieve.

"If you were anyone else, Ronnie, *anyone else*, you'd be wearin' cement shoes right now." The pain in his stare hurts. Angelo has been my family longer than my own was. Our bond is thicker than blood, and I loathe putting the strain of my disobedience on our relationship. However, Genevieve doesn't deserve to get mixed up in her husband's business, and I can't find it in myself to regret my actions.

"And if she were anyone else, she'd be here," I respond quietly. Angelo's expression slackens, shock glimmering in his dark eyes. As long as we've known each other, Angelo has never seen me smitten with anyone. I've entertained many women, but never long enough to keep them in my bed for more than a night.

He scoffs, then turns away from me and links his hands behind his back. Mona Lisa stares at me with disapproval as he paces before me. Alfonso sits in his usual spot in the chair across from his brother's desk, keeping quiet as he stares at us. He's contemplative as smoke billows from his mouth, his cigar nearly depleted.

"Bring John in," Angelo barks aloud.

Two other lackeys, Roger and Samuel, are standing behind me, their chins high, faces slack, always on standby for instruction.

One of them shuffles behind me. There's a click of the office door and silence for a few strained beats before it swings open again. I peer over my shoulder as Roger drags a gagged John into the middle of the room and drops him unceremoniously at Angelo's feet.

Muffled pleas arise from behind the gag in John's mouth, which are promptly ignored. Instead, Angelo pulls out his Colt from the back of his trousers and presses the barrel to John's forehead.

John shakes his head profusely, his indecipherable begging growing louder. Angelo snarls while sobs shake John's shoulders.

Truthfully, the sight brings me such immense joy, I'm nearly delirious from it. Since the moment Genevieve confessed what he did to her, I've been picturing all the ways I'd slowly torture him to death. Make him cry and beg for mercy. Make him suffer in unimaginable ways. Even worse, I can't look at him without imagining the act itself, and a rage unlike anything I've felt before fills me every time.

My hands tremble with the need to whip out my gun and shoot him myself. I clench my fists, focusing on keeping still.

"Your life for over sixteen thousand dollars. Something tells me it's not worth that much, but I'll make do," Angelo spits.

Just as he thumbs back the hammer of the revolver, a melodic voice whispers in my ear.

Promise me you will never play a hand in his death.

I close my eyes, frustration building in my chest. His finger is seconds from pulling the trigger, and guilt unfurls in the pit of my stomach as Genevieve's pleas circulate in my mind.

Even if not for me, please do it for Sera.

Genevieve will be devastated if I stand by and do nothing while Angelo pulls that trigger.

Their *daughter* will be devastated.

And what kind of man am I to make her a promise just to allow it to be broken?

"Boss," I interject, stepping forward, the word tasting like acid on my tongue. The answering look from Angelo could melt the ice caps, but I don't back down.

It's in my best interest to allow John to be shot dead. It would relieve Genevieve of her marriage to her abuser, and I could have her to myself. She would be mine and *only* mine.

However, my mother didn't raise a monster through what little parenting she offered after my father's passing. Killing a young girl's father for my own selfishness isn't a sin I'll allow myself, especially knowing that it would break Genevieve's heart. And while it is not me pulling the trigger, that doesn't remove the blood from my hands.

"He has other uses. Uses that would prove him to be valuable, after all," I say evenly.

"You have two seconds, otherwise I'm firing two bullets tonight."

A threat that I've heard countless times when pulling Angelo off the edge. I *should* be fearful for my life. I've seen Angelo turn his gun on a made man for less.

However, I'm his consigliere for a reason, and it's typically because of my ability to rein him in from making irrational decisions at every turn. Most days, I succeed.

Other days—I don't.

"He's an accountant," I explain. "Despite his terrible poker face, he is exceptional with numbers. It's a wonder he didn't count cards."

John spits out a few words that sound like *I'm no cheat.*

Angelo must pick up on it, too, because he casts an unreadable look his way. I've piqued his interest, though, so I forge on.

"If his life isn't worth his debt, let his hard work be," I continue. "He can work for free until it's paid off. He has the potential to become a big earner for us."

Angelo's a smart businessman, but he's a hothead, and at this moment, all his statues are facing away. Which means I can't trust him to think rationally or be reasonable.

"Are you asking me to give him a pass, Ronnie? You vouchin' for him?"

I grit my teeth. For Genevieve, I'll do anything. Even put my life on the line for her abusive husband.

"Yes, boss."

He studies me closely before turning his focus to John. He sucks his teeth, seeming to contemplate my offer. All the while, my heart thuds heavily. A fraction of a second is all it will take for him to end John's life, and admittedly, I would celebrate his death.

I've done all I could to save his life.

Now, his consequences are his own.

Sweat pours down John's reddened face, and he stares up at Angelo with a fear that only God can put into him. His pleas are silent, but they are mighty because a moment later, Angelo lifts his gun to the ceiling, signaling his acceptance of my suggestion.

His stare stays locked onto John, though he addresses me first. "All right, Ronnie, we'll try it your way. But this deal comes with conditions." After a beat, he continues, holding John's widened stare. "You will work off not only your debt but also the interest you have accrued."

John's words are muffled, though it's clear enough to catch what he says: *What interest?*

Angelo's subsequent grin is smarmy, and he no longer stares at John with contempt but rather hope for an opportunity that may make him far more money than John has seen in his lifetime.

"My wrath is your interest. You will take the omertà and work for me until you become a problem." He turns away from John, the corners of his lips stretching wider as he rounds his desk and takes a seat, adopting a casual stance as he leans back into his chair.

"Believe me, John. You don't want to become a problem."

In other words, John is going to become a made man whether he likes it or not.

And the only way out of this life is through death.

September 16, 1944

Ever since I told Daisy about John, she has been sending letters more frequently throughout the months. She's damn near interrogating me about John, and I've told her everything. How his gambling habits haven't waned. His paychecks go entirely to catching us up on bills, and then we fall behind again. Left with little money for eating or buying ourselves basic necessities.
I also told her about that awful June night. Her response was written so angrily into the page that her pen tore through it in several spots. Some of her words were unintelligible, but I got the gist.
She was seething mad, and begged me to find a lawyer.
But what lawyer would see it as anything other than a marital duty? As John's wife, my body is his.
Even so, I couldn't bear to rip Sera away from her father.
She loves him dearly, and my husband treats her like royalty.
Once I responded with a letter explaining this, she understood my position, though she didn't shy away from expressing her distaste for my husband.
In the end, it does not matter that I am the receiver of all John's mistakes.
Because at least I have Ronaldo.
Wherever he is.

CHAPTER 19

THE RAVEN

September 18, 1944

M y diary sits on my lap, the blank page glaring at me. I
have so much to say, yet I'm unable to string together
an intelligible sentence when my thoughts are racing.

It's been over a week since Ronaldo visited, and I've all but convinced
myself that either he's lost interest or something terribly wrong has
happened.

Throughout the five or so months he's been coming around, I've
gotten used to going days and days without seeing him. Yet there's a
persistent feeling in my gut that something has happened.

I've had my pen poised over the paper for the past five minutes, and just as I touch the metal tip to it, the front door opens.

My heart stalls, and my muscles freeze into solid ice.

Then I hear the familiar cadence of my phantom's footsteps, and it's like adrenaline has been injected into my veins. I shoot up from my chair, the journal and pen scattering across the checkered floor. I pay them no mind as I barrel toward the infuriating man who's somehow stolen my heart.

My arms are around his neck in seconds while his palm warms my lower back instinctively. Instantly, his sandalwood, orange, and tobacco scent brings me comfort. But before I can bask in the relief of seeing him again, a pained grunt slips past his lips.

Pulling back, I gasp, instantly noticing the purpling skin beneath his right eye and several gashes along his cheekbone.

"What happened to you?" I ask, setting a gentle palm on his cheek, my fingers lightly brushing over the discoloration.

"It's nothing, my love," he assures, warming my hand on his face with his own. The touch is affectionate, but I'm unable to appreciate it when I'm nearly choking on my concern.

"It doesn't look like nothing!"

"It's nothing I didn't deserve." What a cryptic answer. No less from a cryptic man. "I'm sorry I stayed away so long. I didn't want you to see me like this but . . . I couldn't endure another day without you."

His words ease my tightened throat like warm honey, though I can't let go of my concern. Someone hurt him, and that hurts *me*.

"At least tell me who did this," I whisper, my brows crinkling as I study every bruise, every cut.

"My boss. He was unhappy with a decision I made."

None of his responses gives me any idea of what happened, but I let it go for now. This man is like a snow globe that has frosted over. It doesn't matter how hard I shake him; he will show me nothing unless I crack him open and his contents spill out.

However, I can be patient. But he can only keep me in the dark for only so long before I'll grow bored with his mysteriousness. I have a husband that has excelled at the craft, and I certainly do not need another man with that skill set.

"Is there anything I can do to make you feel better?" I ask quietly.

A simple question, yet I feel like it will open a door that leads to many complications.

His pale eyes trail over my face and down to my throat, where my pulse thunders beneath my flesh.

Can he see it? How deeply he affects me. How strongly I *feel* him.

Tension gathers in the surrounding air, embracing the two of us like a warm blanket.

His fingers slide along my cheek and into the depth of my curls while my hand drops from his face down to his chest. I inhale a sharp breath, shivering from his gentle touch.

He tugs me closer, pressing his chest into mine. He stands several inches taller, and if I lift onto my toes just a bit, it would be so easy for him to . . .

Nothing could have prepared me for his lips crashing into mine. He wastes no time twirling his tongue around my own in a sensual dance.

While every other kiss was electrifying, this one encapsulates a storm beyond earth's capabilities.

It's cosmic, cataclysmic.

A tinge of copper blooms on my taste buds where the pressure has irritated his split lip. It does nothing to deter me. Rather, our kiss only deepens, just as I fall deeper into the cosmos.

My hands glide down his chest and tear his button-up out from his trousers before diving beneath the fabric. He groans as I familiarize myself with his chiseled stomach and then his defined chest muscles, which are covered in a thin layer of hair.

My pointer finger whispers over his nipple, earning me a deep growl. Invigorated, I fasten his bottom lip between my teeth, nipping sharply and drawing more blood.

I scarcely register his walking me backward until my back slams against a wall. The force of it causes a heavy breath to expel from my lungs. I'm granted one last sip of oxygen before his mouth demands more from me. I'm eager to oblige, giving him every ounce of me I have to offer.

Fingers close around my throat, and he brings me away from the wall an inch just to slam me back against it. He rips his mouth away from mine just as I gasp when he releases my throat. Then he drags his nose along my neck, inhaling deeply.

"You're brave, *mia rosa*. But I'm curious to know *how* brave," he ponders, his tone devilish.

His voice against my throat coaxes goose bumps to rise across my flesh like an evening tide.

"You've never scared me the way you should've," I breathe, my chest heaving and heart pounding. "Whatever gave you the impression that I was a scared little mouse?"

He clicks his tongue as if chiding me. "I would guess the moment I make you squeal like one."

A moment later, his teeth are sinking into the soft spot beneath my ear. I'm unable to control the sound that bursts from my throat. High-pitched, just like a damned mouse.

However, he wastes no time gloating and instead thrusts his hips into mine. His hard length presses into my stomach, expressing a different type of hunger than his teeth did.

"I think you can squeal louder than that, no?" he purrs, his voice dipping impossibly deeper. My mother spoke of a voice like that—said it belonged to the ruler of hell. She warned me of this being's dangerous pull over our will and made me swear to find God during these moments.

She'd be disappointed to know that I'm so delirious from Ronaldo's touch, I wouldn't be able to locate where the hell God is, let alone how to reach Him. I'm convinced she was a silly woman.

How could Ronaldo rule hell if he makes me see heaven?

"Ronaldo," I moan, feeling constricted in the clothing covering my body. It's too much, and I need it off.

As if hearing my silent plea, his hands shred at my blouse, tugging it out from under the waistband of my skirt before ripping it apart, sending the pearl buttons flying. The bite of metal from my zipper coming undone sounds a moment later, and the clothing sluices off my skin like water, leaving me in my undergarments and black heels.

He takes a second to rake his heated gaze over my body. The black bra containing my aching breasts and the matching girdle slimming my waist, holding on to my sheer black stockings, the tops rimmed with lace. It's a different set than I wore last time—a more risqué one. While the other had lace detailing, this one has sheer panels highlighting my curves. Silk conceals the parts of me that are most fun to uncover.

I wore it in hopes that Ronaldo would come, just like I've been wearing other scandalous sets for the last couple days. Until today, they went to waste.

I had bought this one for an anniversary that John forgot to celebrate with me.

And now, I'm glad for it.

It feels right that Ronaldo's the first to see me in these undergarments, especially when they were intended for a husband that never seemed to appreciate me.

Which is the exact opposite of what my visitor is doing. His stare

190 | H. D. CARLTON

ravishes my body, his eyes darting over me like he can't get enough. Like he'll miss a vital part of me if he doesn't scour every inch.

"You . . . are exquisite, *mia rosa*," he rasps, his darkened gaze finally lifting to mine. "I am undeserving."

I lift my chin haughtily. "I believe that's for me to decide."

There's very little in life that I've had control over. My dad was too busy breaking his back as a section hand to notice me, and my mother feared God more than she loved me. When she wasn't berating me about my rebellious attitude—which would surely prevent any respectable man from marrying me—she was hammering God into my head with a vengeance crueler than the spikes that were nailed into Jesus's hands.

But the harder she tried to coerce me into following in her footsteps, the less I wanted to. I didn't want to submit to a vengeful God any more than I wanted to submit to a man.

Yet somehow, I fear that's almost exactly where I've found myself. I may not read the Bible as a bedtime story, but I am an ant ensnared in a circle of salt. I'm trapped in the confines of these walls while my husband leaves me here to wander aimlessly.

I have a life, yet I'm no less a prisoner than the ghosts that haunt these hallways.

Ronaldo—he's a choice. Maybe a terrible one, but one all the same. He's the first selfish decision I've made for myself, and I can't deny how thrilling it feels.

I gather every morsel of courage in my throat, then say, "You should know, this ensemble is just as beautiful on the floor as it is on me."

He nods slowly as if assessing the situation and passes his stare over my form one more time before locking eyes with me. Then one corner of his mouth lifts into a smirk and he . . . he walks away!

My mouth falls open, shock paralyzing me as I watch the infuriating man saunter toward the door. The only thing missing from his gait is a carefree tune whistling from his lips as if he simply does not give a damn about what he's turning away from.

Oh, he will *not* get away with leaving me like this! If he does . . . I swear he will never see me in such a state again!

Just as my feet unglue from the floor, I chase after him. But before I can give him the worst tongue-lashing he's ever heard, he pivots toward the staircase. Craning his head over his shoulder just enough to catch my gaze, he winks, then turns and continues up the steps.

Confused but now more intrigued, I follow him. By the time I reach the top, he's halfway down the hallway.

The click of my heels across the wooden floorboards echoes as I slowly trail after him. He faces my bedroom, flicks one last stare my way, then enters.

Heart pounding, I pass a spare bedroom, glimpsing another figure standing within. The sudden intrusion has the erratic muscle in my chest flying up into my throat. Instinctively, I whip my stare toward the doorway, finding it empty.

It was just a flash, but I know something was standing there.

Likely judging me for my careless decision. Even more so now that I'm willing to entertain another man in my marital bed.

Let the ghosts judge. Unlike them, I have a life to live, and I might as well enjoy it before I join their miserable souls in the afterlife.

Swallowing down the residual fear, I reach my bedroom and find Ronaldo sitting on the edge of the chest at the foot of the bed, staring blankly at the wall before him. My vanity is directly in front of him, offering him a perfect view of himself through the gold-framed mirror. To the left of him and directly opposite me is a full-length mirror, which offers me an uninterrupted view of myself.

Two souls staring into our own eyes, unable to hide from the choice we're both going to make.

I look away from my reflection, and my stare clashes with his.
Neither of us dares change our minds.

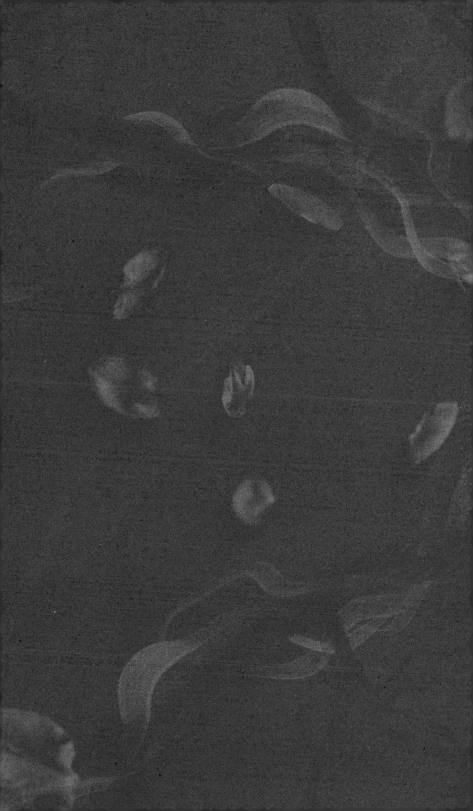

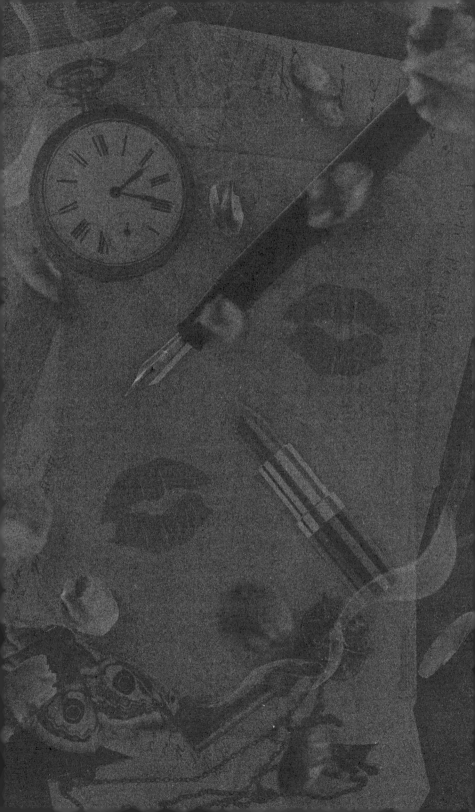

CHAPTER 20

THE RAVEN

September 18, 1944

"Come here, *mia rosa*," he commands roughly.

Fastening my lip beneath my teeth, I sashay toward him, swinging my hips and drawing his hungry gaze to them. Is he imagining holding on to them as he drives himself inside me? Is he picturing me on my back or on my knees? I hope to experience both.

Truly, I'm greedy, but I can't find it in me to release the gluttonous thoughts.

I pause a few feet away from him, just out of reach.

I've done enough pursuing. Enough waiting for him to touch me. If he wants me, he will have to beg.

"Closer," he urges before darting his tongue across his lip. It glistens just as I imagine my inner thighs do.

There's a steady throb there, and I can feel my arousal overwhelming my panties. If I were to spread my legs for him, he'd find just how deeply he affects me. For now, I take a step back.

His stare darts up to mine, a clear warning radiating from his eyes. *Don't you dare.*

Oh, how I dare.

I take another step away, and he slowly rises to his feet, like a predator watching its prey attempt to escape.

"I recall your leaving me in a similar state of undress once before," I remind him. "And I felt so . . . empty when you left. Do you know how that feels?" I cock my head, and he imitates the movement.

"More than you know."

"Yet you would have me feel the same," I shoot back. "I think it would be in your best interest to ask for my forgiveness."

Several emotions flit across his penetrating stare. Surprise, challenge, amazement, and most prominent of all, starvation.

Silently, he removes his fedora, setting it down on the chest with one hand while running the other through his midnight strands.

Of course, we don't talk about the specifics of his secretive job, but for some strange reason, seeing him without his hat and with the bruises marring his face, the first impression that I get is that this man is a mafioso. With his slick black hair, the dangerous look in his eyes, expensive suit, and the gold pinky ring, there's no mistaking his Italian roots—or that they may have granted him access to a troubling lifestyle.

That should warn me away from him, yet I keep still, awaiting his next move.

Holding my stare, he removes his button-up completely. I scarcely contain my gasp as he reveals his beautifully carved body: robust biceps that tighten with power and a stomach that reminds me of the washboard I scrub our clothing on. He's chiseled to perfection, and I'm almost ashamed to admit how my mouth salivates like a hungry dog.

My God . . . he *is* a god.

A knowing smirk quirks his lips while he kicks off his shoes, then removes his socks. Next, he focuses on his belt, kicking my heart rate up a notch. He tugs the entire length from the loops and has his trousers undone in a matter of seconds. His underwear is tight to his skin, making it impossible to miss the hardened length protruding from it.

I swallow thickly, taking another step back—this one unintentional.

He's . . . far bigger than I've seen.

Granted, John has been my only lover, and he's far less endowed. It's . . . God, it's intimidating, to say the least.

"Does my cock scare you, *mia rosa*?" he questions, amusement coloring his dark voice.

"Yes," I admit, forcing my gaze to his. "But unlike the mouse you claim me to be, I don't run."

As if to challenge me, he hooks his thumbs into the elastic waistband and slides his underwear down his thick legs, freeing himself from the confines.

Again, I struggle to swallow. It's so very long, and impossibly thick. Pronounced veins run up his length to the reddened tip, where a bead of liquid drips.

I hadn't thought about it before, but at this moment, I'm faced with the reality that I can't recall if I've ever seen John's penis. My own husband, and I don't know what he looks like.

He's never been so inclined to show me as Ronaldo is.

"That"—I breathe shakily—"is a dangerous weapon."

He grins cheekily. "If only it could win the war."

"It won me," I confess. "Is that enough?"

His long fingers wrap around himself, and I nearly choke from the erotic sight.

"We'll see if you still feel the same way after it makes you scream," he drawls, now approaching me.

Anxiety nips at my nerves, but I force steel into my spine. Even if the threat coming from his mouth is as dark as it is delicious.

He molds his chest against mine, forcing me to crane my neck up to meet his stare. With his length pressed into my stomach, it feels even more unnerving, so I focus on his imposing height instead. Even with my heels, he towers over me. Just as I begin to feel small beneath his predatory gaze, his stare drops to my breasts.

I don't realize his hand has snaked behind my back until I feel the material of my bra tighten a moment before it completely loosens. I catch it before it falls.

"Wait! You— You're taking everything off?"

John always preferred a lights-off, under-the-covers type of lovemaking, and my nightgown has never made it to the floor. The only clothing he removed were the necessary garments. Not . . . *everything!*

"I want to see all of you," he insists, directing my hands to my sides. The bra falls from my limp arms, and while I have the instinct to conceal myself, I force myself to keep still. I don't know if I've ever undressed completely for John before, but something tells me Ronaldo wouldn't appreciate my sudden modesty.

My eyes flutter when his hands palm my breasts and his fingers pluck at my hardened nipples. I bite back a moan, trapping my bottom lip beneath my teeth as little spikes of pleasure zip through my system.

"You are otherworldly, Genevieve," he whispers, his tone full of awe. Then he wraps an arm around my waist and lifts me up against him. My toes dangle a few inches above the ground as he bows his head and catches one of my nipples beneath his teeth.

A sharp cry rips from my throat, his wet tongue eliciting a heady pleasure that shoots directly to my core.

Black strands of my hair fall over his forehead as he moves to the other breast, delivering the same mix of pain and pleasure. Alternating between nipping at the hardened bud and soothing it with his tongue, then sucking it deeply.

I'm lightheaded when he pulls away.

"Do you forgive me yet?" he probes before playfully nipping at the swell of my breast.

"I haven't heard an apology," I say, trying to adopt a stern voice, though it's breathless and shaky.

He hums and gives one final kiss to my nipple before setting me down.

Blinking, I watch him with bemusement as he drops to his knees, holding my stare as he does.

"What are you—"

"Your forgiveness, my love. I ask it of you," he rasps. I'm rendered speechless as he plucks at the garter straps clipped to my stockings. "There is little in life I'm deserving of—little that I allow myself to indulge in. Yet you are the crux of all my selfish desires. I would cease to breathe if I could not share air with you, Genevieve. If I can't live with you, I refuse to at all."

Astonished by his declaration, I can only gape at him.

Taking my silence as acceptance, he unclips the garters from my stockings, though he doesn't remove them from my legs. Then, one by one, he undoes the tiny hooks on the side of my girdle, slowly separating the material, along with any will I had left to resist him.

He slides the material down, catching the edges of my underwear on the way and lowering them both to the floor, prompting me to step free from them.

Panting, I stand before him in only my black stockings and heels, and rather than asking him to remove those, too, I decide to keep them on. The extra height and a bit of lace gives me a boost of confidence I sorely need. They make me feel desirable, and I haven't felt this way in far too long.

His mouth is inches away from my core, and I'm sure a mere glance would betray where my arousal has already begun to leak down my thighs.

"Shall I continue to beg?" he asks, his pale-blue eyes glittering gems as he kneels before me.

Choppily, I nod, still bereft of words. I'm only thankful I can still hear him beneath the deafening beat of my heart.

The first touch of his fingers over my flesh sends electric currents scattering up my spine, and I twitch beneath him. Undeterred, he nudges my inner thighs, prompting me to spread them farther apart.

The second his probing stare drops to my core, the entirety of my body flushes hot, tingles invading the tips of my fingers and spreading down to my toes. Thank God I groomed myself there earlier, shearing my hair to a light dusting. I've heard whispers from wives that men like us to be more . . . well kempt, and while I never needed to worry about such a thing before, I had the urge to test that theory on Ronaldo.

No man's face has ever been this close to the most vulnerable part of me—not even my husband's. I'm unaware of a time he's even explored that part of me with his hands, let alone his gaze.

Whereas this . . . this is far more salacious. And thrilling, no less.

I'm expecting him to use his fingers to touch me—I brace myself for it. So, I'm wholly unprepared for him to lean forward and lash out his tongue over my sensitive nub, sending a shock wave rebounding through my body.

I gasp, my hand flying to his hair.

"Ronaldo! That's— What are you doing?"

"You've never had your cunt licked?" he questions, his words vulgar and . . . unlike anything I've been asked before.

"What? N-no, of course not! Why would he . . ." I trail off, not wanting to mention John at such an intimate moment.

"There is nothing more divine than a cunt that weeps. It would be an honor to taste you, Genevieve."

I sputter, unable to string together a coherent thought, let alone a sentence.

"We can go as slow as you wish, *mia rosa*, but my love is as gentle as it is fierce. And when it comes to your pleasure, my needs are insatiable," he warns. "Even when you're begging for mercy, I will still hunger for more. *And I will take it.*"

My stomach twists with nerves, but his promises only deepen my intrigue and my relentless pursuit to experience a man like Ronaldo. Even if I possessed a morsel of self-preservation, I'd throw it all away for him.

I nod, the movement jerky but eager.

With that, he leans forward and licks along the seam of my core, holding my stare as he does.

My lips fall into a perfect O, instantly overcome with the foreign sensation. It's so wet, and warm, and my *God*, it's heavenly. My knees weaken as he fits his shoulders between my legs, forcing me to widen my stance farther. A small alarm blares in the back of my mind, warning of my growing inability to stand on my feet. But I can't bear to separate myself from his mouth.

As if sensing my impending collapse, he circles one arm around the backs of my thighs, cocooning me in his embrace and keeping me upright. Concurrently, he bars any chance of escape from his prying tongue.

I sway, diving my hands into his hair to ground me and letting my head fall back as he . . . as he *devours* me. Moans and whimpers fall past my lips unabashedly, and after a few moments, I roll my hips to meet each swipe of his tongue—every flick, every swirl, every teasing scrape of his teeth.

He groans against me and mumbles, "You taste like nirvana. I could drown in your pussy."

Through blurred vision, I notice his arm moving up and down. Curious, I grip his hair tighter and force his head back long enough to see his long fingers wrapped around himself, stroking his cock slowly as he pleasures me. My mouth waters. The sight is incredibly erotic, unleashing butterflies in my stomach.

Growling, he dives back in, and I have no qualms with letting him. I've heard whispers of women who give oral pleasure to men—have even heard about how they did it. But I've never understood it or why they'd want to. Now, I understand completely.

I can't entirely see him stroking himself as he licks me, but the image in my head suffices. Never did I think I'd want to suck on something so badly, but that's exactly what I want. I'm certain he'd taste divine.

"Ronaldo," I breathe, "God, I want to taste you, too."

He moans again, eagerly lapping me up until my lungs are bereft of oxygen.

I'm no longer a housewife or a loving mother, but a brazen seductress. Lost to the building euphoria, I hardly notice when he grips the backside of my left knee and hooks it over his shoulder, his other arm continuing to support my weight.

This new angle allows him full access, proven when he proceeds to thoroughly explore my inner walls, causing my jaw to nearly unhinge from the force of my outcry.

My lower stomach tightens into a knot, and the bliss seems to only intensify until I'm certain the pleasure can't get any stronger. But then Ronaldo rallies to prove me wrong, and he suctions my clit into his mouth. I'm dragged to a peak, only for him to forcefully shove me off it.

The tidal wave that passes through me is cataclysmic, and it shatters me wholly. The sound that tears from my throat is so sharp, it nearly shreds my vocal cords. Yet I'm unable to hear it past the storm that has swept me far away. Lightning flashes across my otherwise blackened vision, those electric streaks filled with bright colors. They explode over and over until I'm desperate for a reprieve.

Mercilessly, I grind my hips against his face, both of my hands diving into his dark strands and pulling taut. There's no resistance as I hold him tightly against me, desperate to feel this ecstasy forever.

Soon, it becomes too much. The strength I had to hold myself upright dissipates.

Ronaldo tears himself away. However, there's no hope for my bones to serve me well, and they've grown weary of supporting me. I collapse against him, and he uses the momentum to stand, lifting me in his arms as he does. With a grace only a lion can possess, he hooks my legs over his arms, and every inch of my body molds to him. The new position traps his length directly against my aching core, and like a desperate harlot, I grind against him.

He sucks a sharp hiss between his teeth, and I mumble unintelligibly, "Oh my God."

Despite having come down from that high, I'm delirious. Unable to form a single coherent thought. The only thing I'm sure of is that I want him to do it again.

"Ronaldo," I whimper, overcome with a desperation I would liken to a wolf in a famine. I would do *anything* for him to appease this chasmal emptiness between my legs. And like a starved beast, I'm on the verge of clawing at him and sinking my teeth into his flesh if it would bring me closer to my desires.

"Patience, my love," he growls, but the meaning of his demand is lost on me.

What is patience when I am feral with the need to be filled? I roll my hips against him, evoking a warning groan from him. He climbs onto the bed and drops me onto it, severing the delicious contact.

"Ronaldo!" I whine, lifting enough to lean back on my elbows.

My legs fall apart, and he kneels between them. *Still* so far away from where I need him. His hands pin me to the bed, exposing my core completely to his ravenous stare. It's his for the taking, offered to him with enthusiasm.

I'm an evening primrose, and he is the moonlight. Beneath his touch, I unfurl for him as if he is the sole reason I breathe.

"Please," I beg. "Fill me, Ronaldo. I— *God*, I need it."

Inhaling deeply, he releases my legs to loom over me, bracing his arms on either side of my head. "You beg for me like a whore, Genevieve," he murmurs.

I should be insulted, yet his tone suggests that he's entranced by my brazenness.

I lift my chin, boldly holding his stare as I demand, "So fuck me like one."

CHAPTER 21

THE PHANTOM

September 18, 1944

I'm dumbstruck by such a licentious command.

In my thirty-six years, I've never heard a woman use such vulgar language. Never had a woman demand from me so boldly, either.

She's a marvel—a wonder that I haven't even begun to truly learn yet.

Even so, her brazen words affect me viscerally. My cock swells further, becoming painfully harder than it's ever been. And I'm overcome with the carnal need to make her wish she never asked me to fuck her with a fierceness that will surely send us both into an early grave.

At this moment, I couldn't give a damn.

I lean closer to her, unleashing all those dark desires and allowing her to see just how dangerous it is to challenge me.

"As you wish, my love."

Her straight teeth bite into her plump bottom lip, though the red staining them is now smeared across her face from our feverish kiss. There's also black residue smudged beneath her eyes from her makeup, but the minor imperfections only make her more tantalizing. All this coupled with mussed curls and the sheer black stockings and high heels she dons make her look every bit like a whore, yet I know she has only ever looked this way for me.

It's a sight curated just for me, and only *I* will ever get the privilege of seeing her like this.

And *that* nearly sends me over the edge with an uncontrollable craze. The pride and gratification leaking into my system is toxic, yet there is nothing in this world that could prevent me from relishing in that knowledge.

Unable to hold back any longer, I capture her lips in a deep kiss, diving my tongue into her eager mouth. She moans, and I drink it down greedily, desperate to taste more of those exquisite sounds. I reach between us to position my cock at her entrance, her arousal instantly coating me. She's sopping wet, proven by the lewd noises that arise as I push into her.

Her mouth falls open against mine, halting our kiss, though I refuse to sever the connection and rest my lips against hers. She sharply inhales while a ragged moan tumbles off my tongue, the two of us swallowing down one another's pleasure. Her cunt fists me, slowly yielding to my cock. Despite how soaked she is, she's a virgin to my size, so I force myself to allow her to adjust.

A futile effort.

When I'm halfway, I become impatient. My arms tremble, my body desperate to break free of the restraint coating my muscles.

She ordered me to fuck her like a whore, and it would be terribly rude of me to deny her.

I slam the rest of the way into her, earning a high-pitched squeal. Her warmth is addictive, worse than the drugs tainting Seattle's streets. Her tiny hands fist the quilt, twisting it in her grip as I pull out and drive back into her a second time.

"Oh! Oh my God," she pants, a crease forming between her brows as her eyes pinch closed.

"Too much?"

"Yes!" she huffs against me.

I grin against her lips, letting her feel my approval before I murmur, "Good."

Her eyelids fly open, and she pins me with a weak glare. It's no more intimidating than a mouse, and she struggles to maintain it. The pleasure is overriding any forced ire, especially as I find a steady pace, pumping into her cunt with quick yet rough strokes.

Soon, she's peering up at me with unadulterated bliss, her brows pinched and mouth parted. I move away an inch, allowing me a full view of her expression. Her moans grow higher in pitch as I fuck her harder. All the while, she holds my stare, seemingly as entranced by every expression on my face as I am hers.

Just as I presumed, my need for her is insatiable. I ache for more of her. She's an itch nestled beneath numb skin. No matter how hard I dig, it can't be scratched.

Gripping the backs of her knees, I pin them to her ears, forcing her to lie flat on her back. The new angle allows me to drive deeper into her. Her cries turn to screams, but if she were to beg for mercy, her pleas would go unanswered.

Her nails fly to my back, raking into my flesh without restraint. The sharp bite of pain mixing with the intense pleasure from her cunt is nearly my undoing, but I refuse to succumb to it just yet.

Snarling, I release one leg to reach between us, my thumb finding her clit and applying pressure. Her eyes roll, and her back bows off the bed.

"That's it, baby. I want every soul in this damn house to hear you scream my name," I growl, my vision beginning to blacken from the pleasure.

She's on the verge of coming undone again, and I refuse to unravel without her.

"Oh my *God,*" she chokes out, her body beginning to convulse beneath me. Instead of dragging her nails along my back, she now keeps them in place, piercing them deeper and deeper into my flesh until warm liquid trails down my spine.

I lean closer to her ear. "No, *mia rosa,* not even God can have you," I growl. "You're *mine,* and you will only pray to me."

"Ronaldo!" she gasps a moment before she silences completely. Her back arches farther, and then she erupts. Her release floods past my cock and splatters onto my stomach, and a scream unleashes from her throat. My name becomes a chant as her orgasm rolls through her, and it's all I needed to hear to let go.

I'm helpless as her inner walls tighten around me, and I lose myself to the pleasure instantly. Lightning zips down my spine, and I still inside her as fireworks detonate in my blackened vision.

"Fuck," I groan loudly, unable to contain the word from bursting out of me. The little vixen lets out a breathy, satisfied laugh that mingles with another moan, and if I wasn't already in love with her before, I'm utterly powerless to her now.

My own release fills her cunt to the brim, and for a moment, I feel crazed enough to think it's not nearly enough.

It takes several minutes before the both of us come down. Our bodies are slick with sweat, and the smell of sex permeates the air. She pants heavily, staring up at me with astonishment.

Then a melodic—albeit breathless—laugh spills past her lips.

"You didn't tell me I could have orgasms during sex," she breathes with astonishment.

I grin. "There are many ways to make you come, baby. I intend to show you all of them."

Wonder settles on her beautiful face, and she gazes at me with a look I can only compare to a puppy. "How long until we can go again?"

September 18, 1944

He came back. Ronaldo came back.

He was bruised and hurt when he did. Cuts marred his beautiful face. Bruises discolored his skin. I was so excited to see him, I threw myself at him. Only then did I notice the grunt of pain. I nearly cried when I saw his pain.

He wouldn't tell me what happened. But I think the distance got to both of us.

Because we . . .

I lay with another man. A man who is not my husband.

And I'm finding it very hard to regret it. There's shame, I feel that. But not regret.

In fact, all I want is to do it again.

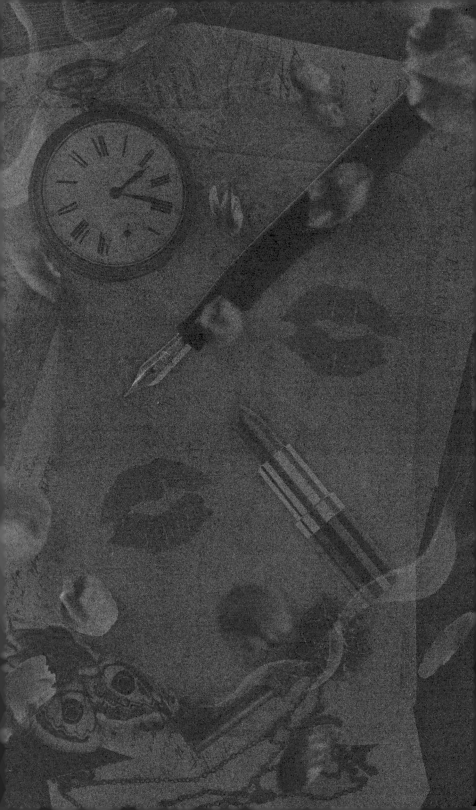

CHAPTER 22

THE RAVEN

September 18, 1944

I s *that* what John has felt for the past sixteen years every time we made love? The notion almost enrages me. How dare he experience something so mind-bending while I felt . . . nothing like that!

How dare he not even *care*!

"*Men,*" I spit beneath my breath, my tone filled with derision as I scrub angrily at the tomato sauce caked on the countertop from tonight's dinner.

"What, Mama?" Sera asks from behind me, startling me so badly I let out a screech and nearly drop dead from a heart attack.

Twirling around, I gasp her name, hand over heart as I try to breathe through the fright she gave me.

She smiles at me sheepishly. "Sorry."

"It's okay, baby," I breathe, letting out a laugh. "I didn't hear you come downstairs."

John appears in the kitchen a moment later, concern etched into the crow's feet around his eyes. His hair is mussed, and I can smell the whiskey leaking from his pores from here.

"Is everything okay?"

"Yes, Sera just frightened me. Everything is fine and dandy," I assure, my annoyance trickling back in now that he's here.

Ronaldo used his mouth on me a second time after we . . . did whatever the hell we did. It was too carnal to call it lovemaking. Too animalistic.

Afterward, he had to leave, though it appeared to pain him as much as it did me.

It left me plenty of time to quickly scribble in my journal about the awakening I had just experienced before locking it in the safe behind a photograph of me in the hallway. Ever since John threatened to read my journal, I refuse to even bring it out around him, and he knows that to be the case. Rather than becoming more suspicious, he's only ashamed. He knows I no longer trust him, and truthfully, I'm relieved that my sordid love affair will never be discovered.

At least not while I'm alive.

After, I bathed the smell of my sins off me, freshened my hair and makeup, and redressed with a more modest set of undergarments—and with my underwear *over* the girdle this time.

Sacrificing my comfort to appear sexy is a privilege only for Ronaldo.

I completed all this by the time Sera came home from the deli after school, oblivious to the awful crime her mother had just committed.

I was floating on clouds all day until John came home hours after his shift should've ended. His dinner on the table had long since grown cold by the time he stumbled through the door, his eyes bloodshot and hair a mess. While he promised he hadn't been gambling, he refused to tell me where he had been, and he reeked of whiskey.

He didn't smell of another woman, but frankly, I would almost prefer he have an affair than waste all our money.

Regardless, it devolved into another fight. Sera was thankfully doing her homework in her room when it got heated, but it resulted in his slamming me against the wall and growling in my face to "mind my own goddamn business."

"Take care of our daughter and be a perfect little wife. Those are your only two duties as a woman."

It was dehumanizing, and I saw red. My palm connected with his face, and in return, the back of his greeted mine.

I shouldn't have hit him first. I know that, yet I was still in shock that he had hit me back. In our entire relationship, John had never hit me. He'd never raped me, either. Yet that's exactly the man he has become.

Despite my budding relationship with Ronaldo, it was devastating to experience the exact moment that I gave up on my husband for good. I loved him for sixteen years. I stood by him in happiness and in turmoil. Through the gift of our beautiful daughter, and the death of any future children.

All for it to crumble away as if it was nothing.

"I don't think I've ever heard you scream like that," John comments, chuckling softly and bringing me back to the conversation.

You would if you ever tried.

I've been seething about that since the moment John suggested we make love tonight to "resolve our tension." The thought of lying with him after having lain with Ronaldo earlier makes me sick to my stomach.

Guilt should be eating me alive at this moment, yet I can't help but look at my husband as if *he's* the intruder.

"I don't think you've ever heard me scream like that, either," I agree, forcing myself to keep the mood light purely for Sera's sake. "Did you need anything, dear?" I direct my question toward my daughter, pointedly ignoring her father.

"Can I have some ice cream?"

I glance at the clock hanging on the wall, noting that it's after nine p.m. Normally far too late for sweets, but I don't have the heart to deny her at this moment.

"Sure, baby. But!" I hold up a finger, pausing for dramatic effect. "Don't get used to this. You know better."

She's too excited to care about my warning and skips toward the freezer with a blinding smile stretched across her face.

Instantly, my aching heart eases, and though I've begun to loathe my husband, I sure do love the little human he helped me create. And for that, I'm grateful for him anyway.

September 22, 1944

"We're going out to celebrate tonight with Frank," John announces as he comes down the steps. I'm in the living room opening up *Frankenstein*, prepared to read it again for the millionth time.

It's been four days since Ronaldo and I first slept together, and he's visited me every morning since. It's Friday night now, and with Sera and John home on the weekends, I'm unable to see him until Monday rolls around again. He promised he'd visit then, and it's all I can think about.

This past week has been full of more pleasure than I've experienced in my entire thirty-five years. It's safe to say I'm addicted to the man, and he has not only invaded my dreams but my every waking hour.

I frown, setting *Frankenstein* down on the stool.

"Celebrate? Celebrate what?"

A wide grin stretches across John's face, and he splays out his hands on either side of him as if presenting a prize. "We're caught up on all the bills!"

I blink, thunderstruck by his declaration. He keeps his position for several moments until he realizes I'm speechless. Excitement glimmering in his eyes, he rushes over to me, carelessly grabbing my book and setting it on the floor so he can take its spot on the stool before me.

He grabs my hands, leaning close as he says, "I told you I was going to fix my mistakes, and that's precisely what I've done, Genevieve. I know I was awful to you these past few months, but things are looking up now. Things are going to be better. *I'm* going to be better."

My mind races trying to figure out how he could've possibly pulled this off. Frank told me how much John owed from his gambling, and I saw how many bills piled up, only deepening our debt. Unless he won a large sum of money, it's impossible for him to have accomplished such a feat.

"Did you win big? From gambling?"

He shrugs coquettishly, deliberately giving me a cryptic answer, which only raises my concern rather than soothes it.

Even so, there's so much eagerness in his gaze, and I don't have it in me to snuff it. Regardless of my growing resentment toward him, I do still care for him. And at this moment, he looks more like the man I fell in love with than he has in a long while.

"That's . . . That's amazing, John," I finally choke out, forcing a relieved smile onto my face.

And I am relieved. Relieved that Sera will continue to have a roof over her head, food in her belly, and a warm bed to sleep in at night. But I'm equally concerned. I have an unsettling feeling that while John may not owe money any longer, he owes something far greater than that.

His life.

John jumps up, tugging me to my feet and dragging me to the center of the living room. He laughs as he raises my arm in the air, prompting me to twirl around on his finger.

When I spin back toward him, he pulls me into his embrace, holding tightly on to my hand while his arm bands around my waist. There, we sway while he hums the tune to his favorite song, "All the Things You Are" by Tommy Dorsey.

I rest my forehead against his chest, hiding the tears welling in my eyes. The faint smell of whiskey clings to his breath and clothes, and my heart breaks a little more.

If things were normal, I'd place a red kiss on his lips, and just this once, he wouldn't gripe about the stain I left behind. I'd even sing the lyrics to this song while he hummed. He always said I had a beautiful voice, but if I were to use it right now, it'd crack into pieces.

I vowed I would love him for the rest of my days, and I took those vows seriously. If I were a forgiving woman, I wouldn't let a few terrible months be the end of an otherwise happy marriage. I wouldn't have betrayed my promise to be faithful.

Yet I struggle to regret my choices.

God, how I wish that wasn't the case. Part of me feels obligated to give John another chance. To forget Ronaldo and invest everything I have into fixing this marriage.

Be a perfect little wife, he had said.

That's what's expected of me.

But I'm *tired* of doing what's expected of me.

Every human on this earth is born pure, and all it takes is one day, one decision to change that forever. And sometimes, the damage can last a lifetime.

John's transgressions shouldn't be forgotten, even if they were a first.

He gambled away everything we had and put our daughter at risk of becoming homeless.

He invaded my body.

He hit me.

And even now, he continues to drown himself in alcohol. Some of those transgressions have already become habits.

So, while I mourn the death of our marriage, I can't find it in me to forgive him. Nor can I find it in me to fall back in love with him again.

To put it simply, John Parsons doesn't deserve my love. Not anymore.

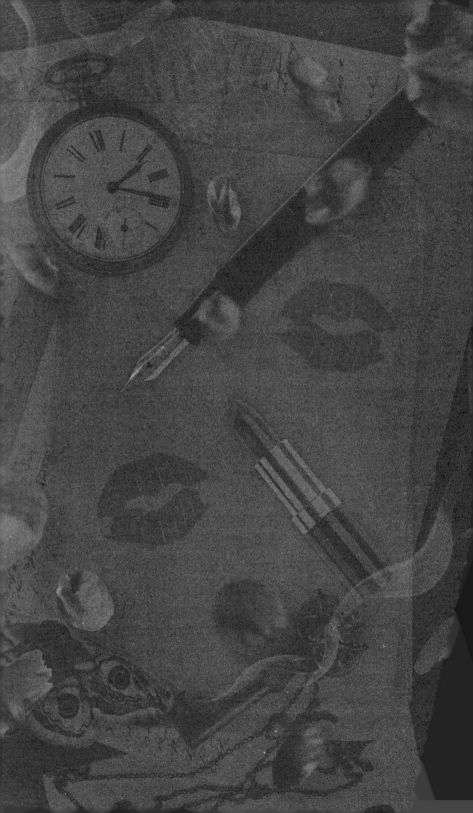

CHAPTER 23

THE RAVEN

September 22, 1944

"You look divine, Genevieve," Frank compliments, his gaze quickly scouring my body as I make my way down the stairs where he, John, and Sera wait in the foyer.

After the small dance in the living room, John led me up to our bedroom and presented another gift to me: a beautiful cherry-red evening gown. He said it reminded him of my lips, and he couldn't bear to not see me in it.

The top half features a sweetheart neckline, accentuating the swell of my breasts. A sparkling jewel pinches the straps right above them, leading up to cap sleeves that barely fall past my shoulders. The soft silk bodice hugs my curves tightly and tapers down to a beautiful lace skirt encrusted with thousands of tiny faux gems.

The dress itself is incredibly rare. Most resources are going toward the war, so the government implemented rations on many things, including fabric for civilians. Inevitably, attire has become very simple. Seeing a dress with this much detail, this much material—I have no idea how John pulled it off.

Even finding a new men's suit is nearly unheard of these days, yet next to my dress was exactly that: a three-piece black suit, the fabric high-quality and surely expensive.

He insisted we had stamps to spare from our ration book and found the clothes hiding in a boutique for a discounted price, but I don't believe that for a second. The man just told me we're debt free yet brings home clothing that surely puts us right back in it!

When I had asked him where we were going, he simply placed a kiss on my nose and told me to get ready. Then he took his black suit and left to change in a spare bedroom, citing that he wanted to be surprised when I finished getting dolled up.

"My God, Gigi, you are an absolute vision," John breathes, stepping forward and inadvertently shoving his friend aside.

I offer them a wide, appreciative smile, praying that my red lipstick hides the tremble in my bottom lip.

Dread has formed in the pit of my stomach, and I'm afflicted by a deep sense of foreboding. Whether it's the extravagant clothing or the secretive location, I'm on edge.

John offers me his hand and I take it, wearing red elbow-length gloves that match the silk of my dress. They provide the final touch to an elegant ensemble. Thankfully, he didn't splurge further on shoes, so I slipped on a pair of black heels.

He escorts me down the last few steps, my black clutch hanging from my arm. I made sure to stash my lipstick and powder in there in case I need an excuse to run off to the ladies' room for a moment alone.

"Holy cow, Mama, you look beautiful," Sera gushes. I release John's hand to wrap her in a hug, desperately needing to feel her warmth. Some days, she feels like the only thing that will get me through. She's getting awfully tall, too, and it pains me that she's growing up so fast.

"I assume you have plans tonight, too?" I ask.

She nods eagerly, tilting her chin up and resting it on my chest, peering up at me with beautiful cinnamon-brown eyes. Such a unique shade, one she inherited from her father.

"I'm seeing a film with Martha and Greta tonight. Daddy gave me a couple extra dimes and said I could even get ice cream after."

I smile and raise a playful brow, imitating a sardonic expression. "A few extra dimes, huh? You don't say. And how are you getting there and back?"

"Martha's daddy is coming to get me at six. We'll walk to the ice-cream parlor after the film and then I'll stay the night with them. He'll bring me home tomorrow morning."

"Okay, sweetie. You have fun tonight, okay?" I place a soft kiss on the tip of her button nose, hating that I'm not seeing a film and eating ice cream with her. "And don't stay up too late, you hear me?"

She wrinkles her nose and grumbles her agreement, though I know better than to believe it. Martha has stayed with us many nights, and the two girls are always up all night giggling.

I'd much rather spend time with Sera than go to some fancy event. She'll always be my daughter, but sometimes life can be cruel, and there could be a day where tragedy strikes, and I won't get those moments with her anymore. I want to soak them up as much as I can.

"Are you ready, my love?" John asks, prompting me to release her.

I nearly choke on the spit I had been swallowing at that moment. *My love.* I can't recall a time John has ever referred to me as such, yet he chooses now to do so. It doesn't have the same effect after hearing that endearment fall from another man's lips. In fact, it makes me sick to my stomach to hear it come from my husband's mouth.

Clearing my throat softly, I force cheerfulness into my tone as I say, "Yes, though I would love to know where you two dreamboats are taking me."

Truthfully, I hardly noticed how John looks in his new suit, but now that I give him and his friend a cursory glance, the two look awfully dapper.

There's a slight stiffness in Frank's shoulders, and as soon as the question leaves my lips, he shoots my husband a poorly disguised, disgruntled look.

"We're running late, dear," John deflects. "I'll tell you on the way."

I narrow my eyes, recognizing his strategy for what it is. He wants to get me in the car where I can't escape before he breaks the news.

It only adds oxygen to the fire, and the anxiety burning a hole in my stomach flares.

I hesitate but ultimately give one more farewell kiss to Sera's nose and follow him out of the house, allowing them to sweep me away.

September 22, 1944

Angelo Salvatore.

That's whose house we're currently pulling up to. I sit next to my husband, tossing glares his way every few moments while Frank sits in the back, having already attempted and failed to make light conversation. Not even the war ending could slice the tension in the car.

I know that my husband has been lying to me. All those unanswered questions clicked into place like puzzle pieces.

His recent influx of money and subsequent lack of debt, and how at times, he'd come home roughed up after gambling, paranoid and consistently checking over his shoulder, even in the safety of our home.

Now that we're being invited as guests to a party hosted by the biggest mob boss, I realize that he's been involved with the Mafia longer than I could have imagined. And the worst part is, I know he'll continue to lie, even when I demand the truth.

If I had the grit, I would strangle my stupid, *stupid* husband.

We cruise up a circular drive with an exorbitant fountain in the middle featuring baby elephants carved out of stone, their trunks serving as the water spouts. At the front of the house, a valet awaits wearing an all-black suit.

Flicking one last glare John's way, I allow the valet to open my door and help me out of the vehicle, his face carefully blank and his stare pinned above my head.

John and Frank flank me moments later as the valet driver hands John a ticket. Then he takes off with our car, disappearing with my only form of escape.

A rock forms in my throat as I stare at the monumental Georgian-revival mansion before us. Erected on either side of the walkway leading to the entrance are intricate twin statues of Saint John. Beyond the open front door, a grandiose chandelier glistens, exhibiting just how much money the Salvatores possess.

John holds out his crooked elbow, and begrudgingly, I accept it. Gossip spreads like wildfire in Seattle, and I'm sure there will be plenty of wives with scrutinizing eyes in attendance who will instantly pick up on the tension between John and me. It's my duty to ensure that doesn't happen, even if I'm tempted to stick out a foot and trip the damn man.

Folks come and go from the entrance, some of them smoking cigarettes and loitering about. Others stand in small groups, sharing stories with animated hands and laughing loudly while they sip champagne.

Uncharacteristically, it's a beautiful September night. Not only has the rain held off for once but the air is warm and the breeze gentle, attracting many of the partygoers outside to enjoy the weather.

John leads me through the front door, where we're greeted by a butler holding a tray of champagne flutes.

The three of us accept one before wandering farther into the oval foyer, taking in the beautiful Rococo ornamentation etched into the walls and leading up to a plafond dome. Intricate gilded edges surround a painting depicting a scene from a Roman myth.

White marble floors extend straight down a wide walkway, illuminated by several more chandeliers. To the left is a sweeping wooden staircase leading up to a balcony that overlooks the foyer.

I swallow, hesitant to take another step. The detail that went into crafting this house is intimidating, to say the least. I'm terrified to touch a single thing in case I ruin or break it.

"Do you think he's got a Bentley?" John wonders aloud.

Frank snorts. "I would bet good money he's a Rolls-Royce type of fella."

The thought of that alone is incredible. Before John's gambling habits, he dreamed about owning a luxurious car. Now, he's ensured it will always remain just that—a dream.

John and Frank appear just as taken with the decadent interior, slowly herding me along as we wander deeper into the house, following other attendees into the great hall.

It's just as opulent, with high ceilings, more glistening chandeliers, warm orange walls, and the familiar Rococo architecture.

In the middle of the room gather several couples, swinging each other around as they dance to the Glenn Miller Orchestra. On the outskirts are several tables covered in white tablecloths and littered with whiskey glasses, champagne flutes, and ashtrays.

The room is robust with chatter and laughter as if we're not in the middle of a brutal war, and certainly as if we're not in the home of the leader of the largest crime syndicate in Seattle. Not only the largest but the most *dangerous*.

"Remind me how you received this invitation?" I ask, forcing myself to take a sip of the bubbly liquid before I do something worse like vomit.

"I helped the Salvatores with a little bookkeeping, that's all," he responds flippantly. If it's not a lie, it's a gross understatement of the truth.

I drag my gaze to Frank, who is staring at the scene with his lips flattened into a firm line. I'm confident that he's privy to John's involvement with Angelo Salvatore, but Frank has always tried to protect me from harsh realities, despite my insistence that I can handle them. I'm not a delicate woman, yet he refuses to treat me any differently.

Now, I regard him with scrutiny. If he knows John is working with Angelo, shouldn't he arrest my husband? How could he possibly be okay with it—he works for law enforcement, for God's sake!

Unless . . . he works with Angelo, too.

"You're a homicide detective. How are you even allowed to be here? Are you okay with this? Shouldn't you be arresting every one of these people right now?" I whisper heatedly.

"It's not that simple, Gigi," he mumbles tightly. "But as a matter of fact, *no*, I'm not okay with this. Angelo is very aware of who I am and only cleared me to join the party alongside John on strict instruction that I'm off the record and cannot use anything I see here against them."

I hum, unconvinced that he's not involved with the Mafia. Even still, walking into a den of wolves as the hunter attempting to kill them doesn't seem very . . . safe. "They're not going to shoot you, right?"

He sighs and mutters contritely, "If they do, make sure they shoot John, too."

Well, now. *That's* not very reassuring.

He sighs and grabs my elbow, leading me several feet away until we're out of hearing distance from my husband. John glances at us, and Frank gives him a stern look, silently relaying something to him that I can't interpret. John apparently can and turns back toward the party stiffly.

"Look, Gigi, I don't want to be here any more than you do," Frank begins, a pleading look in his gaze. I refrain from rolling my eyes, convinced he's going to wax on about how John really does love me, and I just need to give him a chance. The last thing I need to hear is all the reasons why I should forgive his lying best friend. "So, leave with me."

I blink, sure that I didn't hear him right. "Leave?"

"It is John who is required to make an appearance tonight, not us. I can make up some excuse that you're not feeling well, and I will take you home."

I shift as something uncomfortable and disconcerting unfurls in the pit of my stomach.

"And leave him here alone in a pit with dozens of mobsters?" I ask incredulously, keeping my voice low. I glance around, double-checking that no one is listening.

Lord knows what would happen if one of them heard me refer to them as such.

"He's been around these men for months gambling. I think he can handle a party, Gigi," he says, scoffing with condescension.

My brow furrows, and I stare at him with bewilderment, at a loss for what to even say.

"I'll stay with you until he comes home," he continues, his eyes sparkling. "Mark is sleeping, and Ruth is expecting me to stay out late tonight anyway. We can relax, open a bottle of wine, and listen to some tunes until John is finished here."

My mouth flops open, attempting to process that.

Ruth is his wife, and Mark is their eight-year-old son. Mark has spent many summers and weekends over the years at our house, even with his being six years younger than Sera. He's quite the handful and has a bit of a temper. He's gotten violent a few times, which has caused Frank and Ruth a lot of stress. They both have differing opinions on how to correct his behavior. However, Mark has always been attached to Sera, and she seems to keep him calm, so we've never had an issue with the two of them. Though it's something I've watched carefully as Mark's tantrums have worsened with age.

So, I suppose I can understand why Frank wants to continue to enjoy his night away. He and his wife rarely see eye to eye these days. Yet I can't help but feel strange about his request.

"I don't know, Frank. I think it would be best if I stay here. I would be a nervous wreck otherwise."

His jaw clenches, and for a moment, what looks like fury passes over his eyes. Just as quickly, it's gone, and he offers me a defeated smile and a nod.

"Of course, I understand. Let's get back to the party, then, shall we?"

Inhaling deeply, I attempt to shove away the unsettled feeling clinging to my gut, forcing a grin and marching toward my lying husband.

"Would you care to dance?" I ask. I'm still angry with him, but I feel

232 | H. D. CARLTON

the need to separate myself from Frank for a bit, and a dance is the only way to do so.

"I'm afraid I must interrupt," a deep voice cuts in from behind us.

Startled, I turn around, finding none other than Angelo Salvatore before me.

Except it's not the sight of him that makes my heart stop in its tracks.

It's the man standing beside him, and though I keep silent, my lips mouth the question anyway.

Ronaldo?

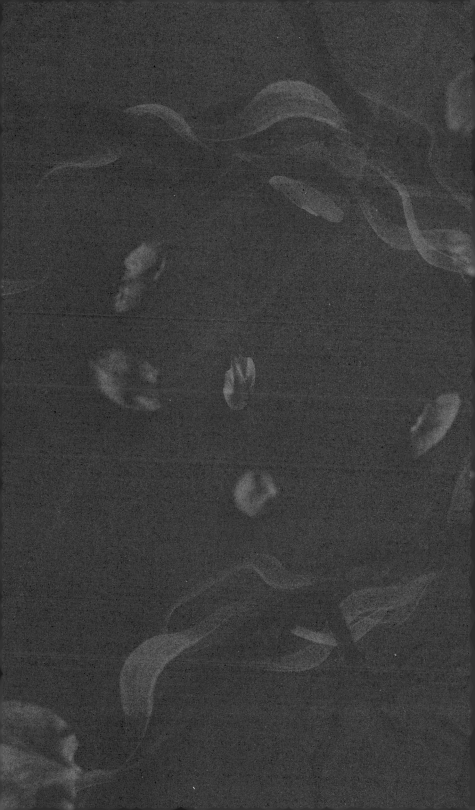

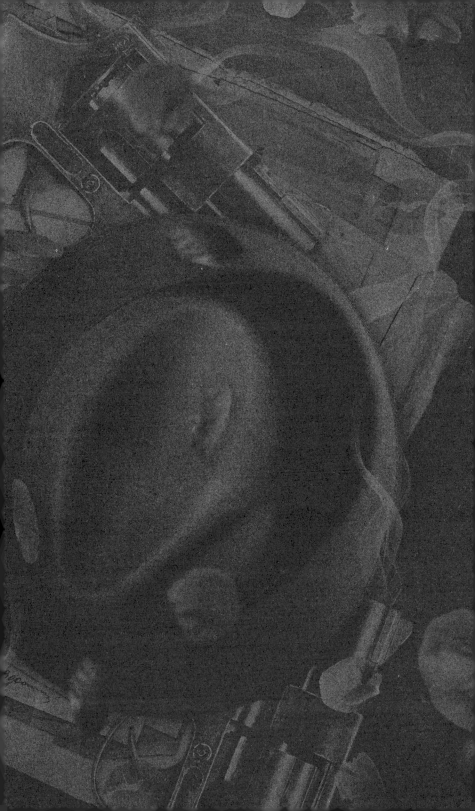

CHAPTER 24

THE PHANTOM

September 22, 1944

S he shouldn't be here.

Angelo's too busy grabbing Genevieve's gloved hand and placing a gentle kiss atop to notice my pointed glare. However, she takes a second too long to drag her thunderstruck gaze away from me before smoothing her expression into a soft smile.

It seems my friend forgot to mention a key detail about inviting the Salvatores' new accountant. I was there when John took the oath of omertà, yet it didn't cross my mind that Angelo would invite him to tonight's festivities.

236 | H. D. CARLTON

More still, I recognize that dress. It belongs to Angelo's sister, Lillian, though I can't deny how ravishing it looks on Genevieve, as if the seamstress stitched it just for her. If I wasn't too busy panicking that she's in a very dangerous domain, I'd steal her away and fuck her in it, only to rip it from her body with my teeth.

John's detective friend, Frank Williams, stands on the other side of her, and he boldly glowers at Angelo for his flirtatious ways.

"Genevieve, Frank, this is Angelo Salvatore and his good friend, Ronaldo," John introduces, motioning toward the two of us respectively.

I meet his stare, but he quickly looks away. Whenever he's in my presence, I know he can feel my hatred for him rolling off me, and I make no effort to hide it.

The *only* reason he still breathes is because I'm deeply in love with his wife.

I hold out my left hand, palm up. She hesitates for a fraction of a second before grabbing hold of it. Holding her stare, I slowly place a kiss over her knuckles, enjoying the way she works to swallow. In those few short seconds, the world around us blurs, and the music fades into white noise, leaving just the two of us alone. At that moment, it's only her and me. No mob boss. No husband. No witnesses to our sinful love affair.

Then I release her, and our surroundings come rushing back. She quickly tucks her hands to her sides, taking what seems to be her first breath since she first laid eyes on me.

Frank turns his burning stare in my direction, his upper lip threatening to curl. The man hates me, and the feeling is mutual. I shoot him a wink, provoking him. I'd love nothing more than for him to flip a wig. It would provide me with the perfect excuse to pop him.

The man is as corrupt as a detective can get and is also the one responsible for getting John into his bad gambling habit to begin with. A point of contention between him and Angelo as of late.

Frank insists he didn't know John would get so bad, yet he kept bringing him back to the tables anyway, knowing that his best friend was digging himself deeper and deeper in the hole. Frank knows what happens to the men who owe Angelo money and can't pay up, especially because he's the one solving their cases after they're whacked.

Something that never quite made sense to me.

Why would Frank push his best friend into the line of Angelo's gun?

The question has burned me up inside since the moment Frank discovered John was a made man. He appeared disappointed by that news and had even picked a fight with Angelo about it, claiming John wasn't to be trusted to handle the Salvatores' money and that he'd put the entire operation at risk.

A declaration that had Angelo questioning my advice, which had my trigger finger twitching. Luckily, John is an ace and has done the opposite of Frank's claims. Already he's introduced a more streamlined method of laundering Angelo's money through the multiple businesses he owns. Not only has he cut down on time to clean the money but he's also increased Angelo's profits.

"I trust the three of you will join in on the festivities?" Angelo prompts.

Frank rips his stare away only for it to land on Genevieve instead. He watches her closely as she eagerly engages with Angelo in conversation.

As I've said before, she's a charming woman.

She falls into a relaxed candor, complimenting Angelo on his beautiful home and even asking him about the artist who painted the scene on the foyer's ceiling.

She's a natural, and without even realizing it, she holds all four of our attentions with ease, all of us completely beholden to her.

"My husband is aware of my eclectic taste in decor. Much to my mother's dismay, I loved reading Edgar Allan Poe as a girl," she explains, a light laugh tinkling from her throat as she affectionately squeezes John's arm. It takes effort not to pull her toward me, then fire a bullet off in the man's skull. He doesn't deserve Genevieve's hanging on his arm as if she's a prize he won. He doesn't deserve her *at all*. "I fear my love for all things gothic never went away, and I've made myself a bit of an outcast."

"Oh, gobbledygook," Angelo bellows loudly, waving a dismissive hand and howling theatrically.

I shoot him a quizzical look, tempted to laugh. I don't think I've *ever* heard him use the term *gobbledygook*, and it sounds ridiculous coming out of his mouth.

"I'm afraid it's true!" Genevieve insists, wearing a bright smile and lighting up the entire damn room. "I tell ya', some of the women think John here is Count Dracula. I'm ashamed to confess that I may have confirmed he was when I overheard them gossiping about it, and well—" She stares up at John sheepishly, and he smiles down at her, deepening my annoyance. "Now they think Seattle is being terrorized by vampires. Little do they know, I loved Mary Shelley growing up, so he's more like Frankenstein's monster."

"Is he?" I drawl lazily, attracting her reluctant gaze. She's tried her best to avoid my burning stare since I kissed her hand. "Your monster?"

Her smile slips for the briefest of seconds. Then she clears her throat, recuperating quickly. "He certainly has the head shape for it, don't you think?"

John shoots her a chagrined look, and another obnoxious roar booms from Angelo's throat. While I've seen him finish a few glasses of whiskey already, he's certainly not sauced. If I allow him to keep it up, he's going to attract his wife's attention, and Carmella is a sharp-tongued viper. She also has a history of pointing a gun at a bird or two, convinced they had lain with her husband.

Truthfully, they probably had, but Angelo is skilled at lying through his teeth.

"John, Genevieve, Frank," I address, pulling their attention away from the conversation. "I'm afraid Angelo and I have some business to attend to and a few other guests to entertain. But please, enjoy the party and indulge in as many refreshments as you like."

I grab hold of Angelo's arm and damn near drag him away.

"You trying to get that woman iced?" I growl beneath my breath, releasing his arm quickly.

"Oh, come on, Carmella is too preoccupied with the gossip and champagne to notice," Angelo defends. "My two sons are leaving me tomorrow to head back overseas. I'm only drowning my sorrows. Do you know how hard it was to convince Congressman Caserta to pull some strings so they could come home for a week? The only reason he allowed it was because I nearly lost my life at his son's restaurant. A place that *guaranteed* my safety."

He's rambling, and I know it's because he truly is heartbroken to see his sons leave. The worst part is not knowing if they'll come home again.

"Well, no reason to make it worse by enraging your very possessive wife," I remind.

He sighs. "You're right. Though I'm a little annoyed you prevented Paulie from stealing that woman away. I daresay she would've been a delight to have around."

"She wouldn't have survived long with the way you're acting," I mutter.

He chuckles. "I can understand why you've taken a liking to her, Ronnie. Just don't cause trouble with John. I'd hate to have to punish you for sabotaging my favorite accountant."

I say nothing and instead direct him to another guest. He's swept away by a conversation while I stew.

It takes a matter of moments to find Genevieve on the dance floor, John's arms wrapped around her.

He wears a large smile, content knowing that Genevieve belongs to him. And while he may never be wise to who she *actually* belongs to, I think my girl could use a reminder.

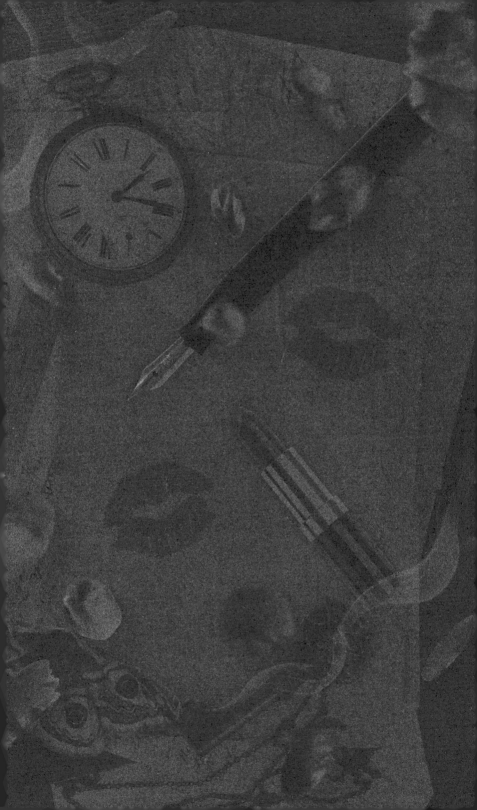

CHAPTER 25

THE RAVEN

September 22, 1944

"Are you working for him?"

"No, of course not. The Salvatores hired one of my employees, Richard, as their accountant. Turns out, he made a huge mistake and made a run for it. I got pulled in because it's my company, and they took me off the damn streets to answer for it."

"Elmer's Tune" by Glenn Miller is playing through the speakers, but I hardly process anything outside the guilty look on my husband's face. John swings me around before pulling me back into his arms, and it takes effort not to send my palm flying into his face.

I would never in a public setting, which is the only thing saving his cheek from blossoming into a tomato-red shade.

The second Angelo and Ronaldo left, he rushed me off to dance, sensing the fury radiating from my pores.

"They were going to kill you for Richard's mistake?" I ask incredulously the second our chests press together again. I attempt to keep a smile firmly pasted on my face, though the words come out through gritted teeth.

"He was my employee, so they considered it my problem, too. The Salvatores had a damn gun to my head," he hisses beneath his breath. "The only thing that kept them from shooting me was Ronaldo."

Surprise thunders through me, and it takes me a moment to find my voice again. "Why?"

"I don't know, truthfully. Ronaldo insisted I have the opportunity to correct Richard's mistake. I was left with little choice, so I did, and Angelo was thoroughly impressed." There's smugness in his tone, and it makes me want to smack him all over again. Even if Richard is a real employee, he'd likely be dead if he crossed the Salvatores, and yet my husband beams with pride. "I helped them one time. I swear to you, Gigi. Angelo's sons are returning to war tomorrow, so they're celebrating their last day. To show his gratitude, Angelo invited me. That's all."

I glance away, focusing on the blurred background as we twirl around the dance floor. I can't explain it, but something about his explanation doesn't settle right and creates a dreadful feeling in the pit of my stomach. Almost as if he's lying to me.

"Please tell me this won't ruin us, Gigi," he begs.

"You're involved in something incredibly dangerous, John. Have you not thought about the implications of this? What if something happens to our daughter—"

"*Nothing* will ever happen to Sera or you. I promise you that." I don't believe him. Truly, I don't. If John couldn't even save his own life, how could he save ours? "I didn't have a *choice*, Gigi. But I'm not involved with them anymore. We only came to show respect."

"How am I supposed to believe that, Johnathan? It feels like all you've done is lie to me or keep secrets. You helped them once, impressed the goddamn godfather of Seattle, and expect to walk away from it? I don't believe that for a second." I didn't mean to get so heated, but by the time I'm finished, I'm outright glaring at him, the smile long gone from my face.

His upper lip curls into a snarl. "*I'm* the victim here, Gigi. Why can't you see that?"

"Then why does it feel like Sera and I are the ones suffering?"

The song ends a moment later. Delicately, I remove myself from his hold, hating the way his proximity feels.

"I'm going to take a powder," I mutter, needing to get away from him as desperately as I need to breathe.

He lets me go, likely not wanting to raise attention, and for once, I'm thankful we're in a public setting.

After a butler points me toward the powder room, I briskly head there, offering smiles to strangers as I pass by, injecting every bit of delight into my face. But the second I close the door and lock myself in, my mask breaks apart like a beaten piñata.

I lean heavily against the door, inhaling deeply, only to release the breath as a staccato exhale. It feels as if the edge of a razor scraped against every one of my nerves.

Then there's a quiet knock on the door, scaring the absolute hell out of me. A yelp slips from my throat, and then I groan, instantly annoyed. Why did he follow me? Can't he give me just a few minutes before I'm forced to put on a happy face for him again?

I swing open the door, prepared to tell John to give me five more

246 | H. D. CARLTON

minutes, but I'm being ushered backward before I can get a word out. Ronaldo stands before me and hurriedly locks the door behind him.

It takes several seconds for my brain to catch up. Once it does, I'm swinging a hand into his chest. He winces but doesn't stop me from stepping up into his face.

"You work for *Angelo Salvatore?*" I hiss, glowering up at the behemoth of a man. My heels offer me a few extra inches of dignity, but he still towers over me.

It's not lost on me that I'm having the same conversation with two different men in the span of a couple minutes.

"I do," he answers simply.

"What are you, his hit man or something?"

Amusement floods his stare, and one corner of his lips twitch. Once more, I'm tempted to smack him.

"I'm his consigliere," he corrects as if I have any idea what that means. "Angelo and I grew up together. We're best friends, and I'm his adviser." I blink, attempting to wrap my head around that. "But I take contracts for him as well. I don't have to, but I enjoy it."

My mouth parts, and my eyebrows fly up my forehead. "You enjoy murdering people?" I repeat incredulously.

"Yes."

"Yes," I echo, laughing breathlessly as I turn away from him. I can't breathe with him so close. Can't think properly.

My phantom is a murderer. Not only that but he also likes it. Funny how I was just berating John for getting involved with the Mafia, and here this man is, boldly telling me he chooses to kill for them. Not even a lick of remorse in his tone, either.

I turn toward him again, my eyes narrowed. That deep, unsettled feeling still swirls in the pit of my stomach, questioning John's story. And if Ronaldo can so boldly tell me how he enjoys murdering people, then surely he will tell me about my husband, too.

"Tell me the truth. Does John work for him, too?"

"Yes."

That one syllable cracks what was left of my heart into pieces, and I hate that he confirmed my suspicions. I close my eyes, attempting to get a handle on my emotions. I had a terrible feeling John was lying to me, but I had hoped it was only my paranoia.

It's not disbelief that sends pain flaring through my chest. It's only sorrow that my husband did exactly what I expected of him, and somehow, that hurts worse.

He told me he was the victim, yet all along, he was the perpetrator.

"Why am I not surprised?" I whisper to myself. Inhaling deeply, I open my eyes, needing to hear the truth. "Tell me everything. How did John get involved with Angelo?"

Ronaldo quickly tells me the story—the *real* story. John's gambling with the Salvatores and owing them money. John continuously unable to pay. Angelo growing impatient with my husband and finally kidnapping him, intent on making him pay with his life. And then Ronaldo's saving him, asking Angelo to allow John to work off his dues as their accountant instead.

It makes me sick hearing what truly happened. That it was John's gambling that got him involved with the goddamn Mafia. And that it was Ronaldo who ensured Sera and I wouldn't be homeless—not my own damn husband.

There's no question whether I believe Ronaldo. While he'd omitted who he was working for before, he has never lied to me. Truthfully, this explanation makes far more sense than John's contrived story.

I'm staring at him numbly, attempting to process everything I've just learned. But instead of dwelling on my husband's lies, I decide to focus on the man before me now.

The man who isn't shying away from his involvement with the Salvatores. The man who confessed he murders people.

"Genevieve," he calls quietly.

"Am I in danger with you, Ronaldo?" I ask softly. "Should I be screaming for my life right now?"

"Yes."

I'm baffled by his response, though I don't even know why. Ronaldo has never shied away from telling me what I don't want to hear.

He prowls toward me, backing me into the wall behind me and pinning his hands on either side of my head.

"I've always been a danger to you, *mia rosa*. You've never been safe from me."

"What does that even mean?" I ask breathlessly.

His lips dip closer to my own, his breath warming them as he speaks. "Did you think I was lying when I said there are things I want to do to you that would make you want to run away? And I told you that if you try, I wouldn't let you. I still mean that, my love."

His voice is incredibly deep and dark, and it stirs the butterflies in my stomach.

"You've lost your mind," I breathe.

"Since the moment I saw you," he confirms.

"If I run away, you can't stop me," I challenge. I'm uncertain I want to run away, but there's a part of me that wants to try only to see what would happen.

It's reckless to provoke a man who just told me about his affinity for murdering people. Yet I know deep in my bones that Ronaldo would never truly hurt me.

Not like John has.

"You're right," he murmurs, cocking his head thoughtfully. "But I can certainly catch you."

The air between us buzzes with static energy, making it incredibly hard to breathe. To think straight. My chest pumps as we stare at one another for a beat, the two of us waiting for the other to make a move.

To hell with it.

I dart to the side, but he's prepared. I barely make it an inch before his hand is cupping the underside of my jaw and slamming me back into the wall before him. I gasp, and it's the last breath I'm allowed before his mouth crushes mine.

His tongue pries my lips apart, diving in and curling against the roof of my mouth. I lash my tongue against his and grip the lapels of his suit, pouring all my pent-up frustration into the kiss.

He releases my throat and grabs at the bottom of my dress, lifting the heaps of fabric until both of his hands are beneath it and pawing at my girdle. He pauses when he discovers that it's crotchless and I wear no underwear beneath it.

When he pulls away, I shrug choppily. "It's hard enough to use the restroom in this dress. I didn't need added complications."

Growling, he grasps my hips and forces me to turn around, roughly slamming my chest into the marble wall. Then he kicks at my feet.

"Spread them," he demands roughly, his voice nearly unrecognizable.

"We can't do this here," I rush out, though I don't move an inch as he quickly unfastens his belt and the front of his trousers.

"Who's going to stop me?" he fires back. He grabs my hips, and instinctively I arch my back. "You?" The question is dripping with condescension, and I'm tempted to smack him for it.

"Only if you don't hurry—"

He's slamming inside me before I can finish, and a sharp squeal replaces the rest of my words.

"Shh, *mia rosa.* Someone may hear you," he whispers darkly in my ear. "What would they think, knowing your husband is still out there?"

250 | H. D. CARLTON

He's retreating and slamming into me again before I can formulate a response. My mouth drops, and my brow furrows as he finds a quick, rough pace. The pleasure rises from between my legs, stealing my breath.

"They might think you're being fucked," he continues, his tone wicked. "And I'd be happy to show them just how much of a slut you are for me."

I'm forced to clamp my bottom lip between my teeth, biting down hard. It's nearly impossible to keep quiet, but somehow, I manage as he drives into me with vigor.

One hand glides over my hip and down my stomach, finding my clit and rubbing tight circles over it. His fingers slip from the wetness gathered there, though it doesn't make it any less pleasurable. If anything, the proof of how deeply he affects me only heightens the bliss.

My eyes roll, a silent scream on my tongue, forcing my jaw to unhinge.

"Don't you dare make a sound," he growls, keeping his voice quiet. Yet the smallest moan leaks past his lips, unable to follow his own orders. "Don't think I won't kill every goddamn person in this house to save you from shame. Their blood would be on your hands, all because you can't keep fucking quiet and take my cock like a good girl."

I'm barreling toward an orgasm so quickly, I'm unable to process it. His fingers stop their ministrations between my legs, only to deliver a sharp slap. He anticipates the inevitable noise that bursts from my lips and covers my mouth with his other hand.

One more slap, and I'm erupting. My knees weaken as the surge of pleasure sends me spiraling into outer space. His hand clamps tighter over my mouth, muffling the screams that demand to be let loose, no matter how hard I try to keep quiet.

I'm somewhere else entirely when another low growl unleashes from Ronaldo's throat, and he trembles violently, pumping his release inside me. He rests his head on the back of my shoulder while his hands fall away from me.

I'm panting heavily, delirious and slowly coming down. My body trembles from the aftershocks still firing off inside of me, and it's a wonder my knees still hold me upright.

Slowly, he pulls away from me entirely. "Hold your dress up, baby."

I keep my eyes closed, resting my forehead on the cool tile while I attempt to process what the hell just happened. The water tap turns on, then off. Then there's a warm press of a towel between my legs as he cleans me up.

When he's finished, he helps me straighten out my dress, attempting to free it from wrinkles.

Afterward, we both tidy up our faces. I reapply my red lipstick while he cleans his face of it. I powder my nose and swipe the black from beneath my eyes. We both straighten out our hair, attempting to put everything back the way it was before he fucked me in the powder room.

When the two of us are done, he grabs me by my nape and tugs me into him roughly, drawing a gasp from my lips.

"My cum will leak down your thighs while you're dancing with your husband. If you dare to wipe it away, I'll expose you in front of everyone and make him swallow it," he threatens, his tone unyielding and savage.

My mouth drops, and I can only stare at him with shock.

"I'll leave first. Wait a couple minutes."

Blinking, I expect him to turn and go. Instead, he places a soft kiss against my lips. Barely a whisper of his flesh against mine.

"Don't test me, Genevieve. I will be watching," he whispers. Another soft kiss. "I love you."

Then he's gone. Just like the phantom he's known to be.

September 22, 1944

I cannot believe what I discovered today.
What has my life become?
I'm at a loss for words. John doesn't know that I know who he's
working for now, and truthfully, I don't even know what to say.
It's the only thing that is currently keeping us from losing our
house and casting our daughter into the streets. It's keeping John
alive so Sera doesn't lose a father.
But that doesn't make it any easier of a pill to swallow.
And Ronaldo . . . I can't help but feel a little lied to, though I
know it's not fair. He made it clear that his boss was dangerous,
but I wish he'd just still told me.
I don't know how I feel about any of this. I'm so incredibly
conflicted.
Is it terrible that this doesn't make me want to stop seeing him?
It should. He said he's killed before and he will continue to do so.
That alone should have me running far away.
Yet I still want to stay.

CHAPTER 26

THE RAVEN

November 18, 1944

"What are you going to do while I'm gone?" John asks, hovering around the kitchen island while I prepare Sera's breakfast.

An anxious energy radiates from his pores, and it's making my skin itch.

He and Frank are leaving for a fishing trip this morning, and they plan to be out until late tonight. With winter approaching, today is a rare day of no rain, so they've decided to take advantage of the weather.

A plan that seems to set John on edge.

Everything has changed between us, and while the two of us try our best to make Sera's homelife as normal as possible, there's a noticeable shift. I don't let him kiss me anymore. A decade ago, we would slow dance by the radio while little Sera would cling to our legs. Even five years ago, we'd sneak away for time alone or giggle and tease each other. Admittedly, it's been years, but at the very least, we *touched* one another. Now, I shift away from even the smallest touch, always keeping a wall between us.

We coexist. While affection for Sera has never waned, not even for a second, it's gone extinct between John and me.

I'm okay with that. However, my husband is not.

He tries to reconnect with me—to reignite the flame between us. I wouldn't dare say John and I weren't happy at one point, but that flame has always burned low.

I'm not a silly little girl, seeking a connection with a man and expecting it to always be fireworks and explosions. It's inevitable for relationships to become boring and monotonous as life goes on, and I've no qualms settling into a life of comfort with my other half.

But that's not what John and I have. We've always gotten along just fine if only to sit in comfortable silence with one other, though I have never truly *desired* John's presence. I don't recall the last time I was overcome with happiness or even a time where I craved him in any capacity. I've felt those things sporadically, of course, but never wholly.

It's become apparent that John and I were young and weighed down beneath the pressure of societal expectations. We were two kids dumb enough to think we were in love; then we were friends, then parents, and now, we're strangers.

I've settled in my discontent, and for years, I constructed some semblance of happiness, first for my Sera's comfort, then for my own.

Nevertheless, it doesn't matter anymore. John spiraled, and as a result, he hurt me in ways I cannot come back from.

If he left tomorrow, I wouldn't miss him.

"Sera and I are going to catch a film around lunchtime, then she's going to Brenda's for her birthday party and sleepover," I answer, keeping my tone pleasant.

"And after?" he pushes. "What will you do when she leaves?"

"I will stare out at the trees and write in my journal," I say evenly. An unnecessary dig, but that comment of his hit a nerve. Since that fight when he claimed I do nothing more than write in my diary, he still hasn't shown appreciation for how I've always taken care of him and our daughter.

My husband is determined to win back my love, but he thinks he'll accomplish that by calling me beautiful or complimenting my dress. One night, he brought home a bouquet of tulips, and when I had asked him why, he said he remembered they were my favorite.

I didn't bother correcting him. During the summer, I place vases of poppies in various parts of the house, keeping them alive for days on end. The flowers fill the front yard, too, and I held a poppy bouquet when I married him. He had one pinned to his suit, for God's sake.

Poppies are my favorite.

Or rather, they used to be. Lately, I've been favoring roses.

"Gigi," he sighs. When I give him my full attention, he seems to struggle for his next words.

Sera comes barreling into the kitchen a moment later, slicing the building tension and effectively ending the conversation.

"Just in time," I chirp, turning to grab Sera's plate, which is piled with a waffle covered in butter, syrup, and a small heap of blueberries.

"I hear you're seeing a film today, princess," John says, tugging on Sera's ear affectionately. "What are you seeing?"

"That new musical comedy that came out earlier this month,

Something for the Boys." She takes a huge bite of her waffle, then swings her upper body side to side in a little happy dance.

She's always been prone to dancing while she eats, and it never fails to make me smile.

John lifts his gaze to mine, where lingering questions still swirl within. I sigh and give in, hoping it will mean he doesn't stress and rush home.

It's sad to say, but I'm looking forward to his leaving for the day.

"I have a stack of books waiting to be read and a bottle of wine waiting to be drunk," I say softly. "Those are the only plans I have."

It's concerning how easy it's become to lie to my husband, yet I can't find it in me to feel an ounce of regret. Shame, maybe, though even that has waned.

His shoulders relax, and he nods. Relieved, I turn around to clean up. The front door opens and slams shut a moment later, signaling Frank's arrival. I peer over my shoulder just as he appears.

"Ready to catch some fish, Johnny-boy?" Frank calls as he saunters into the kitchen, a wide smile on his face. It's rare to see him in something other than a nice suit since his job as a detective requires him to present himself a certain way. Today, he and John both wear simple trousers with suspenders, polo shirts beneath their thick jackets, and panama hats. They appear to be law-abiding citizens, but ever since they brought me to Angelo's, I know better now. John is involved with the Mafia, and I have an unsettling suspicion that his best friend is, too.

"Always," John returns with a forced grin while Frank ruffles Sera's hair, causing her to swat at him playfully with a waffle-filled giggle.

Frank raises his hand, holding up a case of Rainier. "Thought we'd get some cold beers in our system today."

John's smile drops an inch, and the two men's gazes swing toward me. Frank is aware that alcohol has become a sore spot in the Parsons household, yet he brings it anyway. I cast him an unimpressed look, and though he has the decency to appear ashamed, it does little to ease my frustration with him. Before, I wouldn't have thought twice about John's drinking beer. Now, I wonder how drunk he's going to come home, and what will happen if he does.

If Frank truly cared about his best friend's drinking habit, he wouldn't have brought the beer. Yet it's tradition, and I certainly don't believe John has confessed to Frank all the terrible mistakes he's made while sauced. Maybe if Frank knew, he'd be more diligent. However, it would be inappropriate for me to tell him such intimate matters about our marriage.

Still I won't cause any more unnecessary tension. If he does come home drunk, I will just have to deal with it then. Saying nothing, I refocus on piling the dirty dishes into the sink.

Frank breaks the bout of silence, forcing heartiness in his tone. "You ready, Johnny? Let's skedaddle. The fish are just beggin' for some good bait today. I can hear 'em all the way from over here."

I keep still as John approaches from behind, grabbing my arms and leaning in to place a chaste kiss on my cheek. A year ago, I would've met that kiss with my lips. Now, I keep my stare pinned to the dishes and wave them off without turning around.

"You boys have fun. But not too much," I say merrily.

"Yes, ma'am," John says quietly as he retreats.

They're out the door a few minutes later, and relief washes over me. Turning around to Sera, I paste a smile on my face.

"Finish up those waffles, pretty girl. We have a film to catch, and you still need a bath. You have syrup in your hair."

She shrugs haughtily as if wearing syrup in her hair is a fashion statement that I'm too old and decrepit to know. "I don't need a bath. I'll just smell extra sweet."

"So sweet, you'll make all the bees come out," I retort.

Her eyes widen comically. She's always hated bees. "A bath, it is."

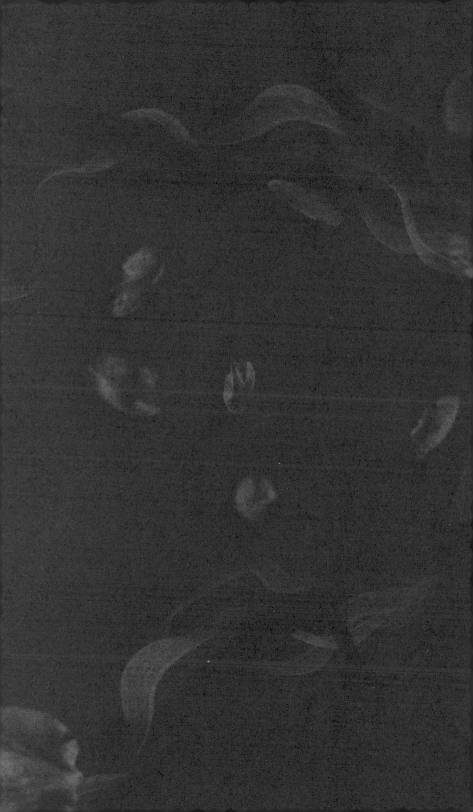

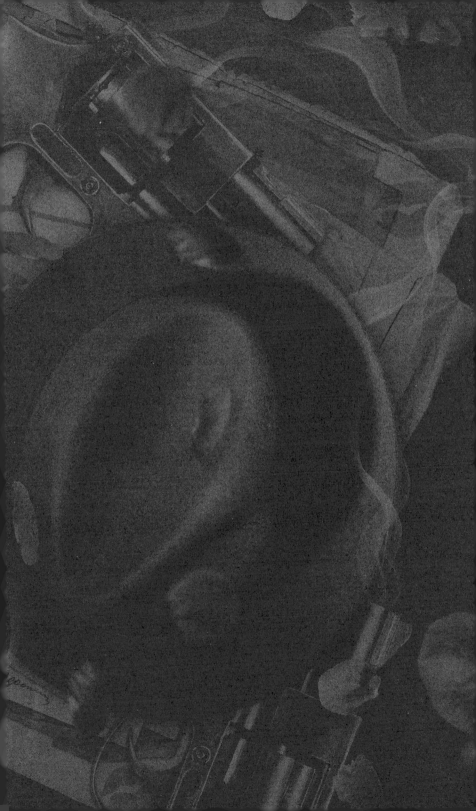

CHAPTER 27

THE PHANTOM

November 18, 1944

"Would you ever let me read your diary?" I didn't intend to ask such an invasive question, but curiosity got the best of me. I lean against the doorframe to the living room, watching her as she scribbles in the leather-bound book. It's midafternoon, and Sera left only ten minutes ago. I didn't waste time coming inside once she had gone, and Genevieve has been studiously ignoring me since.

Or rather, trying to. A wicked little smile has been playing on her lips since my arrival.

I've tucked my hands in my pockets, forcing myself to stay put despite how my fingers continuously twitch with the need to touch her.

Genevieve peeks up at me, a coquettish *you know better* expression on her beautiful face.

"Then you would be privy to all my deepest, darkest desires, Mr. Capello," she teases. "You might find me boring if you knew everything about me."

I raise a brow and smirk. "I don't believe that's possible, my love. I suspect that I'll only grow more fascinated by you."

She hums and leans back into the rocking chair, staring at me thoughtfully, sustaining her impish look. Then she lifts her journal before her face, only allowing me to see her sparkling blue eyes.

Mischievousness sparks within them as she flips a page before her sensual voice rings out. "November seventeenth, 1944," she recites, flicking her stare toward me for the briefest of seconds. "Ronaldo said he'd visit me tomorrow, and it's all I can think about. I wonder if he'll touch me again or use his tongue in all his favorite places." She holds my gaze as she says the next sentence, though appetency swirls within hers. "They are also my favorite places."

My hands in my pockets curl into tight fists as she continues and effectively ignores the way my stare bores into her. "Though I can't help but wonder if he'd like my tongue on him, too. I've thought about it many times over the months. Even dreamed about it. But I've never done something like that before, so today, I decided to practice. I never thought I'd live to see a day where I'm stuffing a banana down the back of my throat, but—"

My mind goes blank, and my vision blurs as I rush to her. I'm across the room in mere seconds. She yelps when I rip the journal from her grasp, sending it flying with one hand and fisting her curls with the other. I'm pulling her to her feet one second, and the next, I'm devouring those filthy red lips.

Never in my thirty-six years did I think a woman's putting a piece of fruit down her throat would threaten to send me to my knees, yet the image of her doing so just to please me has me spiraling.

"If you wanted to practice, baby, I'm happy to oblige," I growl against her abused mouth, my chest filling with fire. My cock is already straining against my trousers, and it throbs painfully from the knowledge that she wants to wrap those pretty lips around it.

"What if I'm terrible at it?" she asks breathlessly.

Clutching her curls tighter, I yank her head back, evoking a little yelp from her throat. I'm helpless to control myself and be gentle with her.

"You are incapable of doing anything wrong, Genevieve. If wrapping your lips around my cock meant suffering, I'd spend the rest of my days at your mercy."

She peers up at me through her eyelashes coyly.

"Then it's fortunate that I only aim to please you." She plants her hands on my chest and pushes away from me, and I let her go, watching her closely as she backs a few feet away.

Her green floral dress cuts into a deep V-neck, dainty buttons trailing down the length of it and holding the fabric tight to her curves. She toys with the top button, right below a hint of cleavage.

My mouth waters as she plucks it free, then the next, and onward until the top half of the dress is parted, exposing her silky brassiere. Instead of removing the dress completely, she slides her arms free of the three-quarter sleeves, allowing the material to droop to her waist.

Next, she reaches behind her and unhooks the bra, letting it fall to the floor.

My God, I'll never tire of the sight of her. Full breasts that are more than a handful and have gone unappreciated for far too long. I've licked and sucked those rosy-pink nipples any chance I could get over the past few months, yet it never seems enough. A conundrum I can't seem to escape, despite how often I ravish her body.

I always. Need. More.

She points to her rocking chair. "Would you sit for me?" she asks sweetly, and I'm tempted to bite her just for playing innocent.

She *is* innocent, in some ways—her mouth, and her plump backside that is begging to be explored. But she certainly has expressed no desire to *stay* that way. And I have no plans to allow her to.

I grin, licking my bottom lip slowly before biting down on it as I pass her, causing those red lips to part in anticipation. I make no effort to hide the animalistic hunger gnawing at the inside of my chest. I want her to see me for the predator that I am. And I want her to feel like every bit of the prey that she is.

First, I move the stool out of the way, allowing her ample space to kneel. Then I adopt a casual posture and sit in her chair, leaning back and keeping my legs spread, my elbows perched on the armrests.

She stands several feet away, and when she goes to take a step, I hold up a palm, stopping her. Her eyes flare wide, but I don't allow embarrassment to settle in.

I nod at her. "Kneel right there."

Her brows knit in confusion, and she hesitates for only a moment before dropping to her knees. The pale skin of her chest is flushing red, and the color slowly works its way up her throat. She's becoming nervous, though she tries to hide it.

Genevieve is a confident woman. Yet all it takes is one look from me for her to squirm beneath my stare.

"Now crawl to me, *mia rosa.*"

She swallows thickly, and I see the decision settle over her gaze as she turns from unsure of herself to a powerful vixen in a matter of seconds. She may act beneath my command, but she knows it is I who am beholden to her.

Licking her lips, she stares at me with a seductive look, her blue eyes bright beneath her thick, black eyelashes—her straight white teeth toying with her bottom lip.

A goddamn goddess, she is. Derived directly from the myths carved into ancient ruins.

I'm enraptured by her as she gets on her hands and slowly crawls to me, her hips and beautiful tits swaying seductively.

A growl works its way out of my throat before I can stop it. I've seen many beautiful sights in my years. But nothing could even begin to compare to Genevieve Parsons crawling on her hands and knees for me.

By the time she reaches me, my hands are clenched around the armrests, and I'm two seconds from exploding. Decades of experience to build my stamina as a man, and one woman is threatening to revert me to a prepubescent boy.

I keep silent as she reaches for my belt, sucking on her bottom lip in anticipation. There's a slight tremor in her hands as she unbuckles the leather, though her fingers are deft. She has my trousers unfastened in seconds, and by the time she releases my cock from the slit in my briefs, it's painfully hard and throbbing in her small hand.

A hint of nervousness rears its head again, and she glances up at me. "You'll tell me what you like?"

"Anything," I rasp, the word damn near breaking apart at the syllables. "I'll love anything you do to me."

My assurance—or maybe how I'm so clearly unraveling—is all she requires to gather her confidence. Keeping her blue eyes pinned to me, she leans forward and wraps her lips around the tip of my cock. I hiss between my teeth, and she studies me closely as her tongue darts out and licks the bead of precum.

It's not her experience with men that keeps her gaze locked on mine—most women know that's any man's undoing. She does so because she strives to satisfy me, and she's devoted to watching my every expression to ensure she does just that. The damn woman has no idea that her eye contact alone is more than enough to send me over the edge.

She reaches her hand up and wraps it around my length, and I'm immediately sitting up. "Nope, you're going to make me come before I get a chance to enjoy it. Put your damn hands behind your back," I demand roughly. She pulls away, blinking in confusion, though she still obeys.

I rip my belt from the loops and then lean forward, wrapping the leather around her wrists and tying them together tightly.

When I lean back, there's an amused smile playing on her lips.

"I'm only to use my mouth?"

"Yes," I all but snarl. I've never been this uncontrolled, and I'm damn near terrified I'll come after mere moments, robbing us both of an incredible experience. If I knew this was going to happen today, I'd have taken care of myself beforehand if only to save myself from utter embarrassment.

"Okay," she says simply. "Am I allowed to continue?"

I thin my eyes. "You have two seconds, Genevieve."

She perks up and doesn't dare waste another instant. My eyes shutter the moment her wet heat is engulfing the tip of my cock again, this time venturing further down my length.

I don't expect her to take all of me, so I let her test her own limits for now. I have every intention of pushing her, but only after she's accustomed to the feel of me sliding in and out of her throat.

She takes her time exploring my length with her tongue almost curiously at first, as if she's tasting a new cuisine for the first time. Then she grows bolder and licks me with more sureness. All the while, we watch each other, entirely riveted by one another's expressions.

As her confidence grows, her cheeks hollow. The first time she truly sucks on my cock, a moan spills from my lips. Her blue eyes flare from the sound, and determination settles in her gaze. It's the moment I know I'm done for.

And she proves me right. With eagerness, she sucks me harder, bobbing her head up and down as she does and flattening her tongue against the underside of my cock. She's intent on pulling more of those sounds out of me, and I yearn to please her, so I loosen my restraint and let her hear just how feral she makes me.

"God, baby, you suck me so pretty," I whimper, losing my mind over the red lipstick smeared down my length. Soon, her lips will be wiped clean of it, and I'd be happy to use my cock to reapply it.

Invigorated, she moans around me and bobs her head earnestly, swallowing as much as she can until she gags, evoking another grunt from my lips.

"Such a good girl," I whisper. "What would your husband think of seeing you like this, gagging on my cock?"

She flicks a glare at me, and I grin in return, my eyelids drooping. "He'd be devastated, watching his innocent wife choking me down like a little slut."

Now, she keeps her watery blue eyes pinned to me again, fire raging within, though she doesn't dare retreat. Instead, she sucks me harder, evoking a groan.

"It would torture him, wouldn't it, baby? Knowing that he will never fill your throat like I do." I manage a chuckle, the sound distorted with pleasure. "He can't even fill your cunt like I can."

A lone tear tracks down her cheek, muddled with eyeliner. I smear it across her skin with my thumb, biting back another grin.

"Don't worry, *mia rosa*. I'll make him watch while I fuck you like you deserve, then I'll cut off his hands and cock so he can never touch you again." I snarl, overcome with the thought. Then I whisper, "Poor Johnny-boy, bleeding out on the floor while I make his wife scream my name."

She makes a high-pitched sound, her cheeks flushed and her eyes fiery. But I know her pussy is dripping wet. She pretends to be affronted by the words, yet she swallows me down until she gags again, and it takes effort to keep my eyes from rolling.

"*Fuck*, Genevieve, keep sucking it like that. You're doing so good."

Eagerly, she obliges, swallowing me down until she gags once more. My balls tighten, and I continue to moan and mutter encouragements, words tumbling from my mouth that I hardly understand. Each time, she seems to become more desperate for the next one.

"So fucking proud of you."

"Swallow it, deeper. Please, baby, I need it."

"Fuck, that's it. That's a good girl."

"Oh, just like that. Please don't stop sucking it."

The pleasure she elicits is astronomical, and it takes every bit of concentration to keep from exploding in her mouth. I'm too goddamn enraptured to let it be over yet.

Especially because I have so much more in store for her.

Deciding that she's practiced enough, I curl a hand into her hair and pull tight. She pauses, yet it's pointless because I'm shoving her head down, her lipstick staining my cock.

A little squeal resounds against me, but I pay it no mind. With her hands tied, she's unable to stop me as I lift her head until the tip pops free, a trail of saliva connecting from her lips to my head. Her eyes are rounded at the corner, and her tongue is hanging past her lips while she pants heavily.

I mourn that I'm unable to take a photograph of her like that. I'd never let go of it, carrying it around with me for my eyes only. And when my day came, I'd ensure it was the last thing I saw before I took my final breath.

I see no way through this life without her. Obsession, addiction, love—they are meager words to describe what I feel for her.

"Such a pretty whore for me, *mia rosa*," I growl.

"If I were your whore," she whispers, "you'd fuck my mouth like one."

I lose it.

She dares tempt a beast, and I'm happy for her to suffer those consequences.

I'm shoving her down on my cock instantly, and she's ready for me, swallowing me down with ease. I pump my hips into her mouth, guiding her head as I do until she receives exactly what she asked for—I *fuck* her mouth.

Unintelligible sounds pour from my throat as I come undone, spitting out words through clenched teeth. "That's it, baby, that's how you suck my fucking cock. Such a desperate little slut for me, aren't you? You fucking love choking on it, don't you?"

Still I've no idea what I'm saying, and maybe later realization will settle in, and I'll be ashamed of the way I spoke to her. Right now, I'm out of my damn mind, and I couldn't care less about what spills past my lips.

Euphoria has my stomach clenching and balls constricting. I feel my length swelling in her mouth, causing her to gag as I hold her head down, entirely lost as the pleasure comes to claim me like a reaper who witnessed my last breath.

"Yes, yes, make me come, baby, *make me fucking come.*"

She gags, and I erupt so forcefully that I sit upright, cradling her head against me as I'm consumed. Distinctly, I feel a shout burst past my lips as I flood her throat, followed by uncontrollable moans and whimpers as I mindlessly rut into her mouth.

The ecstasy is too much—too strong—causing me to bite my goddamn tongue as I'm swept beneath the tidal wave. Colors detonate in my vision, and my cock feels as if it's literally going to explode from the pressure.

It's intense and breathtaking, and *fuck*, is it violent.

Soon enough, it eases, then becomes too sensitive. I pull her head back, needing some type of relief from the sensation.

I'm getting too old to experience something like that, and for a moment, I'm convinced I'm on the verge of having a stroke. My chest is tight, and I can't inhale a single breath.

However, after a few more moments, the constriction around my chest eases, and my lungs loosen. Tremors rack my body as I slump back into the chair, a hand over my mouth as I stare at her in utter shock.

All the while, she stares at me like she was just handed an Oscar for her performance.

"I rather like it when you beg."

"My God, Genevieve," I choke out. "Are you trying to *kill* me?"

She grins devilishly, crimson and saliva smeared across her chin. "How else will we spend eternity together?"

November 17, 1944

Ronaldo said he'd visit me tomorrow, and it's all I can think about.
I wonder if he'll touch me again or use his tongue in all his
favorite places.
They are also my favorite places.
Though I can't help but wonder if he'd like my tongue on him,
too. I've thought about it many times over the months. Even
dreamed about it. But I've never done something like that before,
so today, I decided to practice. I never thought I'd live to see a
day where I'm stuffing a banana down the back of my throat, but
there I was, gagging on a piece of fruit.
My eyes watered instantly, and a tear tracked down my cheek.
And I just knew that if Ronaldo were there watching me, he
would have loved the way I looked.
Now, I don't know if I will ever look at bananas the same.

CHAPTER 28

THE RAVEN

December 22, 1944

There's a deep chill scattering down my spine like tiny little mouse feet, causing me to shudder.

I'm unsure if it's from the snowfall today, the freezing temperatures working their way into Parsons Manor, or because there's a decrepit soul standing behind me.

I glance over my shoulder, wondering: If there is someone there that I can't see, what would they think of my diary? *That you are going to burn in hell.*

Possibly.

My mother always claimed so.

Maybe all this time, she was actually onto something.

If that's the case, I suppose I'll see her there.

I glimpse Ronaldo's form outside the window, wearing all black as he usually does. Excitement thrums in my chest, nearly bubbling out of me as the front door opens, then snicks shut.

It takes effort to keep my behind seated in my chair rather than run to him like a lovesick fool. Even if that's precisely what I am.

However, I am helpless to contain the bright smile from stretching across my face when he appears, a light dusting of snow clinging to his shoulders and fedora.

He pulls off his hat before running his hand through his black strands, and just like every other time he comes to visit, my heart stalls in my chest.

"What are you writing about today, my love?" he asks warmly, a grin on his beautiful face. My diary is on my lap, open to a page blank save for today's date.

He saunters toward me in such a way that my throat tightens. The man is simply *walking*, and I'm damn near quivering.

I shrug coquettishly. "I haven't begun yet. I suppose I have nothing to write about right now."

"Does this mean I should give you something to write about, Genevieve?" he asks wickedly.

I swallow. Or rather, I try to. It feels as if my tongue has swollen to twice its size.

"Maybe so. Your visitations have been rather boring," I tease sarcastically.

His answering chuckle is devilish, and the sound sends chills down my spine. When he reaches me, he flicks a finger at me, gesturing for me to stand.

Frowning, I do so, taking my journal with me. I can only blink at him when he moves me aside so he can sit in the rocking chair, adopting a casual position as he leans back into it. Resting his elbows on the armrests, he smirks up at me.

"Aren't you going to sit?"

Blinking, I move to crawl onto his lap, but he holds up a hand, stopping me.

"You know better," he croons, tsking at me. "Clothes off first."

My heart pounds heavily as I set my diary on the footstool, then unfasten the pearl buttons that line the length of my wool dress. A tremor racks my body, and goose bumps cover my flesh as I shrug it off, left in my undergarments.

The surface of my body is cold, but my insides are steadily heating, warming me from the inside out.

Ronaldo licks his bottom lip before biting down on it, leaning his head back and staring at me like he wants to devour me.

Invigorated, I unhook my bra, my breasts feeling full and heavy as his stare burns into me. Then I unfasten my crotchless girdle and unhook the garter straps, letting that fall to my feet, revealing my lack of underwear beneath. I stand before him in nothing but my stockings, and a groan leaks from his mouth.

The bulge in his trousers is prominent. When he notices my gaze, he quickly undoes his belt and trousers, freeing his cock from the confines.

"Sit on it, Genevieve," he orders. "And bring your journal."

"Bring my journal?" I echo, confused.

"That's what I said."

He doesn't bother to explain himself further, and I'm growing impatient anyway. My knees tremble as I grab my journal and pen from the stool, then crawl onto his lap. He keeps his feet planted on the floor, preventing the chair from rocking as I adjust myself to hover above him.

I wrap my free hand around his length, evoking a hiss from his teeth, and line him up with my entrance.

There's no question whether I'm drenched. I felt myself wetting my inner thighs before I undressed. So, without preamble, I seat myself completely on him, pulling a moan from both of our throats.

When I prepare to lift again, his hands slam down on my hips, keeping me seated.

"Uh-uh. Write in your journal."

"What?" I squeak.

"Did you think I wanted reading material while you ride my cock? No, baby. I'm giving you the material. Now, write."

My mouth flops, and he nods toward my diary, gesturing for me to proceed.

Clearing my throat, I balance the diary on my arm, and with shaky hands, I write: *I'm so full, and he expects me to write when all I want to do is fuck him.*

"The first time I saw you sitting in this window, you were writing in your diary," he begins, his voice husky with desire and so very deep. "You were the most magnificent creature I'd ever seen."

My pen stills, and inadvertently, I clench around him, drawing out another hiss. I'm desperate for even a smidge of friction.

"I watched you for weeks, and most of the time, you didn't know I was there." I glance up at him, a little surprised by his admission. So many days, this man stood outside my house and watched me, and I had no idea.

"There were many times I pictured this moment exactly. Sitting beneath you while you wrote. Your cunt stuffed with my cock and leaking all over my lap."

I bite my lip as I try to write, my handwriting increasingly worsening as he speaks.

"Your beautiful tits on full display, where I can lick and suck them. God, you have no idea how many times I've salivated just thinking about it. How many times I've stroked myself to the thought."

He's. Driving. Me. WILD.

His grip on my hips becomes bruising. There's a desperation in his own gaze, suffering from his own games as much as I am.

"I imagined those pretty red lips begging me to fuck you," he growls. "To make you come all over me."

My God, he has no idea how close I am to defying his orders and doing just that. If I roll my hips the slightest bit . . .

He stops me, a warning growl rumbling in his chest.

"I'm not finished," he bites out through gritted teeth.

But I am.

He wants to play? Then that's exactly what I'll do.

I tighten my walls around him, causing him to twitch.

"Genevieve," he snaps.

"Yes, my love?" I ask innocently, sparing him a glance before I continue writing. Then I squeeze around him again, earning myself another growl.

"Put the journal down."

"I'm not finished," I repeat, quirking a brow. I clench again and keep writing, and his breath stutters out of him. He goes to lift me himself, so I bear down and lock my hips, refusing him as he refused me. His eyes narrow, and he looks seconds away from standing with me in his arms and fucking me anyway.

"Don't you want to hear what I wrote?" I ask coyly. "It's about you."

He opens his mouth, but I continue before he can say *later*. *"I told Ronaldo that I had never touched myself before, and at the time, that was true,"* I read aloud. *"But since then, I've done it many times. Sometimes, even right next to my husband while he sleeps. I'd reach down into my undergarments and feel how wet I was."*

"Genevieve." He speaks my name like a whip cracking in the air, but it doesn't deter me.

"Softly, as to not rouse the man next to me, I rubbed my clit. Thinking of those days where Ronaldo would call me his little whore and fuck me. Whether it was my mouth or my cunt. Or the times he would lick my pussy so thoroughly, I could keep him fed for a week."

"Goddamn it," he hisses.

"It was so hard to stay quiet. Especially when I made myself come, whispering Ronaldo's name."

He tries to move my hips once more, but again, I refuse. Instead, I clench around him, a soft moan spilling from my lips.

"Please, baby," he groans, his chest heaving.

I grin. *"It felt so good, but I was always left aching to be filled,"* I forge on. *"My cunt, my mouth"*—I meet his gaze—*"and my ass felt so empty, so incomplete without him."*

He tears the journal and pen from my hands, dropping them carelessly onto the floor beside us, hellfire raging in his eyes.

"Ride me, *mia rosa*," he orders roughly.

I shake my head, biting back a smile. "Haven't I told you before? I rather like when you beg."

His brow furrows, and his face twists as if he's in pain. "*Fuck*, Genevieve, *please*," he pleads, his voice lined with gravel. "*Please* ride my cock. *Please* make me come. *Please* fuck me. I need it so bad, baby."

I moan. "Good boy. You sound so pretty when you beg."

His eyes flare, raging infernos within. And I roll my hips, giving into what we desperately need.

My head drifts back, and my body takes control, grinding against him with vigor, his pelvis creating the perfect friction against my clit.

"Fuck, yes, that's it. Just like that," he whimpers. "Let me suck on these beautiful tits."

Lost in the euphoria, I have enough sense to lean forward, meeting him halfway. His mouth wraps around my nipple, licking and sucking on it forcefully and sending another shock wave of pleasure straight to my core.

I dive my fingers through his hair, holding him to me as he trades between using his tongue and his teeth.

"Lift your feet up, let the chair rock," I pant, pulling away from him briefly. His legs are long, and it takes effort to maneuver them until he can hook his feet on the base rail beneath the stool.

Once he does, I arch my back and balance my hands on his shoulders. The motion of the chair causes me to wobble at first. It takes a few tries, but soon, I'm able to use the momentum to my advantage, allowing me to lift up and down on his length with ease.

With this new angle, he hits a spot inside of me that takes my breath away. My stomach tightens, an orgasm quickly building.

"Fucking *Christ*," Ronaldo groans, cupping my breasts in his palms and pushing them together, placing open-mouthed kisses and nipping all over. "You fuck me so good."

"You take it so good," I whisper, diving one of my hands back into his hair, tugging the strands tight.

My eyes roll as the pleasure heightens, my hips tightening and stuttering as it builds to a sharp point.

"Ronaldo," I gasp.

He releases my breasts and grabs onto my hips, taking over and guiding me up and down on his cock.

"Yes, yes, that's it," he mutters, urgency in his tone. "Come for me, baby. I want you to milk my fucking cock."

My hips still, then I erupt seconds later, a dizzying wave rushing straight to my head. Then I'm grinding mindlessly against him, no rhythm to the way I move. Ronaldo explodes soon after, a hoarse shout bursting from his throat before he descends into madness alongside me.

Our bodies are no longer ours to control. They're not even one another's. We can only succumb to it, as if God has sent a flood to sweep us away—the waves too powerful to survive.

For several moments, I'm cast into blindness and silence, my senses useless. My lungs, too, as it's impossible to draw in a breath.

I'm drowning, and it's so peaceful.

Finally, the orgasm retreats, and I'm able to come up for air. We embrace each other tightly, his face in the crook of my neck while I slump over him. I tremble violently in Ronaldo's hold, and my throat feels raw as little gasps and pants uncontrollably rush out of me.

"Oh my God," I heave breathlessly, aftershocks causing me to twitch and jolt.

I pull away enough for him to tip his head up toward me.

"What the fuck did you just do to me?"

December 22, 1944

"Since I won't see you on Christmas, I brought your present today," he tells me quietly.

We're lounging on the couch, the two of us completely nude now but keeping warm thanks to the crackling fire a few feet from us. I lay my head on his chest, my fingers tracing invisible pictures on his skin.

I frown, tilting my chin to look up at him. "You said no presents."

"I said no presents for *me*," he corrects. Another grin ticks up the corners of his mouth. "I never said I wouldn't get you anything."

"Ronaldo," I whine. "That's not fair."

"Then I suppose it's a terrible time to confess that it's also my birthday today."

I gasp, sitting up on my elbow to glare at him.

"Why didn't you tell me? I would've—"

He rests a finger over my lips, silencing me.

"Right here, right now, this is all I could ever want from you, Genevieve. Nothing else."

I frown. "But I could have done something special for you."

"Baby, the only thing I want for my birthday *and* Christmas is your love." He pauses. "And maybe your pretty cunt on my face. Otherwise, I want for nothing else."

I roll my eyes, though I can't help but chuckle. I'm incapable of berating him for his vulgarity and insatiable appetite when I'm no better.

What we just did . . .

There are never any words for it.

He reaches beneath the cushion behind him and pulls out a small box, holding it in his palm. I hadn't even seen him hide it there when we lay down.

My stare pings between his glittering eyes and the black box he's presenting to me. Sighing, I take it, flicking him one last indignant glance before opening it.

I gasp. A beautiful red rose brooch shines from within, the petals encrusted in glittering rubies. I sit up, balancing on my elbow as I stare at the piece that surely cost way too much.

"Ronaldo," I breathe. "It's exquisite. But it's simply too much."

"It's not nearly enough. If I could, you would have a ring on your finger," he rebuts. "But I will settle for a brooch for now. I figured it may be something your husband would assume you've had for years."

Emotion clogs my throat as I set the box on his stomach and wrap myself around him. He cradles me to him as I brush my lips against his.

"Thank you," I whisper against his mouth, also hating that his ring doesn't decorate my finger. Maybe one day, but today, I am only happy he's here.

"Just be careful," he murmurs between soft kisses. "It could prick you."

I grin against him, my chest so full, I can hardly breathe. "I would gladly bleed for you."

He groans his approval against my lips, and butterflies flutter in my stomach as an idea strikes me.

Pulling away, I sit up on my knees, watching him carefully as he stares at me with confusion. Now that I'm no longer in the throes of ecstasy, taking control in such a way has my nerves prickling. But if I am anything, I am brave.

"The least I could do is make all your wishes come true," I say, staring at him with a half-lidded gaze. "It would be awfully rude of me not to."

His expression slackens as I straddle his chest, prompting him to readjust a little and give my legs room on either side of him. Then I climb over his face and watch as his mouth parts in awe and a savage hunger ignites in his pale eyes.

"You wanted my pretty cunt on your face. And now I want you to eat it."

"Fucking *Christ*," he curses, not wasting another second before he does exactly as I ask.

December 22, 1944

I'm so full, and he expects me to write when all I want to do is fuck him. God, I can barely concentrate, even as he speaks in that deep, gravel voice of his.

I need to move, but he won't let me. And the filthy words pouring from his lips.

He's. Driving. Me. WILD.

I told Ronaldo that I had never touched myself before, and at the time, that was true. But since then, I've done it many times. Sometimes even right next to my husband while he sleeps. I'd reach down into my undergarments and feel how wet I was.

Softly, as to not rouse the man next to me, I rubbed my clit. Thinking of those days where Ronaldo would call me his little whore and fuck me. Whether it was my mouth or my cunt. Or the times he would lick my pussy so thoroughly, I could keep him fed for a week.

It was so hard to stay quiet. Especially when I made myself come, whispering Ronaldo's name.

It felt so good, but I was always left aching to be filled. My cunt, my mouth, and my ass felt so empty, so incomplete without him.

I never got to finish, he tore the journal out of my hands and crumpled the pages. It was worth it.

I found out it is his thirty-seventh birthday today, yet he was the one gifting me. I felt terrible at first. Of all days, I did nothing for him except make him beg and climb onto his face.

It definitely will not be the last time.

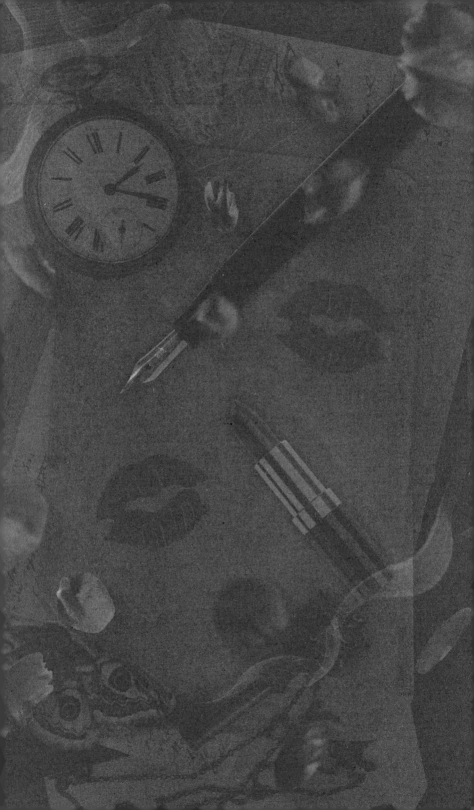

CHAPTER 29

THE RAVEN

January 13, 1945

I'm in so much trouble.

The front door slams, and I wince. Dread weighs down my bones as Ronaldo storms into the room, fury in his eyes and his fists clenched.

He's livid.

It's the first time I've truly seen him look at me with anything other than love and affection.

I realize now I've been spoiled, having gone this long escaping his ire.

"Why did you let him kiss you?" he asks quietly, his tone rough.

"I didn't *let* him. He took me by surprise!" I defend, my hackles rising.

Ronaldo was hiding within the tree line this morning when John and Sera left for a day trip to a few markets. I was standing at the door, calling out to Sera to behave today when John swooped in and stole a kiss. He caught me off guard, and I couldn't react quick enough.

John was halfway to the car before I realized what had happened.

And the first thing I felt was shame. I hated how he did that. I knew it was wrong to feel so disturbed by a kiss from my husband, yet it felt like he took something from me without permission all over again. A pit had formed in my stomach almost instantly, and I had hoped Ronaldo didn't see.

"Have you been kissing him all this time?"

"No!" I shout, my nails forming crescent moons in my palms. "I haven't let him kiss me since—" My throat closes, but I force the words out anyway. "Since before what he did last June. We've hardly touched since you started coming around. That's why I wasn't expecting it, Ronaldo."

His chest deflates, but the anger clings to him. And truthfully, I can't even blame him. It's not hard to imagine a woman kissing him, and the burning anger that accompanies that image is undeniable.

I understand his wrath, but what would he have me do? Divorcing John when we have a kid together . . . that's almost unheard of.

As if sensing my thoughts, he swings his thin gaze toward me. "I could kill him," he growls. "I would have no qualms ending his pathetic life, Genevieve." He takes a step toward me. "I *dream* about it. And the only reason I don't is because of *you*."

"Because of Sera!" I correct. "I am not like you, Ronaldo. I don't wish harm on the man, but make no mistake, it is only Sera I think of."

He snarls, turning away from me as he paces the checkered floor. I feel incredibly helpless. And suffocatingly trapped.

Worse yet, I can't find it in me to regret my marriage to John. Not when Sera resulted from it. And there isn't even the smallest part of me that could *ever* wish she didn't exist.

I love Ronaldo, but my daughter will always come first.

"Do you have any idea how hard it is to only love you in the dark when you deserve to be loved in the light?"

My bottom lip trembles, and tears well in my eyes, blurring my vision. My heart feels like it's been dropped into a blender, each word slicing until there's nothing left.

"I do know. You deserve that, too, Ronaldo," I whisper. "I want to love you openly. I . . . I want Sera to know you exist and get a chance to love you openly, too. But what court would grant me that?"

"Have you tried? Maybe they will allow it, and you'll only have society to deal with. But you've already ostracized yourself from them with this house, haven't you? What's one more decision to truly set you apart from the rest of them?"

He takes a step toward me, conviction shining in his eyes. "Do you understand what it's like knowing that when I leave here, another man takes my place? Or having to wait for him to leave to take his?"

I don't, but I can imagine, and it hurts.

"He sleeps in your bed. He is the first person who sees you when you wake and before you sleep. He—"

"But he is not the one I dream about," I insist. "He is not the first on my mind when I wake. And it's not he who owns my heart."

I had hoped my declaration would placate him in some way, but he doesn't look appeased. Torture fills his eyes, and it feels as if he stabbed my heart with a needle and injected his pain directly into it.

"Believe me, Ronaldo. You are not the only one who suffers when he is near," I whisper, my voice as broken as a future with Ronaldo by my side.

We stare at one another silently for a few moments, both of us mourning what could be but what will likely never come.

"I am destined to love you from the shadows, *mia rosa*," he says quietly. "I will never be more than your phantom."

My chest cracks, and tears well over the rims of my eyes.

And I can see it. I can see how he stares at me with a hint of bitterness deriving from a fantasy I refuse to allow him. He wants to murder John and rid me of the man who unknowingly shackles me to a life of discontent.

It would be so simple for him, too. To hide in the shadows, wait for John to come home, then fire a single bullet into the back of his head. With the snap of his fingers, I would be free of my husband.

But how could I live with myself afterward? Lying to my daughter every day, insisting that some random criminal broke into our home and took her father's life, when all along, I'd be sleeping next to his true killer. Slowly inviting him into our home hoping she would accept him and love him as a stepfather.

However, her heart would always have a hole in it, and her sorrow would be my sorrow. How long would she have to suffer just so I don't have to? Only my suffering might never actually end at all if I had John's blood forever staining my hands.

I couldn't live with myself.

I couldn't look her in the eyes and tell her such lies.

It's a life that would only bring us more pain, not any relief. And I hate that Ronaldo can't see that as I can.

Even without words, I know he thinks that time will heal our wounds, and as years pass on, Sera would find happiness again. She would all but move on from her father's senseless death and settle into a future with

Ronaldo as her father.

But it's a farce, and he knows it, and the thought of it makes me ill.

John isn't the greatest of men, but he doesn't deserve to die.

Even if he did and I *could* live with myself, there's another important component that is impossible for me to ignore.

"You work for one of the biggest criminals in the country, Ronaldo," I remind him, forcing stoicism into my tone. "You *are* a criminal—something I've overlooked because I know you are also a good man. But you could not guarantee safety for my life or my daughter's. Even if I could forgive you for taking John's life, I would never—*could* never—forgive you if your crimes resulted in Sera's death, too."

The muscle in his jaw pulses, and I only know I've struck a nerve because it is a fact that he cannot defend himself from.

He knows as well as I do that if I were to have my husband killed and marry him instead, I'd be unchaining myself from a life of discontent only to chain myself to a life of terror instead.

I'd die before I could truly live because surely my heart would give out from the fear of seeing my daughter hurt or murdered.

"I would never let anything happ—"

"It is not always up to you, Ronaldo. I trust you would protect us with everything you have, but that doesn't mean you would succeed." The words are as sharp as a whip, but I still mean them.

He winces, feeling the sting. But is it because of what I said or because he knows it's true?

His expression smooths into cool marble, though the muscle in his jaw still pulsates. My heart thuds heavily in my chest, a strange kind of fear arising. This conversation has been distressing for both of us, but watching him wipe his face clean of his hurt is like watching him wipe his heart clean of *me*. And that . . . that is simply devastating.

"Would you have me leave you alone?" he asks, his tone rough yet quiet.

Even if my words could escape me, my voice would fail. I shake my head, wanting him to stay as desperately as I need air.

"Then what do you want, Genevieve? Because whatever it is, I will grant it to you. At the cost of my heart and my sanity, I will give you whatever you ask of me."

Another tear trails down my cheek. "I—I just want *you*."

He nods slowly, his teeth clenched and his fists tightened. "So then it is your phantom I will be."

January 14, 1945

The cold, dreary weather is putting me in a mood that rivals the ice clinging to my windows.

Frank even noticed my sour state when he stopped by today.

He tried to cheer me up with bad jokes. I'll admit I laughed at one or two, but I can't seem to muster much more than that.

Ronaldo and I argued yesterday.

He said he can't stand that I'm still with John. He's incredibly jealous, and I can't say I entirely blame him. Not when the thought of him with another woman nearly makes me blind with rage.

But Ronaldo's life is still far too dangerous. How could I give up stability for my daughter for a man whose life could get us killed?

I'm at a loss.

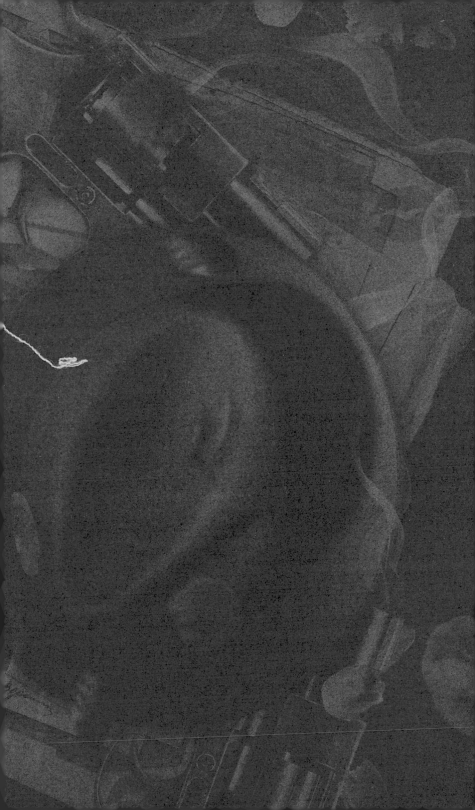

CHAPTER 30

THE PHANTOM

January 14, 1945

"Manny Baldelli has been spotted outside of Seattle," Paulie informs Angelo while standing next to his desk with his hands crossed behind his back.

Alfonso and I are sitting in the plush chairs, the three of us puffing on our Cuesta-Rey cigars.

Normally, I would've turned down the tobacco, but with Genevieve's words from yesterday still clouding my mind, I needed something to release some of the tension.

Angelo's fist slams down on his desk, sending pens clattering off the wood and rattling the crystal decanter.

"What do you mean, he was spotted? Ronnie shot him!"

Angelo's face is beginning to purple while red and white splotches form in my vision.

"It wasn't fatal," Paulie affirms. "I saw him with my own eyes and clocked him all the way to Don Leonardo Saputo's estate."

A snarl curls my upper lip.

"Fuckers," I mutter, my fingers beginning to twitch uncontrollably.

My mood has been as dark as the sight in my left eye, and even Angelo has trodden carefully with me.

The need to kill . . . it's like a parasite beneath my flesh, taking control over my bodily functions until the only thing I'm capable of is death.

The Saputos have made their allegiance to the Baldellis clear, so it's no surprise they're housing him. Which could mean they're planning something, likely banking on the fact that Angelo's growing comfortable again after believing Manny to be dead the last five months.

But Angelo did not become the *capo di tutti i capi* without reason. When the media gifted him the name, they also gifted him a paranoia that no drug could emulate. He doesn't take a single step without glancing over his shoulder.

I grind my teeth and keep my glare pinned to Mona Lisa. If it was possible, the paint composing her face would melt beneath my stare. That slight smile she dons feels as if it's just for me, like she knows something I don't.

Whether it's about Genevieve or Baldelli, she'll never tell me.

"I'm going to the Saputo estate and taking them out myself," I declare stoically, puffing on my cigar as Mona Lisa's smile blurs.

The three men's stares land on me at once.

"Not alone, you won't," Angelo argues.

I arch a brow. "Paulie can come if he'd like," I say. "But I'm more familiar with the Saputo estate than anyone."

Angelo grins. "Ah, yes. You fancied his sister at one point, no?"

The only thing I fancied was her lips wrapped around my cock. But that was years ago, and though Lucia would've loved it if I had asked for her hand in marriage, I couldn't stand to hear her high-pitched voice. Which is why I could only tolerate her when her mouth was plugged. My fling with her didn't last more than a few months, but it offered me plenty of time to familiarize myself with their estate.

Back then, the Saputos were loyal to Angelo, and Don Leonardo was happy to show me around and entertain me over a glass of whiskey. He had hoped I would marry his sister, too—even he couldn't wait for her to find a husband and be out of his hair.

"Last I heard, she finally got married," Alfonso offers.

"I don't care if Lucia is buried six feet under," I bark. "If she finds herself in the house, she will wear a bullet no differently than her brother."

Angelo whistles, amused by my sour mood. His own spirits are lightening now that I plan to handle the problem instantly.

Angelo trusts no one more than me to complete a contract. Manny may have gotten away with his life once, but that won't happen a second time.

"Boss, I can confirm that at least fifteen men occupy the Saputo estate," Paulie cuts in. He keeps his tone even and his face expressionless, but I know him well enough to sense that he's not fond of only the two of us walking into that fight.

But Angelo knows me well enough to sense that I'm not waiting for the rest of the crew to show up. There have been many moments in my life where I need nothing more than to feel blood on my hands. And when those moments arise, not even Angelo can get in my way.

"We'll come heavy," I clip, taking one last puff of my cigar before putting it out. "Or I go alone."

Paulie dips his chin as I stand from my chair, restlessness holding my muscles hostage. My fingers twitch with the need to fire bullets into as many brains that dare get in my line of fire.

"I'll always fight beside you, Ronaldo."

Walking into a den of wolves with only one man beside you is no easy decision, and at this moment, Paulie has my utmost respect.

"Then let's go. I'm not waiting any longer."

January 14, 1945

Return with Manny's head.

These were Angelo's parting words, though I didn't bother to respond.

The Saputo estate is nestled in northern Seattle, nearly taking over an entire block by itself. Leonardo Saputo owns the largest paint-manufacturing company in the country, with locations in nearly every city across-the-board. He uses the business to wash the tens of thousands of dollars the family makes transporting guns.

I hope Leo has picked out a suitable heir.

The entire car ride to the house was silent save for Paulie's double-checking that we had enough bullets to win the goddamn war.

I park far enough away from the front gate to stay undetected. There, two guards are stationed. The second they see us at the gates, Paulie and I are firing off one shot each, our bullets sluicing through their brains before either of them can reach for their pack sets.

Only a heavy chain and a padlock keep the gate secured, just as it was all those years ago. Paulie hands me bolt cutters, and I make quick work of clipping the chain and sliding it free, tossing the tool aside when I'm finished.

The outside of the estate is quiet. Trees rustle in the chilly winter air above a light dusting of snow on the ground.

I forge ahead and Paulie keeps to my left, as he always does—an unspoken arrangement between us. Since the moment he found out about the blindness in my left eye, he started stationing himself on that side of me, understanding the vulnerability with my lack of peripheral vision.

As we approach, one man walks out onto a balcony on the second floor. Paulie takes aim and fires off a shot instantly. The body slumps over the railing before plummeting onto the pavement below.

If they didn't hear us before, they surely have now.

Shouts arise from within the house, and I waste no time grabbing my tommy gun strapped to my back before I barge in, my finger pulling the trigger before the door fully makes it open.

Paulie opens fire only a moment later, the two of us quickly taking down three men standing in the foyer. Straight ahead is a hallway and a stairway on the left wall. Entryways to other rooms are on either side of the foyer right before the staircase, so we split up, taking cover behind our respective walls.

Chaos ensues. Return fire zips in our direction. Wooden chunks fly in my face from bullets nicking the edges of the doorframes.

While they shoot, I glance around, finding myself in a grand living room. Another entryway is opposite me, so I wait patiently, keeping my eye on it.

It takes only a few more seconds for Lorenzo Saputo, Leonardo's firstborn son, to appear in the opening. Our guns are both raised, but I pull my trigger faster.

Bullet holes riddle his face before his finger can twitch, and then he's tumbling to the floor.

I turn back toward the entryway facing the foyer, and the moment the Saputo bullets cease, Paulie and I are stepping out, unloading our magazines and taking out two more men.

In the middle of the massive foyer is a fountain constructed of baby angels, water spouting from their mouths to create a serene ambience.

I don't like it.

I turn toward two of the bodies strewn on the tile floor, grab them by the collars, and drag them toward the fountain. Then I throw their bodies into it, and their blood slowly pollutes the water until crimson is spitting from the angels' mouths.

Much better.

Paulie cocks his head, staring thoughtfully at my creation. "Nice," he mutters, a grin ticking up one corner of his mouth.

Then he turns and zips down the hallway while I climb the stairs, taking two steps at a time.

Leonardo's office is on the third floor, and I have a feeling it's where he and Manny currently are.

The second floor is comprised of another expansive living area with a few other large rooms branching off from it. I check each area, ensuring no one is hiding. After deeming the floor empty, I head toward the far back wall in the main area, where the second staircase is. The third floor is an open concept, the middle completely exposed and allowing a view of the second level. Closed doors are littered across all four walls, though several of them open just as I reach the final step, loud shouts ringing from their pack sets and alerting them of my arrival.

I'm firing before I can process who spills out from the rooms.

While spraying bullets with one hand, I fumble for the nearest doorknob to my left and rush into the room, scarcely missing a bullet that whizzes past my ear.

I'm greeted by a startled scream and a man shouting something indiscernible beneath the gunfire.

Lucia kneels on the bed between her new husband's spread legs, entirely nude. Her wet mouth hangs open as she stares at me in utter horror. She still grasps his hard cock, and the man whom it belongs to is just as astounded. These upper rooms are soundproof, and they were unaware of the carnage going on inside the house until this very moment.

I don't give them any more time to react. I laugh, aim my weapon, and unload several bullets into the two of them. Their screams quickly die out as blood sprays from multiple points of their body.

"He's in Lucia's room!" a man shouts.

I turn and take aim toward the open doorway, instantly realizing I've depleted my bullets. Footsteps are pounding toward me while I quickly switch out the magazine.

I take aim just as a man appears, the two of us firing at the same time. My shoulder jerks; intense pressure erupts, followed by burning pain.

Luckily, my aim was true, and the man drops to the floor.

Ignoring the searing agony, I wait for the rest of the men to appear. Their shadows stain the doorway right as the telltale sign of a needle catching onto vinyl sounds from the depths of the house, followed by a familiar tune.

Cesare Andrea Bixio's composition "Mamma son tanto felice" plays, and Beniamino Gigli's voice belts out the lyrics, which causes enough of a distraction for me to step out and unload several bullets into the last two men. They drop like flies. All the while, I wear a wide grin.

Paulie mentioned once before that he likes to play music when he completes contracts, so I'm confident he's the culprit for the melody playing from below.

And I can admit, it adds a nice flair when watching blood paint the walls.

I head straight into Leonardo's office. He stands in front of his desk, holding his own tommy gun, while Manny Baldelli stands beside him. They glare at me with beady eyes, though sweat slicks their thinning hair and the weapon trembles in Leo's hold.

"You shouldn't have come here, Ronnie," Leo calls, attempting to choke down his fear. "Come on, you're already hurt, and I don't want to see you dead, but I will if I must. You're a good man, but you're blind to your friend. You know as well as I do, Manny is the rightful godfather. The Salvatores stole his birthright from beneath him, and any man with honor would never respect that."

"You speak of honor, yet you refuse to acknowledge that the Baldellis' great-grandfather had no ties to the Mob. He was a *cafone* and an empty suit, desperate to belong to something that was never his to claim."

"That's not true!" Manny roars, his face reddening and spittle flying from his mouth.

Maybe. Maybe not.

But it doesn't change the Baldelli roots.

They've always been simple men playing dress-up in mobster clothing.

"You move exactly like he did," I respond stoically. "Undermining authority and laying claim to something that was never rightfully yours. Seems it runs in your bloodline."

Absolute rage overtakes Manny, and he's reaching for the tommy gun in Leo's hand, intent on shooting me himself. I don't let him get that far, though. During their struggle, I lay my finger down on the trigger, the vibrations from my gun filling my body and sparking euphoria.

In a matter of seconds, metal fills Don Manny and Don Leo's bodies, their eyes wide in disbelief as they fall to the floor.

Approaching the two men cautiously, I mumble a few of the lyrics alongside Beniamino Gigli.

Leo's eyes are wide open, devoid of life and destined to rot inside a body that decayed his soul years ago.

Manny is still alive, though, his breath whistling from his punctured lungs as he glares up at me. How poetic that he spent five months recovering only to find himself in front of my barrel once again.

He coughs up blood, his red face violently trembling as he attempts to reach for the fallen weapon beside him.

I kick it aside, and his dilated eyes sear into me. "Fuck . . . *you*," he spits, hardly managing to get the words out.

I crouch over him, ensuring my pleased smile is the last thing he sees before his entire body deflates, giving out on him and releasing his soul to the pits of fire below.

This time, I leave no room for error. I stand and unload my gun into the two men again, my bullets decorating their faces until they're nothing more than meat and bone.

There will be no surviving me a second time.

When I'm satisfied, Paulie's voice rings out from behind me. "Didn't Angelo tell us to bring Manny's head? There's nothing left of it now."

Staring down at the corpses, I hum, adrenaline coursing steadily through my veins and numbing the pain in my shoulder. Even still, my finger is still itching to unload a few more magazines.

I turn and meet his stare. As usual, he wears a blank expression, but there's a gleeful glint in his eyes.

I chuckle quietly. "No, there isn't. And maybe it's just me, but it still doesn't feel like enough, does it?"

The slightest smirk plays on Paulie's lips. "Not nearly enough."

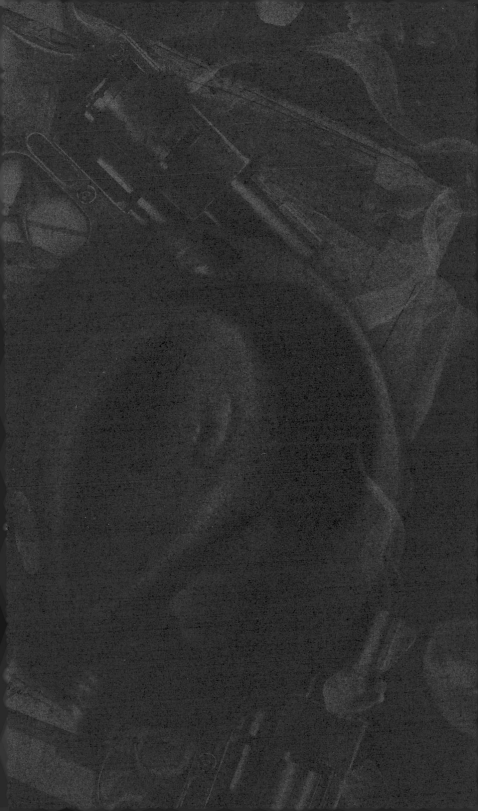

CHAPTER 31

THE PHANTOM

January 16, 1945

"Tell me about her."

Alfonso has just left, leaving me sitting before Angelo's desk while he puffs on a cigar, the two of us alone aside from the small pile of cocaine before him. He stares at me calmly, but there's a hint of challenge in his eyes, as if he's daring me to lie to him.

I tap my fingers on the armrest, contemplating how much I should divulge.

"You may be my consigliere, Ronnie, but I would hope that you didn't forget you are my friend—my *brother*—above all else."

I sigh. "She's the love of my life."

He nods slowly, his gaze studious. "I knew there was something deeper between you two when you defied my orders and prevented Paulie from taking her. Even more so after the party when I saw you sneak after her to the powder room."

I tighten my lips, disappointed I wasn't as sly as I had thought I'd been, but certainly not surprised. Even inebriated, Angelo has always had a sharp eye.

"I've left you alone on the matter because I had hoped you would come to me if it ever became serious. But I see I was wrong."

"Angelo—"

"Do you know there's a certain look to a man when a woman is taking care of him? Since I've known you, you've always had this"—he twirls his hand, searching for the word—"hardness about you. And for as long as I can remember, I've been waiting for the day when a woman would come around and soften you."

He takes another puff of his cigar. "It appears that day has arrived. And it's the wife of my accountant, no less."

"She was mine before he was yours," I grumble.

"Which is why you saved him. For her."

I nod once, grinding my teeth. Angelo and I rarely discuss our feelings. While we hide nothing from one another, we rarely discuss our feelings, only divulging emotions that are necessary.

I shift, discomfort wrapping its claws around my bones.

"You love her," he states plainly. "Since when?"

I sigh and grab a damn cigar from his table, deciding I'm going to need it to get through this conversation. My nose will never touch cocaine, so tobacco it is.

"Since I first saw her, truthfully. We've . . . Our affair has been going on for quite some time."

"And John? Does he know?"

"Of course not. He would—" I clench my jaw, fury constraining my vocal cords for a moment. "He would likely hurt her if he did."

That has Angelo raising a brow, unimpressed with that new knowledge of John. While my boss hasn't always been the most faithful, he retains respect for his wife. He'd never lay a hand on her, and despite his occasional infidelity, he treats her like a queen.

"You know Judge Jones would accommodate anything I asked of him—"

"They have a daughter."

Angelo has a few judges in his pocket, as a matter of fact, and it's an advantage I've considered before. Yet it's one I haven't brought up to her, considering how adamant she is to keep her family together. I've threatened to kill John on many occasions only because my anger got the best of me and I can't stand the thought of him drawing breath. But after our argument a few days ago, I don't know that she even *wants* to divorce him.

"It's frowned upon to be a single mother. And she wants Sera to grow up in a home with both parents. She can only think of her daughter, and I can't blame her," I continue.

Angelo cocks his head. "Is that the only barrier between you two? She knows what you do, correct?"

"She knows my position, though I do not divulge our business to her. But yes, my job is another point of contention. My lifestyle is dangerous, and she fears for her daughter's safety."

He's quiet for a few beats, staring at me thoughtfully while he takes another puff of his cigar, the jewels of his ring glinting off the overhead lights.

"You understand you're only my consigliere, yes?"

I frown. "Yes."

"Which means I do not require you to complete contracts or put yourself in more harm's way. You've made your bones, Ronnie."

I sigh, understanding where he's going with this. It's not my job to whack people, but I do it anyway because of the release it brings me. I enjoy it more than any normal man should. But handling the contracts personally puts me—and my loved ones—in more danger of retaliation.

This life is not one I can leave, but it is one that will allow me to retreat into the shadows, where it's not only safer for myself but also a family, too.

"Having a family is a strain on the heart for those of us in the position we're in. We both understand that. But that also means that we make sacrifices to ensure our families stay safe. We make sacrifices to ensure our own *happiness*." He finishes his cigar, stubbing it out while piercing me with his stare through the smoke billowing before his face. "Killing offers you relief. But you must decide if ending a life is better than experiencing your own, my friend."

January 17, 1945

I've always enjoyed watching Genevieve squirm.

There's something innately satisfying about making her nervous.

I haven't visited since our fight. Mostly because I've been busy with work since I cleared the Saputo estate. But partly because I'm injured, and I know the moment she realizes, it'll only prove her point about why we can't be together.

"I've missed you," she breathes, twiddling with her fingers. She stands before her rocking chair, shifting anxiously, waiting for me to make a move.

I am a little displeased that she didn't run to me as she usually does, but I also can't deny my enjoyment from watching her.

"I missed you, my love," I say softly, slowly approaching her.

She swallows, attracting my attention to where her throat bobs. I'm certain her pulse is hammering beneath the delicate flesh there, and my teeth clench with the urge to bite it.

She's always felt so much more alive between my teeth.

"Ronaldo, I don't want to fight," she says, nearly vibrating by the time I'm within a foot of her. The tension between us is thick, and it tastes as sweet as her pussy after she comes for me.

"Then let's get the first one out of the way," I say. I remove my trench coat, then my button-up, allowing her to see the large bandage over my shoulder.

While I undressed, she seemed enraptured, but now that her stare is locked on my injury, only concern shines through. She gasps and closes the gap between us, faintly brushing her fingertips over the bandage.

"Tell me what happened."

"I was in a terrible mood after our argument," I confess quietly, the words rumbling out of my chest. "And the next day, we spotted a long-time enemy on our territory—someone I thought I had killed before. So I went there and iced them all, but they did manage to hit me."

There's a tremor in her bottom lip, and I know she's picturing the scenario I laid out for her. Imagining the moment a bullet sliced through my shoulder. The danger I immersed myself in the very day after she said that my job could get her and Sera killed.

"Was it worth it?" she asks, her words cracking at the seams.

"Yes."

"Would you do it again?"

"Yes."

"Will you *keep* doing it?"

This time, I hesitate. "I don't know. Maybe not."

Her blue eyes finally flick to me, unshed tears within.

"This isn't a life I can walk away from, my love. But as Angelo told me, it is one that will allow me to retreat into the shadows. And for you, I would do that. I may not be able to guarantee that things will always be safe, but I can guarantee that as long as I breathe, I will always stand between you and a bullet. Sera, too."

She's not entirely satisfied with my answer, but she nods, deciding that it is good enough. At least for now.

"And I may not be able to divorce John right now . . ." She hesitates for a split second, licking her lips. "But maybe I can when Sera turns eighteen. She won't be young forever, and there will come a time when she moves on with life and creates one of her own, and then I won't be so beholden to John."

Just as Genevieve was unsatisfied by my response, I'm not entirely pleased about having to wait four more years to make her my wife, but it's enough. And regardless, my heart sings. It feels like for the first time in nearly a year, there just might be a future for Genevieve and me.

One that doesn't end with either one of us suffering.

"Angelo knows a judge. When you are ready, I believe he will grant you a divorce."

Shock flashes through her gaze, then happiness. And when a few tears finally spill from her eyes, they're complemented by a bright smile.

"Yeah? D-do you think he'd let me keep Parsons Manor?" she asks, staring at me with the hope of a little girl asking for a brand-new pony.

I grin. "If he knows what's good for him, he will."

A shaky laugh reaches my ears, and I can no longer withstand the distance between us, small as it is.

Ignoring the flare of burning pain in my shoulder, I dive my fingers through her curls and pull her into me, crashing my lips against hers.

She opens for me earnestly, a soft moan greeting my tongue. She tastes divine, and I'm unable to restrain myself from devouring her, licking her eager little mouth and biting her delicate lip.

Her hands flatten against my stomach before slowly gliding up to my chest, taking her time exploring the surface of my bare flesh. All the while, it sends tremors throughout my body, her touch dismantling my restraint inch by inch. My cock firmly presses against the zipper on my trousers, hard enough to crack ice in the South Pole.

Our kiss grows hungrier. We feast on each other, yet it only leaves us even more starving.

"Fuck, Genevieve, I love you so much," I groan against her mouth. I bite her bottom lip and drag it through my teeth, savoring her taste before diving back in for more.

She whimpers against me, scarcely getting out her breathless response through impatient kisses. "I love you, too."

Bullet wound be damned, I grab the back of her thighs and lift her in my arms, carrying her to the couch and dropping us both onto it.

Our hands tangle and fumble as she unfastens my belt and trousers, releasing me from the confines and wrapping her hand around my cock. Meanwhile, I shove her dress up past her waist, fumbling with her undergarments.

I growl, growing impatient with her girdle and straps and instead tear her underwear from her body. She gasps, and instead of dropping it on the floor, I rip myself away from her lips and stuff the shredded fabric in her mouth.

"If you want to know how good I make your pussy feel, then I expect you to fucking taste it, too," I growl.

Panting, she stares up at me with rounded eyes, utterly shocked. Yet she makes no move to spit them out and instead watches me closely as I line up the tip of my cock with her opening and drive inside her.

Her eyes roll, and her scream is muffled, though the sound is no less erotic.

Pinning her knees to her ears, I fuck her quickly and roughly, enraptured by the sight of her tight pussy gripping my cock as I slide in and out of her.

"Look how desperate your cunt is for me," I snarl. "But I don't think you know what true desperation is like, do you?"

She nods, adamantly disagreeing. But my little rose has gone through life without ever being plucked from her place of comfort. Before her husband turned to the bottle, he treated her delicately, those thorns keeping her safe in gentle hands. How unfortunate for her that I'd gladly bleed if it means crushing her beneath my fist.

"Hold your legs right there, baby. If you let go, I stop."

Confused, she replaces my hands on the back of her thighs, keeping her legs spread and knees up to her head.

With one hand, I rub her clit in tight circles until her eyes flutter and her back arches. Once she's comfortable in her pleasure, I close my other hand around her throat, triggering another stunned expression.

A tinge of unease bleeds into her stare, though my cock and fingers keep her distracted enough. However, I quite like the way she wears fear, so I squeeze tight, a squeak slipping through before I sever her oxygen.

Instantly, her cheeks redden, and her body shudders beneath me. Yet another moment where I wish I could photograph her staring up at me just like that.

Bright-blue eyes filled with pleasure and panic, her brow furrowed, and those pretty red lips stuffed with her soaked underwear.

"Fuck, baby, you look so goddamn pretty when you're desperate," I groan, my balls tightening from the view alone. "My needy little slut."

She's unable to make a noise, but her body speaks plenty. Violent tremors overtake her, and her nails claw at her own skin, leaving behind red marks as I pound into her.

Red-faced, she squeezes her eyes shut and slides her hand over to my wrist, her arm barred across the back of one of her thighs. Crescent moons form in my skin, her thorns surfacing and drawing blood. As if it's not enough, crimson trickles down the same arm from my shoulder injury, though the pain is indiscernible beneath the ecstasy holding my body hostage.

My own moans make up for her forced silence, pouring from my throat like water from a spigot. If anything, my pleasure makes her wilder.

"This is true desperation, *mia rosa*," I bite out through clenched teeth. "This is what I feel when you are near. So completely taken by you that I can't fucking breathe."

Her cunt clamps down on me the moment the last word leaves my mouth, and I release her throat, allowing her to belt out a broken scream.

"Ronaldo!" Her outcry is muffled from the underwear in her mouth, and she seizes beneath me as the pleasure contorts her body. Even her fingers stiffen and splay wide, her hands sightlessly fluttering around, unable to grasp onto anything solid.

She clenches around my cock tightly, and instantly my vision blackens and I see stars. The orgasm rushes through me unexpectedly. I thought I had it under control, but her pussy is too goddamn tight, and it rockets me right over the edge.

"Oh, *fuck*, baby," I shout, becoming lightheaded from the dizzying rush of pleasure coursing through me. "Fuck, *yes*, milk my fucking cock."

Hips gyrating, she does exactly that. My release pours into her in rivulets, filling her until it leaks from the sides and spills onto the couch.

My body trembles violently, even as I come down. The aftershocks are persistent, and I twitch endlessly while waiting for my vision to return.

When it does, I'm resentful of my limited sight. More than anything, I'd love to have a full view of her heaving below me, still shaking as I do while little sounds ripple from her throat uncontrollably.

Her chest, throat, and face are still flushed tomato red, but her expression is slack with exhaustion.

Panting, I sit up straight and am briefly confused when I notice we are not in the same spot as before. It takes a few seconds to process that I fucked her so hard, I moved the couch a good foot from where it had been.

She notices, too, glancing around before turning her bright gaze back to me, her astonishment evident. "If you wanted to rearrange my furniture, you could've just asked me."

February 12, 1945

John came home from work sober, and with a stack of new books in hand for Sera. She loves reading, like I do, and when she saw them, she lost her mind with excitement.

She's gotten used to seeing him less. First, because of his drinking and gambling. Then because of his second job. He told her he is now working for a big client on top of his business, so she understands his new hours now. Though we didn't dare tell her who the client was. I would be beside myself if Sera knew who John's boss is, but John and I are both well aware of how children overhear all sorts of gossip from their parents.

After gifting her the books, he challenged her to a dance competition.

For the first time in so long, we turned on the radio and danced and sang together as a family. And when Sera grew tired, John had her step up onto his feet and he swirled her around the living room. Sera was so happy, and she stared up at her father with so much love that it made my heart ache.

If I knew that he would come home like that every night, it would make staying with him easier. My heart has long since been stolen by another, but at least Sera's would stay intact. Until she turns eighteen, that is.

Because then I will be the one to break her heart.

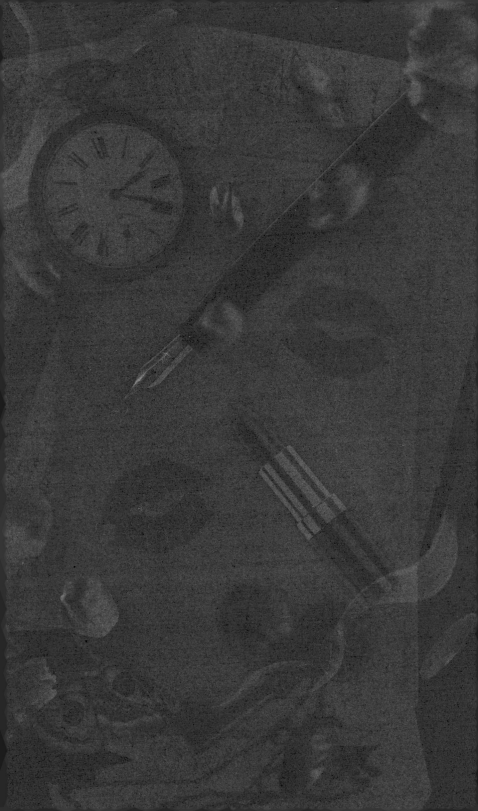

CHAPTER 32

THE RAVEN

March 9, 1945

"I'm going to miss you," John whispers in my ear from behind me, startling me damn near half to death.

I screech and whip around only to be pinned to the counter by John's arms gripping the edge on either side of me.

My heart is racing, and I stare at him with residual terror as I lean away from him, despite his being my husband. A hint of beer lingers on his breath, though it's admittedly better than the sour stench of whiskey that usually greets me.

After all this time, I hoped I would grow used to the awful smell, yet it doesn't get any easier. His drinking, his loosening temper . . . none of it has gotten any easier.

"You nearly killed me," I whisper, hand over my chest.

"I could never kill you," John says, chuckling. "That would mean I would have to live without you, and that simply will not do."

I force a smile and lightly push at his chest. He resists, and my discomfort grows.

"Well, of course not. You couldn't cut a tomato without slicing open your finger, let alone cook anything," I tease, though my voice is tightening. He still won't release me, and it feels as if a wet blanket is constricting around me, preventing me from moving or breathing.

The man is many things, but he certainly is not a quitter. I've evaded further romantic touches between us, and since his stolen kiss back in January, I've told him I wasn't ready to go back to the way things used to be.

It led to another fight, of course. I told him that unless he ventures to take advantage of me again, then he does not have access to my body. And if he *does* disrespect me as he did before, then there will be no hope of my ever forgiving or loving him again.

So while he doesn't dare kiss me or try to engage in any intimacy at night, he persists in winning back my affection.

"Your culinary skills aren't the only reason I need you, Gigi," he berates lightly. "I don't know how I would survive if anything were to happen to you."

I roll my eyes and push him away again, this time firmly enough for him to comply. Subtly, I inhale a deep breath, grab Sera's breakfast plate, and set it on the kitchen island despite her not being down here yet. Still the gesture offers me a bit of space from him.

"I'm going away for one weekend, John. I think I'll be fine," I assure. "I don't believe there is much to kill me on the Oregon coast."

Sera barrels into the kitchen before he can respond, with her hair unbrushed and crust still clinging to her lashes. She's been an absolute nightmare getting up this morning for school. Her bottom lip is protruding into a pout, and her brow is furrowed.

"Mama, do you *have* to go away?" she whines, sliding onto the stool at the kitchen island and slapping her *Schools at War* journal onto the surface along with her rucksack. Then she slumps and rests her chin on her hand, her frown deepening.

Ever since I construed my little lie about going on a girls' trip with Daisy this weekend, she's been in a mood. Sera undeniably favors me over John and tends to get moody if I'm away for too long. I have gone on trips in the past, and I'm always met with the same attitude beforehand.

"Yes, my dear," I sigh, leaning on the counter before her. I hate that she's so upset. "You know I go on one every year with Daisy."

She bangs the tip of her shoe against the island, pouting further. "It's stupid," she mutters, picking up her fork and flapping it through her scrambled eggs aimlessly, clinking the metal against the plate.

"You're hurting my feelings over here, princess," John teases, placing a hand over his heart dramatically. She flicks an annoyed glance his way, radiating teenage angst. "What if I sneak you ice cream later?" he bargains. The sullen look on her face doesn't disappear, but he has her attention.

"How much ice cream?" she asks, glancing at him. Sera rarely takes advantage of situations, but with her father, she will bleed him dry any chance she gets. Only because she knows he's the only one who will let her get away with it.

I give John a look, but he ignores me. "Until your tummy hurts."

"How many flavors?"

I narrow my eyes at the two of them as they still ignore me.

He taps his finger against his chin, pretending to contemplate it.

"How about three?"

"Fine," she mumbles, though one corner of her lips sneaks upward. "Don't forget that I have to get my war stamps after school. But then I expect to be drowned in ice cream."

John does a mock salute, earning an eye roll from our daughter, though it lacks heat.

"It'll only be two days. I promise I'll come home first thing Sunday morning," I tell her.

"Will you bring me back something?" she asks, staring up at me with puppy dog eyes.

"I always do," I sing. "Now quit playing with your food and eat it. You leave for school in ten minutes."

"Fine, but I expect a really cool present. Expensive, too. None of those touristy gifts."

I grin. "Brat."

March 9, 1945

This is the first time I've been in Ronaldo's car, and something about the way he uses his palm to control the steering wheel is tantalizing. I squirm, clenching my thighs as he drives us down 101.

Once John and Sera left, Ronaldo picked me up. Usually, Daisy drives us on our trips, so it wasn't unusual for me to need to wait for my ride to arrive.

There's an undeniable thrill that I'm sneaking away from my friends and family to spend a weekend with Ronaldo. For the first time, there will be no time constraints, and we will be able to enjoy one another freely and fully for these couple days.

Since the moment he picked me up this morning, I haven't been able to stop bouncing in my seat with excitement.

"What do you think you'd do for work if you weren't a mobster?" I ask, breaking a tension-filled silence. It's not that I'm not comfortable with him; it's that I'm tempted to mount him at every turn, and *that's* not very ladylike.

He twists his lips, contemplating. "I don't know, to be truthful. You may find it odd, but I would have loved to research snakes."

I blink, entirely taken aback by his response.

"*Snakes?* Why on earth would you research snakes?"

He grins, casting a mirthful glance my way.

"They're quite fascinating. I used to pick them up as a little boy and carry them around everywhere. It was one of the few times I got a reaction out of my mother. I always thought I'd work with them some day."

I scoff. "Well, then you should know, I will have a fit if you bring one of those to me," I warn playfully. "But I suppose I can see why you would find them to be fascinating creatures. If I set aside my fear of them, I can admit they're quite magnificent."

It's rare that I see Ronaldo take on a boyish expression, but at this moment, that's exactly how he looks.

"I could tell you all about them, but I won't bore you with the details. However, don't be surprised if I confess to bringing one or two home one day," he tells me.

"Fine, but I will *not* be holding them."

He hums, his tone changing from joyful to something more seductive. "I will just have to dream about you naked in my bed then." He groans, and my core pulses. "A python wrapped around your throat and holding you still for me while I feast on you and fuck you. It would be a dream of mine."

My mouth dries, and I stare at him almost blankly since I hadn't expected him to say something so dark. So . . . alluring.

I try to swallow, to speak, to do anything but flap my lips soundlessly, but he's moving before I can, silencing me further. His left hand grabs the steering wheel, and his right slides to my thigh. I bite my lip as he hooks his fingertips beneath my brown wool coat and red dress, gliding his hand over my thick stockings. Midway, my stockings end, and his palm connects with bare flesh, sending a tremor throughout my body.

"So where does Daisy think you are?" Ronaldo asks, changing the subject and deliberately acting as if he didn't confess a profane fantasy to me. There's a satisfied glimmer in his eye, and I'm tempted to dare him to make good on it, as terrifying as it would be.

"I wrote her a letter a couple weeks ago telling her that John and I ran into some troubles and that I'd be staying home this year," I respond, deciding to let it go. My voice is cracking with desire, but I refuse to be embarrassed about it.

I like how he teases me. And it'll only be so much sweeter if I make that dream come true for him.

"What if she and John run into each other?"

"She lives far enough away that I needn't worry about that happening. She never did care for John, anyway."

We've been taking these girls' weekends for over a decade. During summer, we're always so busy with the kids, and the dead of winter is an awful time to travel, so every March, Daisy organizes a girls' weekend for the two of us and a few other gals from her town, all of us desperate to get away from the snow. We drive down to the Oregon coast, where we rent a little cabin in the mountains and enjoy the misty rain while we gossip and relax by a fire, just enjoying one another's company.

I'm saddened I won't see her this year, but it was the perfect opportunity to get away with Ronaldo, allowing us uninterrupted time to explore each other thoroughly, without fear of being caught.

"Why's that?" he asks, keeping his tone neutral.

Since our first argument back in January, he's kept a cool head when it comes to John. We're still hopeful for our future, but we agreed that while our situations may be temporarily binding, our love doesn't have to be.

"My mother was very strict and wanted me out of the house the day I turned eighteen. She expected me to be married and on my own and pushed me to marry the first man I came across. I resisted at first and would flirt with all the boys, but then John came along, and he showed an interest in me that didn't begin and end with my body. He was stable and consistent, and his family was wealthy. I hated going home to my mother, so I gave in and married him within the year. Back then, Daisy was my best friend, and I think she could tell that I settled, even if I convinced myself I was in love. And as we grew older, our marriage became very monotonous. Daisy said the day I married him, the sparkle in my eyes dimmed. I never knew what she meant, but I think I understand now."

Ronaldo squeezes my thigh, his touch now more comforting than provocative.

"Were you ever happy with him?" he asks.

I shrug. "I thought I was. We got along perfectly well, and I think I was just so happy to be out of my mother's house that I would've been ecstatic to live in a cardboard box. Then we had Sera, and my time was so full of her, I thought little about our marriage. We were always comfortable, and he was happy to accommodate my odd taste in decor when we built Parsons Manor. Then again, John never had an opinion on much. He was always the go-with-the-flow type, and I ended up making all the decisions over the years." I shrug again. "We had a routine, we never fought, and I didn't know any different. Until I met you, that is."

"Do you think Daisy would like me?" There's a smug little smirk on his face because he already knows the answer.

I roll my eyes. "She'd probably love you."

"Even though I have ties to the Mob?"

I raise a brow. "Daisy was wilder than I was. That'd probably make her even more intrigued. She had a thing for danger and thrills back then, and even though she's married with kids, she still loves an adventure."

He grins, clearly pleased with my answer.

"She'd think you're more handsome, too," I tell him. He squeezes my thigh again, his approval detected in the way his fingers slide deeper between my legs.

"Is that what you think, *mia rosa*?"

Truthfully, there isn't even any competition. John isn't a bad-looking man by any means. But he is not Ronaldo.

"Yes," I whisper.

He hums, the tip of his middle finger sliding over my clit.

"Then maybe you should spread these legs so you can show me how pretty you look when you come for me."

March 9, 1945

I almost got Ronaldo and I killed, and the only thing I can do is giggle about it like a schoolgirl.

On the drive to Oregon, he insisted on playing with me, and something about being so alone with him in the car yet knowing that at any moment someone could look over and see the ecstasy on my face . . .

It did something to me. It made me feral, if I'm being honest.

He made me orgasm, but it did nothing to abate the burning need in my lungs. So I leaned over, unfastened his trousers, and took him down my throat.

The car swerved and curses fell out of his mouth, yet there wasn't a single second I thought to stop. To even fear for my life. I was ravenous, and I swallowed him down like he was my only source of oxygen.

And when he erupted, I drank from him like I had gone weeks without a drop of water. He took one look at my face afterward, swerved the car across two lanes to take the nearest exit, and found a rest stop.

I have never even considered having sex in a public building before, but at that moment, there was no question in my mind. I was drowning in lust. So we found a restroom, and he fucked me against the wall, his hand over my mouth to keep me silent.

I shouldn't have come as hard as I did, and I should be ashamed. But I did, and I'm not.

CHAPTER 33

THE RAVEN

March 10, 1945

"Oh my— *Ronaldo*," I gasp, my eyes rounding at the corners as I take in the monstrosity before me. Yesterday, he brought me to a beautiful log cabin nestled in the Oregon woods, offering us privacy and a breathtaking view of the mountains surrounding us. The rain held off this morning, so he took me to a quaint coffee shop that served the most delicious croissants I've ever had.

After, he said he wanted to introduce me to one of his favorite views on earth. We had been walking on a trail for only a few minutes when the sound of rushing water arose. The second I saw the massive waterfall to my left, I lost all function to breathe. Mist clung to the air as we approached a small cement bridge, and I recognized it immediately from photographs I'd seen.

"Is that the Benson Bridge? Is this Multnomah Falls?" My voice pitches higher with each passing syllable, excitement taking my insides hostage.

"It is," Ronaldo confirms quietly, an amused grin tugging up his lips.

"It's the most beautiful sight I've ever seen!" I marvel when we stop in the middle of the bridge, my hand cupping over my mouth as I take it all in.

"I couldn't agree more," Ronaldo murmurs from beside me.

A laugh tinkles from my throat, and I drag my wonder-filled stare to him, finding his gaze already on mine. "This is incredible," I breathe.

His answering smile is devastating, and maybe I misspoke because, truly, the sight of him at this moment is paralyzing.

I force myself to look around before I do something silly like tackle him, the love I have for him nearly boiling over.

"How is no one here? This is such a famous location," I ask, frowning over the lack of tourists. If I didn't know any better, I'd think the place was abandoned.

"I convinced the Forest Service to allow us the day here to ourselves," he explains, tucking his hands in his trousers casually.

My eyes nearly pop from my head, and I glance around, finding a lodge in the distance yet not a single person in sight.

"How?"

"I can be pretty convincing," he deflects.

I narrow my eyes. "Mr. Salvatore wouldn't have had an influence now, would he?"

He grins, confirming my suspicions. At this moment, I can hardly be ungrateful for his boss. The view is absolutely astounding, and I'm relieved that it's just the two of us. While it's unlikely anyone will recognize either of us here, there will always be a niggling doubt in the back of my mind that someone will expose my affair to John.

I hate that we must hide, but rather than dwelling on that right now, I'm embracing how thrilling it is to be alone with him. *Outside* of Parsons Manor.

For the first time in sixteen years, I feel . . . free. Right now, I'm not a mother. I'm not a wife. I'm just *me*. Genevieve Matilda Parsons. A woman who has an unhealthy obsession with Gothic architecture, who wears red lipstick like it's armor, who pours herself into a journal lest she go mad, and a woman who is helplessly in love with a made man.

But what else do I love?

Do I love nature? This waterfall is beautiful, and I hadn't thought to explore other wonders of this earth. Do I love long walks on the beach at sunset, or do I prefer to watch the sunrise? Am I afraid of the ocean? Or do I dare swim out into its depths and let it welcome me in?

I love the written word, but what other forms of artistry do I enjoy? Am *I* an artist? Can I paint? Draw? Play an instrument? I can sing, sure, but what if I want to sing to thousands and not just a family of two?

There are so many questions I have about myself—questions I didn't realize I desperately need to know the answer to. I had never thought to ask them before because so much of my life revolved around being a mother and a wife.

Even with Daisy and the girls with our annual trips, we were so happy to be away from our houses that we settled into a temporary one, content to relax in a cabin and gossip about the homes we were desperate to escape. Rather than exploring the world and trying new things and discovering who we were outside the roles we were bound in, we locked ourselves in an emptier cage and called it freedom.

But here? Now? I am a woman who wants to discover herself. And I want to do it alongside the man standing before me, introducing me to a new world outside of the walls that had begun to feel more like a prison than a home.

"You know what that means, don't you?" Ronaldo questions, pulling me away from my thoughts. He holds out his hand for me to grab hold of, and I take it without hesitation, grinning as he tugs me into his firm chest.

It's cool outside today, yet I burn beneath his gaze. The sun could extinguish from the sky, and his embrace would still keep me warm.

"What does it mean?" I ask, my heart beating in my chest as his stare grows hungry.

He leans in, his lips a hairbreadth away from mine. "No one will hear you scream," he whispers.

I can only manage a blink before he's grabbing my elbow and guiding me to the railing, pushing me against the thick cement. However, I continue to peer at him over my shoulder with confusion.

"What are you—"

He's dropping into a crouch, distracting me from airing the rest of my question.

"Face forward and enjoy the view, Genevieve," he orders. I gasp when he grips the edge of my dress and lifts, exposing my thick stockings all the way up to my girdle and underwear.

"Ronaldo!" I chastise, quickly glancing around again despite his affirmations that no one is here.

He pins his crystal-blue stare on me, a stern expression arranged on his face.

"The only waterfall I'm interested in is the one I'll be drinking from between your thighs. Now face forward and bend over the railing, *mia rosa*. I won't ask you again."

The man has lost his mind! He flattens his palm on my lower back and applies pressure, encouraging me to lean over the railing. My heart races, and it's impossible not to notice the steep drop to the pool below us.

He makes quick work of unclipping the garters from my crotchless girdle and tugging down my underwear, letting it fall to my feet. I jerk beneath his touch, his fingers cold as he spreads me wider apart.

Biting my lip, I glance behind me, my dress draped over his large body, concealing him and his devilish act. He turns around before fitting his broad shoulders between my legs, his back to the railing so I'm straddling his face, his hot breath warming my throbbing core.

"You're going to make me suffocate you!" I berate. He hardly has any room between my thighs, for God's sake.

"Does one stand beneath a waterfall expecting to breathe?" he retorts, clearly unconcerned. "I beg you to suffocate me, *mia rosa*. I'll die a happy man."

The first brush of wetness gliding up my slit has my mouth parting, and I force my gaze to the thunderous waterfall before me. It's far out of reach, yet it feels like it is mere feet away, the power of it as breathtaking as Ronaldo's tongue spearing inside me.

A moan builds in my throat as he thoroughly explores me, licking the inside of my walls before focusing his attention on my clit. My eyes cross, flutter, and roll, utter euphoria consuming my body as he eagerly devours me.

My knees grow weak, and he stiffens his tongue into a point as he lashes at the bundle of nerves, both persistent and relentless.

I make no effort to quiet the cries pouring from my lips, panting them out in staccato bursts of air. I'm unsure if even Ronaldo can hear them beneath the crash of water, and I don't care, anyway. It feels too good, and at this moment, I am convinced I'd do anything in this entire world for it to never cease.

If I could live with his head between my thighs, I'd keep him fed for as long as he breathes. He'd never go hungry with me in his mouth, that I can be sure of.

My lower stomach tightens and my knees quake, the ecstasy mounting and mounting until I'm pushing my hips into his face and rolling them mercilessly, forcing him to grab hold of them to keep me still. My head is light, and if I were to tip over this railing, I don't know if I'd know any different. It already feels as if I'm teetering on the edge of a cliff, seconds away from free-falling.

Sensing my looming climax, he sucks my clit into his mouth while simultaneously plunging two fingers inside me, evoking a sharp outcry as I tumble straight over the edge.

Despite the hand on my hip firmly grounding me on the bridge, I'm as certain of my fall as I am of the water cascading over the cliff hundreds of feet above us. There is no end in sight for me or the falls; we will drown anyone who dares stand beneath us.

Just as Ronaldo wanted.

He drinks me in while pumping and curling his fingers inside me. All the while, I lose myself to the stars detonating in my vision. It feels as if it takes hours to reach my landing, and even then it feels like I'm floating.

The only thing that brings me somewhat back to earth is Ronaldo's sudden absence between my thighs.

Panting heavily, I blink, willing my vision to fully return. His touch reappears before my sight, and he's once more pushing the fabric of my dress and wool coat over my hips, the cool air a balm to my heated skin.

He allows me no warning, and in a single thrust, he's seating his entire length inside me. I choke, my eyes popping wide from what would've been damn near a violent invasion had I not been sopping wet. A vulgar noise arises when he slowly retreats, then drives back inside me again, earning a sharp cry.

A hand curls into my hair and fists tightly, his mouth inches from my ear as he growls, "How cruel it is that Mother Nature spent millions of years forming such a beautiful sight only for you to exceed it within mere minutes."

If he wants my words, then he will not get them.

I'm only capable of strangled noises as he savagely fucks me, my back arching and allowing him to drive deeper inside me. It's almost too much, and it feels as if the tip of his length is hitting the inside of my stomach. However, the bliss supersedes any discomfort, and I allow myself to embrace the fact that I'm being openly ravished on a bridge over a hundred feet in the air. The mere thought of it is so thrilling that a dormant side of me takes over.

Any semblance of modesty bleeds out from my pores, replaced by a woman overcome with lust and shamelessness.

I rest my chest on the railing, crane my head over my shoulder, and reach behind me, grasping each cheek of my backside and spreading myself wider for him. A loud moan erupts from his throat at the sight, and when he lifts his molten stare to mine, I let him see just how wild he makes me.

There's so much happiness inflating my chest, so much freedom, that I boldly smile at him, a laugh mixing with another lascivious moan. His eyes round at the corners and his hips stutter, seemingly taken aback by my behavior yet equally enraptured by it.

"You make my pussy feel so good, Ronaldo," I breathe, biting my lip when his expression morphs from shock to ferocity.

Within the blink of an eye, he's no longer a man but a beast. His hold on me grows bruising, and any regard for my well-being extinguishes. There's no sympathy as he lifts my upper body by my hair and shoves me forward until my hips slam against the railing. He pushes my head far over the safety of it until my feet lift from the bridge.

The roar of rushing water swallows my startled scream, my arms flailing before I desperately grab the balusters, gripping them painfully tight as if they'll prevent me from teetering over the edge completely. A glittering pool a hundred feet below expands across my vision, my only reprieve from the frightening sight being the backs of my eyelids.

We must be over a hundred feet in the air, and he's forcing half my body to hang over the edge!

"Ronaldo!" I squeal, but he either doesn't hear me or doesn't care.

My feet kick, finding purchase on the base rail and giving me some type of balance right as he resumes his thrusting, pounding into me with ferocity. With his towering height, my position only makes it easier for him to hit all the right angles that have my eyes threatening to cross.

Yet the terror overrides my common sense, and I thrash against him, desperate to get back onto solid ground.

"The harder you struggle, the more you tip over the edge," he warns roughly. "You wanted to act like a whore, baby, so you're going to take my cock like one."

One hand presses firmly onto my back, refusing to allow me to sit up, while he uses the other to grab my backside, squeezing almost painfully before delivering a sharp slap, moaning loudly as he does. I gasp, fear and ecstasy battling ruthlessly in my brain. The war between them becomes so violent that they merge as one, and I cannot feel one without the other.

Instead of fighting, I coerce my muscles to relax, allowing him to unleash himself and me to eagerly take all he has to give. I force myself to embrace the mix of heady terror coursing through my system, and rather than cowering from the danger of falling, I lean into it.

Somehow, it only heightens the pleasure, and I think I quite like the thrill of death.

His pace is merciless, his moans unrestrained.

"Such a perfect fucking cunt," he bites out through gritted teeth. "This pussy was made for me. To fuck and fill with my cum as much as I goddamn please."

I couldn't deny that even if I wanted to. Especially when I feel as if I was made just for him, too.

"Yes, yes, Ronaldo," I chant. I'm unsure if he can hear me, but it matters little.

"I'm going to claim all these tight little holes," he growls right before I feel pressure on my backside.

My eyes pop wide, and I stiffen, though he doesn't relent.

"Ronaldo!" I screech, attempting to wiggle his hand away.

He delivers a sharp slap on my cheek, then returns his thumb to the tight ring of muscle.

"You're *mine*, Genevieve," he snarls. "I dare you to fight me. I'd love nothing more than to show you just how helpless you are."

He's right. I *am* helpless as he slowly inserts the tip of his thumb inside me, evoking a foreign sensation that has me squirming.

However, as he goes deeper, my pleasure heightens, and when he begins to pump his thumb in and out, I'm unable to deny how good it feels.

"Oh," I whimper, my eyes fluttering and the glittery pool beneath blurring. I feel so . . . full. Almost *too* full.

There's a pressure building in my lower stomach, and between that and his thumb, it's almost a frightening feeling. My body is reacting to him in ways that I can't control, and I'm powerless to stop it.

"I will be stuffing my cock in this tight hole soon, baby. By the time you go home, you'll be so fucking full of my cum, it will leak through your pores."

My eyes are rolling, but he doesn't relent on his filthy words. "What excuses will you make for yourself when you can't walk, huh, baby? Let's hear how you'll lie through your teeth."

"I—" I can't get another word out, too overwhelmed with what he's doing to me, what he's *saying*.

"Your pussy and ass are going to be swollen when I'm finished. What will you tell your husband?"

"Maybe I'll tell him the truth," I bite out breathlessly, struggling to get the words out of my constricted throat. "That I was your whore and let you fuck me anywhere you wanted. Then maybe I'll tell him I much prefer your cock over his."

The sound out of his mouth is a cross between a dark chuckle and a deep groan, emanating pure satisfaction.

"That's my good girl," he croons. "You're so good at being my whore, aren't you? So fucking eager to please me. So desperate for my cock."

"Yes," I cry, the pleasure becoming too much now. "Ronaldo, don't stop. I-I'm going to . . ."

I'm unable to finish, another orgasm washing over me as suddenly as a tidal wave, and I'm swept away.

I feel rather than hear the scream leave my throat, my mind quickly held hostage to the euphoria rushing through me. At the same moment, his hips still as his release floods me and his moans turn into whimpers.

By the time we both come down, Ronaldo's knees threaten to give out on him, so he gently pulls me back onto the bridge and then down onto the ground.

I don't care that the cement is wet and dirty; stars are still floating in my vision, and adrenaline is still coursing through my veins. I feel high, and my chest is so laden with joy that I feel like bursting at the seams.

A laugh trickles from my throat, breathless and cracked but still so full of life.

Ronaldo tucks himself away before lying flat on his back, heaving, his own smile stretched across his face.

I lie beside him, a few more choked giggles disturbing my unsettled breath.

Tears well in my eyes as I stare at the overcast sky, and I'm unsure of the exact reason, but I do know that it stems from happiness.

"Thank you for showing me a love for waterfalls," I whisper. "I never knew I loved them."

I feel his gaze burning into the side of my face, where a lone tear leaks down my temple. His index finger swipes the tear away, but he doesn't coddle me or demand I tell him why I'm crying. Instead, he whispers, "There are so many more I can take you to."

My bottom lip trembles, and my heart squeezes painfully. Without telling him, he understands my emotions. He knows it isn't often that I learn something new about myself—at least, not before he arrived.

"I want to swim in one," I tell him, keeping my voice quiet. "Can we do that, too?"

"If you promise we can climb it, too," he answers, his tone warm and gentle.

I grin, liking the sound of that.

"Will you take me to the Atlantic Ocean? I must know if sunrises or sunsets over the water are better."

"Then you shall know."

"Can we take classes together? We can learn to paint, or sketch, or maybe even throw pottery."

"You'll master all of them in no time."

Another tear wiggles free, and it feels like my heart is soaring. "Will you take me to the desert? Where it's hot and sandy, and there isn't a single tree in sight? I've only ever known the mountains and ocean."

"Only if we bring lots of water."

I bark out a laugh because his response is both unexpected and everything I needed to hear. My face hurts from how hard I grin, and I turn to look at him.

A knowing smile graces his wide lips. He stares at me as if he already has all the answers, and the only answer is me.

"Could we do these things with Angelo as your boss?"

"We could do anything you dream of, *mia rosa*. He owes me his life—more than he has to give—which is why he will grant me my own."

I chew on my lip, tracing over every inch of his skin. "What about the . . ." I trail off, attempting to find a delicate way to put it. "The contracts?"

"Undoubtedly, I will miss them. But there is nothing more fulfilling than you, Genevieve. I will gladly wash my hands clean of blood if it means your hands will replace it." Butterflies unleash in my stomach, and I am at a loss over how this villainous man became my hero.

"You've never known a life outside of it, but maybe you will learn new ways to satisfy that part of you," I murmur.

"I already have," he returns, a sly grin blooming on his face. His eyes are heated as they trail over my disheveled state.

I laugh, though my insides warm and thighs clench. "Though I must admit," he continues, "I can't say with certainty that I will ever be fully satisfied. I have a terrible feeling it will never be enough and I'll always demand more. Are you prepared for that, my love?"

"I'm prepared for anything, so long as it's with you," I whisper, lifting my pointer finger and trailing my red-painted nail over his soft lips.

He nips at it, trapping the tip of my finger between his straight teeth. I bite my lip, tingles spreading throughout my body as he stares at me through thick lashes, fire raging within.

Releasing me, he nearly growls, "We better leave before I take you here again."

I arch a brow. "Would that be so terrible?"

"Of course not, my love, but there's so many things I have yet to show you. And so many places with beautiful views to enjoy while I pleasure you."

My cheeks flush, and I lift my knees, preparing to sit up. Only then do I realize my legs are still trembling, and I'm unsure how on earth I'm going to stand.

I scoff, finding his gaze locked on to my shaking knees. "I suppose you were right, my dear," I say, chuckling. "I don't know if I can walk."

"I'll carry you. You don't need your legs when you're with me," he rasps.

"No? Won't I need them to ride you?"

He growls, though it quickly bleeds into a groan. "Keep it up, Genevieve. This day has only just begun."

"I know, and you've already nearly sent me plummeting into a waterfall," I chuckle while rolling toward him, bending my arm to rest my head on my hand. We have more adventures to be had, but I'm content to stay here just a little longer, basking in the moment of lying on a bridge with a rushing waterfall as our backdrop.

"You could've killed me, you know," I tease lightly.

He grins, and though he radiates happiness, there's a seriousness to his stare as he proclaims, "I would have followed you."

"You shouldn't," I say softly. "You have so much life to live, and maybe enough room in your heart to love another."

He's shaking his head before I can finish. He raises his fingers to my lips as if to silence me, staring at me with so much love, I can't help but lean in and place a kiss on his calloused flesh.

"There will never be another, nor will I live a life without you. Death awaits us all, Genevieve. Even still, it will not keep me from you."

There will never be sufficient words to respond, so I capture his lips in a passionate kiss, content that no matter what happens, he will always be with me.

In life. And in death.

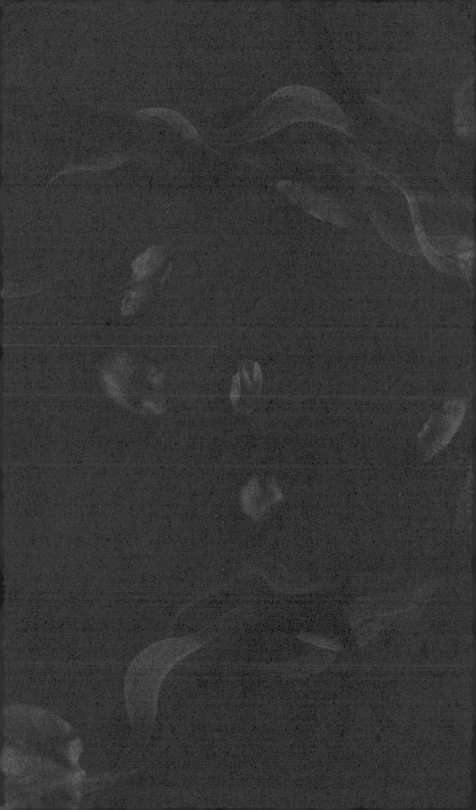

May 16, 1946

I love you, Ronaldo.
With every beat of my heart and every fiber of my being,
I love you so much.
Not even death can take that away from us.

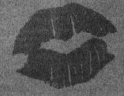

ACKNOWLEDGMENTS

To all my beloved readers, thank you endlessly. This book made me really nervous, and I really hope you all find it somewhere deep in the caverns of your hearts to love it. Or maybe even tolerate it; I won't be picky. But really, thank you all for continuing to support me through all these crazy endeavors. I love you all so much.

Victor, as always, I'd die without you. You already know this. And I love you.

Sami-kins, thank you for being my soulmate, and I love you.

May, Amanda, Tosh: Thank you for STILL being by my side. There are no words that suffice, but I'm eternally grateful for you three, and I love you ladies from the depths of my heart.

Nicki, Ana, Janine, Taylor, and Autumn: You guys are a dream team, and I thank you so much for being on this journey with me. You are appreciated so very much.

ZADE AND ADELINE BONUS SCENE BY H. D. CARLTON

SEPTEMBER 14, 2022

ADELINE REILLY
THE MANIPULATOR

The second I try to blow the dust off the radio, I instantly have a face full of regrets. The mites billow before me just as I inhale, and immediately, I'm bent over coughing, which is then promptly interrupted by a series of sneezes.

"What did we learn?"

Zade's mocking voice from behind me has me tempted to send my fist flying into his face.

"Shut up," I mutter before falling victim to yet another sneeze.

He chuckles, so I swipe at my snotty nose, then proceed to wipe my hand across Zade's chest. His mouth drops, and he looks down at his shirt.

"That was just savage," he mumbles.

Feeling much better, I refocus on the old radio in the corner of the basement. It's woken Zade and me up in the middle of the night several times now, playing on its own accord despite not being plugged in.

I'm not even sure if it truly works anymore, but if the ghosts want to listen to music, then who am I to stop them? I decide to bring it up to the living room so at least then I can utilize it, too.

"All right, big guy," I say to Zade, waving toward the radio. "Bring 'er up. I'll be waiting at the top, comfortably sipping my wine while you do all the heavy lifting."

Mirth ignites in Zade's stare, though something darker accompanies it.

He's so going to get me back later. And I'm probably going to like it. Probably.

Grinning, I escape back up the stairs while Zade sighs and heaves up the heavy radio. I pause midway, long enough to croon, "Good boy," before booking it the rest of the way up the steps.

His answering growl is devilish, and if I had any goddamn sense, I'd lock him down there with the rest of the demons. He'd be right at home, and I'm positive they'd be under his command within a day.

Just as I promised, by the time Zade makes it up the stairs, I'm sipping on my wine in the living room, pointing him toward the cute black stand I found at Goodwill today, stationed right by the fire. It's all metal, with several prongs twisted into a filigree shape beneath the flat top, a skull right in the middle.

Zade cocks a brow as he brushes past me, and my heart flips, fully understanding that I'm pushing his buttons. But in true Addie fashion, I jam my finger onto it ten more times purely because I can't help myself.

He places the radio down onto the stand, and just as he goes to turn away, I speak up.

"It's not centered."

Slowly, his stare slides to mine, challenge and warning swirling in the depths of his irises. He slides the radio an inch to the left, and I purse my lips.

"Too far. Move it back toward me a couple centimeters."

His eyes narrow, but he complies. His silence is as dangerous as it is unnerving, and it sends heat coursing through my veins.

I cock my head, taking my time as I study the radio. It's definitely centered, but I'm having so much fun.

Meeting his gaze after several moments, I take a slow sip of wine, butterflies unleashing in my stomach. His stare has only sharpened, and there's no doubt that I should've locked him downstairs.

I've never done what I was supposed to, though.

Only when I swallow do I say, "It'll do."

One menacing step from him is all it takes for me to squeal, set my glass down on the coffee table, and run.

The sound of static stirs me out of a deep slumber.

I jerk upright, looking around the living room in confusion. The radio still appears dead, and I'm half-convinced I dreamed up the noise.

The fire is still crackling, and according to the clock on the mantel, only an hour has passed since Zade and I fell asleep on the couch, naked and spent.

He did exactly what I knew he would and thoroughly punished me. He said since I wanted to drink my wine so bad, I had to hold the sweet alcohol in my mouth while he fucked me. If I dribbled or swallowed any of it, he stopped.

Too many times, I nearly choked on it, and after my third orgasm,

I couldn't hold it in anymore. He saw it coming and placed his mouth over mine, quickly repositioning us so the wine poured from my mouth into his.

He swallowed it down while I screamed.

Still asleep, Zade shifts behind me, drawing my attention over my shoulder to his naked form scarcely hidden beneath a fleece blanket that was draped over the back of the couch.

My chest tightens from the view of him so relaxed, so vulnerable. His expression is slack, and his full lips are slightly parted as he softly breathes. Seeing him like this is a privilege I get only at night or during moments where it's just the two of us sequestered away from the rest of the world and all its problems.

And every time, it makes my heart ache with how infinitely I love Zade Meadows.

There will always be a small part of me that resents him for it—that hates this man for burrowing beneath my skin so deeply. I lived a much simpler life when I wasn't constantly fearing for his safety or that he'd go off on a mission and not make it home to me.

Yet there isn't a single atom in my body that regrets it or wants for anything else. He may be a goddamn psycho, but these days, I might be considered one, too. And I'm okay with that.

Zade twitches, and I smile softly. The firelight creates the most tantalizing shadows across his form, his packed muscles riddled with ink and scars. If I wasn't aching between my legs, I'd wake him up again. But even the smallest of movements sends a twinge straight to my core.

Phantom music begins to play from the radio, ripping my attention away. My mouth drops as an undeniable melody emits from the speakers. It's fucking creepy, considering we hadn't gotten the chance to plug it in yet.

I grin, an excited smile stretching across my face.

After nabbing Zade's black T-shirt from the floor and slipping it on, I quickly approach the radio, my brain taking several seconds to recognize that Frank Sinatra is crooning from the speakers.

Cautiously, I turn the knob just the slightest and smile when the volume increases.

It's impossible for it to be playing anything, yet I'm confident this isn't a dream.

With a grin, I step away.

The ghosts wanted to dance, so they shall dance.

I still have the taste of the wine lingering on my tongue, and my throat feels quite raw, so I pad toward the kitchen for a glass of water, the checkered tile chilling my bare feet.

I'm too busy rubbing my eyes to notice anything at first, but just as I approach the island, my stare catches on the window directly ahead of me.

The reflection offers an unobstructed view of the living room behind me, where I can still see Zade sleeping on the couch.

However, he's not alone.

My hand drifts over my mouth, astounded by the two figures before him, embracing one another as they twirl in front of the fire.

I gasp when I lay eyes on a woman with curled black hair and bright-red lips, smiling up at a man much taller than her. He wears a hat and a black trench coat, and he stares down at her with unequivocal love.

For a split second, I wonder if it's my great-grandfather, but then I glimpse his face, along with the gold ring glinting on his pinky finger. I recognize him instantly from an old picture of him standing behind Angelo Salvatore.

Ronaldo.

Gigi and Ronaldo are dancing to Frank Sinatra in front of my fireplace, gazing at one another with so much love, it makes my heart ache.

It's the first time I've seen them together, though admittedly, Gigi has only shown herself to me once before. I always wondered if Ronaldo was here with her. Seeing them now—knowing that he is—sends tears rushing to my eyes.

It's been decades since their passing, yet still they remain together in the afterlife. Even death could not tear them apart, their love surpassing the inevitability of their mortality.

One day, hopefully far in the future, Zade and I will join them, and I am so excited to meet them.

ABOUT THE AUTHOR

H. D. Carlton is a *New York Times*, *USA Today*, and internationally bestselling author. She lives in Oregon with her husband, two dogs, cat, and Bigfoot. When she's not bathing in the tears of her readers, she's watching paranormal shows and wishing she was a mermaid. Her favorite characters are of the morally gray variety, and she believes that everyone should check their sanity at the door before diving into her stories. For more information, visit www.hdcarlton.com.